RUMBLE IN THE JUNGLE

RUMBLE IN THE JUNGLE

SANTANA SOKOLOV™ BOOK THREE

MICHAEL ANDERLE

DISRUPTIVE IMAGINATION®

Copyright © 2021 by Michael Anderle
Cover Art by Jake @ J Caleb Design
http://jcalebdesign.com / jcalebdesign@gmail.com
Cover copyright © LMBPN Publishing
A Michael Anderle Production

LMBPN Publishing
PMB 196, 2540 South Maryland Pkwy
Las Vegas, NV 89109

Version 1.00, December 2021
ebook ISBN: 978-1-68500-590-0
Print ISBN: 978-1-68500-591-7

THE RUMBLE IN THE JUNGLE TEAM

Thanks to the JIT Readers

If I've missed anyone, please let me know!

Daryl McDaniel
Dave Hicks
Zacc Pelter
Rachel Beckford
Dorothy Lloyd
Deb Mader
Diane L. Smith

Editor
The Skyhunter Editing Team

DEDICATION

To Family, Friends and
Those Who Love
to Read.
May We All Enjoy Grace
to Live the Life We Are
Called.

— Michael

CHAPTER ONE

The world outside was still, unusual for a city like Atlantica. The incessant hum of traffic had fallen to a gentle hush as a soft patter of rain fell on the streets and caused the streetlights to bleed.

The moon was bright and almost full. The Atlantica fog created a fuzzy glow in the sky.

Inside the apartment, Gyles Forde slept.

He shuffled on the couch. A small trail of drool pooled in the corner of his lips. He'd gotten used to the lumpy old sofa, able to find the contours and shape that provided him the most comfort. Things hadn't been much better back in his former life, sleeping on a rock-hard bed. Life was about little improvements, bit by bit until you no longer recognized the misery you once lived in.

He dreamed of apartments, his head swirling with memories of the last few days and the places the agent had shown him around during daylight hours. He saw kitchenettes and small bedrooms, many of the dwellings not too dissimilar from where he slept now, only more central to the city, and with the heightened pressure of meaning that he'd live alone.

He wasn't sure how he felt about that yet. Especially when his dreams over the last few weeks had often featured cameos of people he once knew from his time as part of the Order of the Scythe. In his visions, he'd be testing a couch or opening a closet when a black-hooded figure would step out from the shadows and raise a scythe high in the air, creating a near-perfect replica of the Grim Reaper.

That was over now, wasn't it? He had to remind himself as he awoke in the dark, forehead peppered with sweat, that it was over. That life was behind him now. Sure, he'd abandoned the Order, but they weren't tracking him, were they? Santana was right. She had to be. Otherwise, how was he ever going to live like a regular person again?

He shifted on the couch, lying on his back. Behind his closed lids an agent with fiery red hair was showing Gyles and Therese around an apartment far from his price range. Glass work surfaces covered island kitchens. Golden sunlight broke through the slatted wooden blinds. An en suite bathroom contained a bubbling jacuzzi, complete with sparkling glasses of champagne and a silver bowl piled with strawberries.

In the real world, a wry grin appeared on his lips, a steady stream of night air filtering through the open balcony doors and kissing his face.

Therese kissed his face. He was in the tub now, with bubbles piled high around them. He was butt naked, and he didn't care—so was Therese.

She snuggled beside him, her dark hair swept onto one shoulder, a hand on his thigh. Movement stirred in his loins, and his breath caught. From the doorway, the red-headed agent continued spouting information about the listing, her words muffled and far away.

Why couldn't it be like this? Carefree and fun. Gyles allowed himself to fall deeper into the dream as Therese's lips found his—lips he hadn't yet kissed in life. They were soft, smooth, supple. He lost himself in the kiss as his eyes closed.

Bubbles popped and roiled around him, the warm water

enveloping him in a heady mixture of steam and massage. The agent's voice wore away until it no longer existed, and all that Gyles knew was the taste of Therese's tongue and the map of her mouth. His hand cupped her cheek. Her hand squeezed his thigh, snaking high up his leg as things began to stir and...

"Mind if I join you?" Santana's voice woke him from his reverie.

Gyles pulled back to find Therese no longer there, and in her place was his host, Santana Sokolov. He recoiled, springing back to the other side of the tub, which appeared to have grown several meters long.

Santana sat in the water, fully clothed, head cocked to the side. She laughed, shaking her head. "It's okay. Therese doesn't mind. Do you, Therese?"

She looked at the doorway where the agent had stood. In her place was a new version of Therese, the one he'd eaten pasta with and walked through the gardens. The Therese who came home with Gyles to find a naked Santana strolling around the apartment and fled before he had a chance to explain.

Therese looked at them both aghast. She spun on her heels and slammed the door shut behind them, leaving Gyles naked and blushing with Santana.

"Oooh, that's going to be an awkward conversation in the morning," Santana offered. "I suppose I'll leave you to it."

She climbed out of the bath, not a drop of water clinging to her supple frame. Gyles found his gaze lingering on Santana's ass before shaking his head and scolding himself. He glanced at the bubbles, only to find that they, too, had stopped.

"What are you waiting for?" Santana's voice crooned again.

Gyles looked up, finding himself in Santana's bedroom. She lay beneath the covers, wrapped up to her shoulders. They were now bare, catching the milky moonlight shining through a window that didn't exist in his real life. He stood at the end of the bed in only a thin pair of briefs, his heart racing fast. His gaze lingered on Santana's lips, and he fell into her eyes. Against his better judgment, he rested a leg on the bed, ready to crawl toward her, unable to stop himself.

He hovered over her, unblinking, drawn by a power he didn't understand. He leaned closer, her scent strange, a mix of lilac and honey. He closed his eyes, puckered his lips, could feel her breath...

She was gone. Gyles sat back on his knees, skin prickling. Something was wrong. Something was desperately wrong.

A scream sounded from behind him. He whirled, finding Therese on the edge of the shadows. Someone was behind her with dark arms wrapped around her throat and waist. Her eyes bored into his, imploringly searching for help as the awful sound escaped her lips. He froze as the shadow coalesced into a figure with a black hood. The gleam of a knife winked in the black.

Gyles sat up sharply and inhaled with a sharp gasp. He brought a hand to his tacky forehead, only vaguely aware of the chill in the air. He drew a couple of steadying breaths, allowed his heartbeat to slow, and let his brain process the confusion of his dream and the mixed feelings that settled in his loins.

Gyles only had a brief moment of relief before he spotted movement in the shadows beside him. Before he could utter a single word, a hand covered his mouth, stifling his shouts of protest.

CHAPTER TWO

The first Santana became aware of the intruder was the dull *thud* in the living room.

She hadn't been sleeping. Caught in the strange line between consciousness and slumber, she'd laid in the dark and let her body take a moment of respite. A long journey was ahead of her, and if her last trip into the jungle with the others had taught her anything, it was that trips taken into the wilds among company were often the most tiresome.

At least alone, Santana could be agile and responsive to a situation. If enemies approached in the middle of the night, she could get out of their way, hiding in the treetops or simply slipping out of sight. With a troop, you had to herd the flock, and often they were slow to respond.

She rolled onto her side, her hair standing on end as the dull *thud* sounded. One of Santana's greatest superpowers had been her ability to remain a light sleeper no matter where or when she slept. Something was wrong. As a muted scuffle followed a second later, she sprang out of bed, one hand gripping the pistol beneath her pillow, the other grabbing the knife that lay on her nightstand.

She navigated silently through the dark and stopped by her bedroom door. For a moment, she wondered if Gyles was having another of his more active dreams. She'd grown used to his flailing since the poor guy occasionally hit the pillows or kicked out as old memories flooded back. She felt sorry for him and wished she could somehow help him. When she asked about his dreams, he often closed up, growing awkward as he mentioned a cloaked specter and their scythe.

Poor guy.

With a gentle touch, she twisted her door handle. She eased the door open and let her eyes adjust to the living room. After a moment of quiet, she eased it a few inches wider, able to make out the soft silver light from the moon and the empty couch in the center of the room.

Empty couch?

Santana slipped through the door, pistol raised. She kept the knife ready, crossing it over the top of the pistol like a cop with a flashlight. She tiptoed into her living room, sweeping her gaze across the place.

The faintest of sounds tickled her ears. Santana spun, finding herself face-to-face with a wide-eyed Gyles. Behind him, a figure clutched him tightly, the mouth of a gun pointing straight back at Santana. She caught the glint of beetle-black eyes and the faintest trace of ruby shining back at her.

Santana exhaled, and her shoulders softened. "Really? You couldn't use the door like a normal person?"

The figure stepped into the moonlight, the silvery glow catching the crimson hue of Valentina Winters' long leather jacket. Her red hair rested on her shoulders, her lips the same color as pretty much everything else she wore. Valentina's gaze was intense, burning into Santana, although Santana felt no fear.

"You're one to talk," Valentina replied softly. "The number of balconies and fences I've seen you scale over the last week. It's like you've forgotten how doors work." She moved the mouth of the pistol to Gyles' cheek, bringing her lips next to his ear. "No screaming. Do you understand?"

Gyles turned his gaze to Santana.

"She's okay," Santana replied. "She's with us."

Gyles carefully nodded. Valentina lifted her hand from his mouth and gave him a gentle prod forward. He stepped away from her, putting as much distance between himself and the Crimson Countess as possible before patting himself down and adjusting his pajama pants. He ran his fingers through his messy hair, attempting to add some order to his life.

"So what *are* you doing here?" Santana asked. "I thought we'd arranged a meeting time and place? I have things to prepare. Things to get sorted ahead of our...expedition."

Valentina holstered her weapon and straightened up. "We did."

"Then are you averse to sticking to plans and schedules?" Santana prodded.

Valentina considered this. "No. I just prefer things to be on my terms. Besides, you planned to meet in daylight. As much as I like swanning around Bon Vivant Valley in the waking hours, I'd much prefer to stick to the darkness where possible. I don't know about you, but it offers something of a cloak that lends well to my particular profession."

Gyles snapped his fingers as wonder appeared on his face. "You're the Crimson Countess." His hands shook as he pointed at her. "You're...her."

"In the flesh," Valentina coolly replied as she took a step toward him. "Although I'd appreciate you keeping your voice down. Life as Atlantica's top mercenary requires some kind of composure and secrecy. You babbling like that isn't going to help my cause."

"Oh, turn it down a little," Santana replied. "Gyles is harmless, by anyone's standards. He's not going to put your precious profession in jeopardy."

Valentina narrowed her eyes at Gyles. He wilted under her gaze.

"What do you mean I haven't used a door over the last week?" Santana cottoned on to Valentina's words. "Have you been spying on me?"

"Always," Valentina returned, as if there was any other option but "Yes."

"How *dare* you?" Santana balked, heat rising in her chest. "Haven't you got better things to do than to stalk an adventurer on her week off?"

"A week off?" Valentina seemed to grow in the gloom, her anger swelling around her as venom leaked from her words. "My brother is lost out there in the forest, taken by assholes who have him hooked up to a *goddamn* machine, and you have the *audacity* to tell me you deserve the luxury of a week off?"

She took a step closer. Gyles shifted uncomfortably. "Santana, you were out there. You know what we're facing. I *trusted* you to find him because you're the only person who has any semblance of decency and honor on this godforsaken island who also knows how to navigate the wilds. Of course, I monitored you. I *need* you. I can't do this one alone."

Santana deflated, sensing the urgency in those dark eyes. Not all that long ago the pair of them had worked their way through the Atlantican wilds in search of Valentina's brother.

Valentina had hired Santana to be her guide, and though they both riffed off each other out in the wilderness, the danger was ever-present. They'd found Archie's secret hideout and worked their way to the top. As they were about to free Valentina's brother, Archie had found a way to disappear beneath the earth and vanish.

Tracking Archie was no small task. The Atlantican wilds were notorious for signal disruption and faults in scanning. There wasn't a soul alive on the planet who understood the jungle's mapping and topography, with surprises around every corner and much of the underground network of caverns and lairs remaining unexplored.

With Taylor Yungheim's aid, however, Santana had managed to confirm a location. Well, once Taylor gave her the final coordinates, they'd be ready to get on their way.

"There was nothing I could do," Santana replied. "You know this. I kept you updated."

Valentina's nostrils flared, but her anger lessened. "I need him, Santana. You don't understand what it's like to have your brother clinging to life and taken by a psychotic billionaire."

Santana gave an understanding nod, taken aback by this sudden show of emotion. In her experiences with Valentina, the latter had composed herself and played the character that the media had created for her to perfection. "I might not know what it's like to be in your situation, but I know what it's like to lose a family member."

Thoughts of her mother's passing flooded her mind and stung her eyes with tears. She saw newspaper clippings and funeral agreements. "I will not let that happen to you. If there's one thing I can promise you, it's that I'll do my damnedest to make sure we can find him, and we bring him home."

Valentina held her gaze for a long moment in the darkness. Finally, she turned to Gyles. "You realize that I'm going to have to kill your friend, don't you?"

Gyles spluttered.

Santana cocked an eyebrow. "Why?"

"He knows too much." Valentina reached for her pistol.

"No, please!" Gyles protested, hands held in front of him as he retreated. "I won't say a word. I promise."

Valentina raised the gun. Santana placed a hand on the barrel and pushed it down. "Val, no. He's a good one. He won't say a word, will you, Gyles?"

Gyles shook his head emphatically.

Valentina hesitated. After a moment, she holstered her gun. "I will find you."

"I know," Gyles replied. "I know."

"Get your shit together," Valentina commanded. "It's time we get going."

Santana sighed. "We're not ready."

Valentina frowned. "Excuse me?"

Santana clarified, "I'm waiting on the final coordinates from Taylor. I also need to stock up on provisions. Once we've received the final location, and I'm packed and set, we can go."

Valentina's fists clenched.

"You need me," Santana reminded her. "You know me. I'm not trying to fuck you over. We're doing this properly. We're getting him back."

Valentina whirled, her jacket fanning behind her as she made her way to the balcony. She stopped in the moonlight, a specimen of dark beauty as she fixed her gaze on Santana. "We leave at nightfall. Tomorrow. No excuses."

Before Santana could add anything else, Valentina climbed onto the balcony rail. She deftly balanced on the edge before spinning and stepping off into nothing.

Her body plummeted from sight. Gyles raced to the balcony, fear in his eyes, knowing how far down the fall from the top of the apartment building was. Santana met him at the rails, and the pair stared down into the misty fog.

"She's insane," Gyles offered softly.

A hand clamped around his ankle. He gasped, then looked down at Valentina's cocky grin. She hung from one hand off the underside balcony rail. "Don't you forget it."

This time she did plummet. She spun, letting her body speed through the air and out of sight. The *clanging* of metal on metal sounded, and Santana wondered what tool she'd used to save herself from the ground.

"You want to be careful around her," Santana informed Gyles. "Highly unpredictable. I won't always be around to make sure you're alive and breathing."

Gyles gave a slow nod as he swallowed dryly.

CHAPTER THREE

"I want to come with you," Gyles stated.

Morning had dawned, and a mystical haze of golden sunlight filtered into the apartment. Santana was in her usual outfit and ready, her pack fixed to her back, bullwhip at her side. Her hand rested on the front door handle. She'd attempted to sneak past Gyles and into the city.

"Your ears are getting good," Santana offered. "Soon they'll be as sensitive to noise and approach as mine."

"So take me with you," Gyles repeated. "Santana, I have nothing keeping me in the city. I'm useful to you. We've been through adventures together, and I want to help you. Let me come with you."

Santana grinned. "It's too dangerous out there."

"I don't care. I like the danger. It gives me purpose. At least I know I'm helping someone. Anyone." Gyles looked at her earnestly from under disheveled hair. He also had bags beneath his eyes. "I have a lot to offer."

"I know." Santana sighed. "There's only one issue..."

"What? I'll do anything."

"Well, two issues." Santana touched her chin.

"What?" Gyles insisted.

Santana chuckled. "Number one, you have a lady friend in the city, and I'm sure she wouldn't appreciate you taking more time out of your empty schedule to assist me for several days—possibly weeks—on this mission."

Gyles considered this as his head hung low.

"Number two," Santana continued, "is that I'm not heading off yet. I'm collecting supplies."

She laughed at Gyles' reaction. He smirked, realizing how presumptive he'd been. "I'm sorry."

Santana removed her hand from the door and sat beside him. "Look, I know you're eager to help, and I can't thank you enough for it. Honestly, without you, I don't know how I'd have survived the last few weeks. Don't get me wrong, I'm looking forward to getting my place back, but I'll miss you when you're gone."

Gyles offered a wry smile. Was there something else in that look?

"But this is dangerous," Santana finished.

"I don't mind danger," Gyles replied. "I've told you."

"It's a different kind of danger," Santana returned. "This could mean life or death."

"As opposed to the other walks in the park where people shot at us, and bloodthirsty animals attacked us?" Gyles quipped.

Santana chuckled. "Right."

"If you're worried about Therese, don't be," Gyles continued. "Do I like her? Sure. I do. But I barely know her still. We haven't even had a third date yet. She'll understand if I say I'll be busy for a couple of weeks. Please. I'm in this with you."

He laid a hand on top of hers. Santana broke out in goosebumps, her throat going dry. She eased her hands from beneath his and rose to her feet. "Let's discuss this when I'm back, okay?"

"Are you going to come back?" Gyles asked.

Santana met his gaze, a part of her wanting to say yes, even though she didn't intend to. But could she use the help? Would

Gyles benefit their party? She already had Valentina coming with her. Would Gyles contribute in a positive way?

"I'll consider it." Without waiting for an answer, she headed out the door.

The metropolis was hopping, the smell of last night's rainfall fresh in the air. As she made her way across the city, Santana thought of Valentina. Flashes of her late-night visit and the fear she'd stoked in Gyles filled her head. Her stomach roiled with discomfort, hating the fact that it reminded her about her mother's passing.

It'd been years since Santana received the news of the cave-in that buried her mother and her expedition team—events that weren't all that uncommon on Atlantica—but there'd always been something that irked her about it. In the days leading up to that final expedition, her mother had been alive, excited, buzzing with energy over the possibility of her future discovery. She'd never seen her mother so sure before that they were on the cusp of unveiling something huge.

She'd never shared what it was with Santana. When she questioned her father, he had little to say on the matter, too.

"You know your mother," he would offer with devastation in his voice. "She was always chasing some golden carrot or another."

Santana hadn't admitted it out loud, but the recent months had kicked up much of her past. Everything from a stranger bequeathing her mother's pendant and turning up murdered a day later, tracking the jewelry through the city with John Chambers after someone stole it, all the way to her recent visits to the Atlantican wilds.

Something was out there, waiting for discovery. She felt it in her bones. Something truly magical that would justify her mother's passing and shed light on the island's ever-expanding mysteries.

As she stared out the window of the driverless cab, she

scoffed. *Sure, Santana. Or it's all a pipe dream. A way to hold on to your mom and not properly let go...*

She wondered if this was how Valentina felt right now, terrified of her brother's passing, trusting in a powerful stranger to keep him alive and breathing.

Valentina hadn't told her much about Archie, and Santana had never expected her to. All that she could glean from their snippets of stolen conversation through the last few weeks was that her brother had been sick, on the cusp of death, and Archie had employed experimental techniques to keep him alive.

It looked as though things were working, too. Or, at least, they were before Archie vanished from the face of the planet. Now, it was anyone's guess. Would Archie risk all of his work to let the poor guy die?

Santana stepped out of the car, narrowly avoiding a businesswoman with a cell phone fixed to her ear. She scowled, hating the narrow-mindedness of those in the city who thought that working on the top floor and counting your happiness in currency was the best way to live. Shaking all thoughts of her mother and Valentina from her mind, she stepped into the Pet Emporium, satisfied by the tinkling bells that sounded above the door.

The familiar humidity met her skin. Animal grunts and screeches welcomed her into the room. She turned her gaze to the wall on the far right where terrariums were stacked atop one another, a selection of domestic snakes and insects and other invertebrates stored inside. She saw lizards and stick insects. Not too far from those were fish tanks vibrant and alive with schools of tetra and goldfish and Japanese fighting fish.

A flash of brilliant color drew her eye as a great green macaw swept across the room, seeking its perch next to the counter where Emily sat and played with something out of sight in a cardboard box.

Santana made her way to the counter. "You're up early."

Emily peeked above the box. "Benefits of insomnia."

"Benefits?" Santana echoed but didn't receive a reply. She neared the box and craned her neck to see inside. "What have you got there?"

Emily sat up to her full height with a wry grin. Shredded cardboard strips lay scattered across the container's bottom, and a smaller box with Spanish text written on its length was propped on its side, the top open and something moving inside. "Fresh in this morning. A real beauty."

Santana leaned closer. The shadow retreated farther into the box.

"Give her some room." Emily shooed Santana with a gentle hand. She reached beside her with a wide pair of tweezers and picked a cricket from a clear plastic box. They were still, and Santana guessed either dead or frozen. Emily deftly placed the cricket at the opening. "Now we watch." She retracted her hand.

For a minute, they were still. The macaw screeched, and creatures shuffled and played in the store, but there was no movement in the box.

Finally, a leg appeared. The shadow grew. The leg was slender and midnight black, covered in a fine layer of hairs. Another leg appeared, then a third, and a fourth. The tarantula crept forward, drawn by the cricket. She had tiny black orbs embedded in her dense black body that looked dark enough to swallow light.

"Ahh...there she is," Emily whispered. Her face lit up.

The tarantula wrapped its legs around the cricket and quickly dragged it back into the box. The cardboard gently shook as the spider attended to its meal. Emily sat straight and beamed. "A Brazilian Black," she explained. "The latest addition to my arachnid collection."

"Poisonous?" Santana asked.

Emily shook her head. "Not really to humans. They're mostly scaredy-cats that would retreat rather than attack. They have venom, but the most you'd get is a little irritation for the day." She tipped her head toward the box. "Super cute, eh?"

"I think half of the world would disagree." Santana chuckled.

"I've never understood it, y'know? Arachnophobia. Spiders—tarantulas in particular—they're big softies. They sell like hot cakes in this place. Half of Atlantica has or wants an exotic beast as a pet, and these guys are remarkably easy to keep once you've got your terrarium set up."

Emily motioned to the wall where glass fronts displayed beds of wood chips, broken logs, and moist foliage housing several arachnids. "And this one...did you see her color?"

"Black," Santana replied flatly.

"Black," Emily echoed with adoration in her eyes.

Santana followed her gaze, spotting a single black leg appear near the opening as the tarantula occupied itself with its meal. "So this one is reserved for someone? A fresh shipment?"

"Hell yeah, it's reserved. It's mine."

"Huh."

"What?"

Santana shrugged. "I guess I never figured that you'd keep pets. I thought all of these guys were for sale."

"We should hang out more."

Santana laughed. "Agreed." Her mirth slipped as she thought of her mission ahead, wondering, as she always did, what the jungle had in store for her this time.

Emily turned her attention away from the tarantula and rose from the stool. "What are you in the market for today, then? I'm guessing this isn't a social visit."

"How could you tell?" Santana smirked.

Emily made her way to the back door and motioned for Santana to follow. As they were about to slip from the room, Santana asked, "What about the tarantula? Aren't you worried about her climbing out?"

Emily turned up her lip. "Nah. She's too frightened at this point."

They left the room to the *squawk* of the green macaw.

The temperature dropped several degrees as they entered the back room. A fine mist hung in the air. Santana's breath fogged before her face.

"How did you find our little venom pouches from last time?" Emily asked proudly, as though she knew the response.

"Perfect," Santana replied. "Got us out of a few little scrapes along the way."

"Us?" Emily asked, an amused look on her face. "I thought Santana Sokolov rode solo."

Santana sighed. "It's a long story. One that I'll go into one day. Suffice to say that it's been a trialing few weeks." She leaned against the counter, watching as Emily inserted keys into locks and opened doors to reveal several poisons and toxins and paraphernalia. "You got anything new?"

"Not at the moment. Business has been booming these last few weeks. There were reports on the news about an extinct creature roaming around the city, and now everyone has decided they need to stock up on exotic pets." She cast a knowing look at Santana. "You wouldn't know anything about that, would you?"

Santana gave a sheepish grin, then turned to the door where a fuzzy gray creature stalked into the room, tough claws *clicking* against the solid floor.

"Meeka, I've told you about this," Emily scolded and shooed the raccoon out of the room. The fuzzy lump squeaked affectionately, unmoving. Emily rolled her eyes, then picked up the raccoon and deposited her out of the room before closing the door. "I swear, that one wants to follow wherever I go."

"Meeka?" Santana asked.

"Mmhmm."

"From *Pocahontas*?"

Emily nodded. "Great film."

"Isn't it *Meeko*?" Santana pressed.

Emily chuckled. "Had to change it for copyright reasons."

They both laughed as Emily returned to the lockers. "So what do you need, Santana? Your wish is my command."

Santana emptied her bag on the countertop, and together they worked through restocking her provisions. Santana examined her weaponry, including her tranquilizer gun and her modest pistol, ensuring that everything was clean, maintained, and functioning while Emily saw to stocking her ammunition. She provided her with vials and potions and toxins that could help along her journey, as well as resources to create a fire in the wild, and several antivenoms and balms to counteract and soothe stings, bites, and rashes.

As they worked, the store's front bell rang. Emily crossed to a monitor on the wall and flicked it on. They spotted the young man exploring the shop, examining all the animals as he worked his way to the feeding aisle. The green macaw swooped low over his head. The man flinched. Soon he left the store empty-handed.

"You not worried about losing the business?" Santana asked.

Emily scoffed. "That's Brian. He's always browsing, but he never buys. I think he's lonely. He likes coming in here and seeing what's on offer."

Santana raised an eyebrow. "You mean he likes checking you out?"

"That, too." Emily narrowed her eyes on the screen. "Oh, shit."

"What?" Santana asked.

"Leeroy's got her." Emily raced out of the room.

Bewildered, Santana loaded the remaining items into her backpack, pleased by the additional weight inside. She shouldered the pack, then headed out the door, almost tripping over the fluffy gray creature that sprinted past her feet.

"Jesus, Meeka," she whispered.

When she returned to the store, Santana's vision filled with emerald green feathers as a rush of wind blew past her head.

Emily shooed away the macaw that had taken a special interest in the Brazilian Black and now hovered over the box.

"Shoo, Leeroy!" Emily reprimanded, sweeping an arm. The flesh was pink with several claw marks. "A little hand, please?"

Santana moved quickly, approaching the macaw from behind and pinning his wings to his sides. She gripped him firmly, bringing him down to the countertop where his feet rested, though his beak still reached for the tarantula.

Emily, now flustered and a little sore, examined the box, looking for the spider. She drew out the smaller cardboard and tilted it onto her hand, relief flooding her face when the weight of the arachnid dropped into her palm. "Thank God."

She brought the tarantula closer to her face. The creature had curled up in a black ball. Leeroy screeched with excitement as he strained toward the spider.

"His cage is over there." Emily pointed.

Santana took the fidgeting macaw to the far side of the store and locked him in his cage. He struggled against the bars, a racket exploding from his throat as Santana returned to Emily. "Is he always like that?"

"No. He's usually remarkably docile with the other animals." Her eyes remained fixed on the black ball that was slowly unfurling. One leg unwrapped at a time until the tarantula was at its full size, crawling slowly up Emily's arm.

She took the arachnid to the far wall where an empty display cage was waiting. Carefully, she scooped the Brazilian Black inside and placed the Perspex lid on top. The arachnid crawled away and disappeared into the decorative wooden cove that was waiting. The moment it entered the shadows, it disappeared.

Satisfied, Emily turned her attention to Leeroy. "What the hell has gotten into you?"

"I think we've discovered that green macaws enjoy Brazilian Blacks," Santana replied.

Emily examined her arm, the skin pink and tender where the

macaw's claws had scratched. "He's never been like that before. I'll have to get some iodine."

Emily disappeared from the room, leaving Santana with the animals. Santana moved to the tarantula's new home and peered through the glass. The creature was impossible to see in the shadows, the perfect camouflage for a creature of the night.

Soon, the shop owner returned with a white cotton bandage around her arm. She placed her hands on the counter and smirked. "Sorry about all that fuss. Did you get everything you needed?"

"I believe so." Santana's eyes narrowed on the exhibit that now appeared empty, even though they both knew better. "Are you okay?"

"I believe so," Emily parroted.

Santana offered a soft smile and laid a hand on her shoulder. For the first time, it crossed her mind that Emily might be the closest thing she had to a real friend in Atlantica. Well, apart from Terra and Gyles. "You were right."

"Always," Emily agreed. "But what specifically do you mean?"

"We should hang out more."

Emily nodded. "You free Friday?"

Santana let out a weak laugh.

"Right," Emily continued. "It's adventure time."

"How about when I'm back?" Santana asked. "I'll give you a heads-up and we can go out for a drink. Maybe some food?"

"Sounds perfect." Emily scanned the store. "I'll have to find someone to watch this madhouse for a few hours."

Leeroy squawked in response.

CHAPTER FOUR

Santana couldn't understand the strange feeling in her stomach.

She shifted uncomfortably in the leather seat of the driverless cab as they rolled gently through the city. She felt uneasy and out of place. The titanic structures of the buildings around her seemed even more foreign than they often did. She studied the civilians walking along the sidewalk and knew that she was different—hell, she always did. What was magnifying this feeling?

The sky overhead was light, the golden sun attempting to filter through the thin ceiling of Atlantica fog. Traffic was dense, and the passage across the city took longer than expected, yet Santana didn't experience the urge to rush. She knew that wherever they were heading next, she needed to preserve her energy. This was the big one. She could *feel* it.

Why wouldn't she? Over the years, Santana had learned of the powerful forces at play outside of human consciousness. Instinct played an enormous part in the survival of every species on the planet. The mouse knew to run ahead of the swooping owl. Great schools of fish know to congregate in the empty places of the world to breed and multiply.

Santana had always wondered about humans. She tried to

understand if their instinct was still as honed and keen as it had been thousands of years ago. Or had millennia of living at the top of the food chain and domesticating in cities dulled their sharp edges and made them soft?

This feeling...

It sharpened her senses. Her ears perked up at every horn blare and AJS siren. Gulls cried above her, swooping low over the city to investigate heaped trash cans. Every *click* and rumble of the driverless cab magnified until she could only hear the city's orchestra.

When she slid her key into her apartment door, she could already hear Gyles inside, the TV playing something that sounded like one of his video games. A weak smile flickered across her lips as she remembered the time she'd lived alone and the numerous traps she had to set to protect her property. Now she had Gyles, the ultimate guard dog.

He smiled at Santana as she entered, sat upright, and paused the game. She was unsurprised to find the freeze-frame displaying the familiar brunette that often appeared when he was gaming.

"Having fun with Lara?" She rubbed her eyes before heading toward the coffee pot.

"Figured I'd play a speed run. I found some guy online who managed to complete the entire game in under three hours."

"Great use of time," Santana mocked playfully. She brought him over a coffee, then settled on the edge of the coffee table.

Gyles accepted the drink. His eyes never left Santana's as he sipped. "Have you thought about it?"

Santana sighed. Her gaze strayed to the window. Up here the fog was thick, and it was easy to pretend that they were alone in a world that existed on top of the clouds. "Yes."

"And?"

Santana chewed her lip. Her gaze found the multitude of traps and wires set near the balcony door, the gadgets and gizmos that circled the apartment walls. Gyles might be a great guard dog, but he'd also proven useful on their adventures so far. Besides, it would be nice not to be entirely alone with Valentina when they re-entered the jungle.

Goddammit. Who have I turned into? "You can come."

Gyles hopped off the couch and threw his arms around Santana. Black drops of coffee spilled from both of their cups, but Santana didn't mind. She chuckled at his enthusiasm.

"You won't regret it."

"I hope not," Santana shot back. "Have fun telling Therese."

Color flushed his cheeks.

"What?" Santana asked.

"I've already told her."

Santana smirked. "Why am I not surprised? You realize this means you'll have to go without your precious video games for a while, right?"

Gyles nodded. "I do."

"I have no idea when we'll be back," Santana added.

"Yep," Gyles agreed.

"We might be heading into certain death. I can't guarantee we'll return."

For the slightest of moments, Gyles' eyes betrayed him. "Fine by me."

Santana drew a long breath. "Then it's settled. I've got nearly everything I need. I have to let Valentina know where and when we'll meet her. Then I have to run one more errand before we set off. Will you be ready by then?"

Gyles looked around theatrically. "I'm ready. What else is there for me to prepare?"

Santana scoffed. "I wish you'd been able to act this fast when I asked you to move out. That process seems to be taking a lot longer than planned."

Gyles looked up guiltily. "I want to find the right place."

"Well, if we don't return, you won't need to," Santana replied.

They laughed together. It felt nice. It felt normal.

Gyles' brow wrinkled.

"What is it?" Santana sensed the question before he asked.

"What makes you think Valentina doesn't already know when and where to meet you?" His gaze strayed to the balcony, and his voice raised a little. "What if she's clinging to the underside of the balcony listening?"

They both waited as though a beautiful woman clad in red was about to appear before them.

Santana shook her head. "Maybe she does already know. Just in case, we'll set up the meet." She drew out her cell and typed the message. Her finger paused for a second before she hit "Send." A chime confirmed the communication had gone. "Pick up your stuff," Santana instructed. "I have one more thing to grab, and we can hit the highway."

She disappeared from the living room, leaving Gyles to attend to his things. He produced a small backpack from behind the couch, then pulled on his shoes.

Santana entered the darkness of her room. Faint light filtered through the closed curtains on the far side. The room was quiet. That strange sensation lingered in her stomach and magnified the silence. There was a slight chill in the air as she made her way to the closet and opened the door.

A rail lined the top of the closet, abundant with hangers that held no clothes. The small amount of clothing she owned was squished to the right, barely taking up a tenth of the space inside. At the bottom of the closet were a few empty shoeboxes and a small security vault protected by a fingerprint scanner.

She crouched with her eyes fixed on the vault. She'd been on dozens of missions before, heading out into the wilderness where she might never return, but not once had she ever felt the need to unlock this vault and take the effects with her.

Instinct...

She pressed her thumb to the panel. Gears *whirred,* and a *beep* sounded. She opened the door and reached inside.

The bottle of vodka was travel-sized, intended to fit neatly within a purse or pocket. A golden circle logo sat on the front with a warped X across its center. The writing read, "Khortytsa."

A nostalgic smile played across Santana's lips as she spun the bottle between her fingers. She slipped it into her inner jacket pocket, then reached for the final item inside.

It was still soft to the touch. The scarf unspooled in her fingers, as light as a cloud. Made from Scottish Hebridean wool and knitted in a tartan pattern, the scarf transported Santana back to when her world was completely different.

She brought the wool to her nose and inhaled deeply, her smile growing into a wide beam as her mother's scent filled her nostrils. No matter where she went, and no matter what her mother was doing, she was always careful to ensure she'd applied her perfume. There had always been a bottle of Yves Saint Laurent's Black Opium in her bag, despite her father's protestations of how the scent would often invite bugs to her flesh.

Santana couldn't remember the last time she'd removed the scarf through fear of losing the scent, but here it was, the smell filling her head with warmth and kindness and memories of a life long lost. She allowed herself a few moments of recollection before she opened her bag and tucked the scarf inside.

Her eyes were a little damp with tears so she wiped them with the back of her sleeve. She turned her attention to the wooden floorboards beside the vault, took out her knife, and slid the blade between the cracks. The panel levered up, revealing the shadows inside.

She reached into the hole, expecting to clasp her final item…

She found nothing.

Her brow creased as she leaned farther into the closet. She shone her cell phone's flashlight on the floor and confirmed the emptiness.

Her stomach tightened.

Instinct.

She'd put it here. Once John had found and returned the pendant, she'd hidden it here for safekeeping. She'd confirmed that it was still here only a couple of days ago, and now...

Her blood boiled. She stormed out of her bedroom, and the door slammed behind her.

Gyles looked up sharply. A *click* confirmed he'd loaded a magazine in his pistol. "Santana, what's wrong?"

She knew straight away that it wasn't Gyles who'd taken the pendant. She could tell from the innocence on his face.

"Santana?" Gyles pressed.

Santana tried to calm her breathing as her mind worked a thousand miles a minute. She closed her eyes, the blackness behind her eyelids filling with the face of one man. A man she didn't want to have to rehire to recover the item she'd lost again.

CHAPTER FIVE

"This is how you spend your days off-duty?" Doug Nevill brought the foaming Guinness to his lips and took a long sip of the dark ale. As he lowered the glass, a white mustache remained on his upper lip. He dragged a calloused hand across his face, then licked the remainder off.

Dick Chambers cocked an eyebrow, his concentration taken from the two playing cards he held in his hands. His gaze strayed across the table to the three other players, each one waiting for Dick to take his turn.

Dick placed his cards facedown on the green mat, then rapped his knuckles on the surface. "I'm never off-duty. Not really."

"So this is work to you?" Doug observed as a man with narrow eyes and a scarf covering the lower half of his face threw a couple of red chips into the center of the table.

Dick ignored him, focusing on the game at hand. The tavern was sparsely populated—of course, it was at this time of day. The sun had barely passed its zenith, and its warmth filled the room and made Dick sleepy. Smoke swirled around him, kicked up by the handful of other patrons puffing on their cigarettes. Dick's lip curled, wishing that he'd remembered to buy some on the way in.

"Hardly quality time spent with a friend," Doug mocked from the sideline. Dick knew he was kidding. Ever since the two had reunited, they'd had less and less time to spend together.

They'd served together in the Army many moons ago but got separated during combat. Doug had believed Dick abandoned him to die and spent years searching for his old comrade to exact revenge. However, time and memory are often deceitful mistresses, and the truth came out. Dick never abandoned his friend but was forced to believe that he'd died.

Their reunion had been messy, but the truth prevailed. Now, Doug grew ever busier with his job while Dick's investigation business continued to grow. Atlantica knew how to divide and conquer, how to swallow its citizens and ensure that they never left, that only the thickest-skinned could band together and rise.

By pure chance, both men had discovered that their calendars aligned, and finally they could have a drink together, something they hadn't managed in weeks.

"If you don't like it, either fuck off or get involved." Dick smirked. He tossed some of his chips on the table, leveling the bet. "This is how I choose to unwind."

Doug scoffed. A woman with shining silver hair cast him a sideways glance.

"How do you like to unwind?" Dick asked as the dealer set the next card in the center—a jack of hearts.

The woman shifted in her seat. She twisted her bracelet.

Dick grinned.

"Usually with a good book and a bubble bath," Doug snarked. "I'm currently knee-deep in the latest Patterson novel. Thrilling stuff. Add some strawberry bubble bath, a Pinot Grigio, and I've got myself a perfect night in."

Dick held the woman's gaze as he tossed a green chip into the table. She snarled and bowed out, her cards quickly recovered by the dealer.

"Really?" Dick directed his question to Doug. "Didn't have you down for the lavish luxuries of bathing."

Doug rolled his eyes and sipped his drink. "Of course not."

"Then what *is* your perfect night in?" the man with narrow eyes asked. His words oozed like toxins through the cloth.

Doug smirked. "I'll let you know if I ever have one. Most I ever get is a quick snatch and tug on my own dangly bits before I clock out for the night." He shook his head. "Atlantica."

"Atlantica," the group chorused, sharing his exasperation.

The round continued, chips piling high. Dick managed to cash out a broad man with bulging biceps on the other side of the table. His rash of stubble was white, and his skin was dark. Soon, the only ones who remained were Cloth Man and Chambers.

The dealer's deft hands dealt the final card. Silence settled over the room. Even Doug shut his mouth as he monitored the table.

Cloth raised the stakes.

Dick watched him closely. The man was difficult to read since the cloth masked any tells involving his lips.

Dick raised even higher.

Cloth raised again.

Dick held his gaze, waiting for something, anything to tell him what the guy was holding. He'd already proven himself a great bluffer, but there had to be some weakness, a single point of vulnerability.

There it was. His ear twitched, rising ever so slightly as he sneered behind the mask.

Doug shuffled uncomfortably behind Dick.

Silver Woman had left the table.

Salt Stubble held his breath.

Dick raised the stakes, throwing another three blues on the pile.

Cloth held his breath, then pushed all his chips into the center. Dick matched and still had chips in reserve.

"Reveal," the dealer announced.

Dick turned his cards, showcasing three of a kind and a pair for a full house. Cloth grimaced before slamming his cards on the table. "This is bullshit." His drink fell to its side. Amber liquid soaked the green table cloth as the beer snaked over to Salt Stubble.

Salty hopped up, his lap darkening from the drink. He growled, and without waiting for an explanation, slammed his fist into Cloth's face.

Cloth's eyes rolled back in his head, and he fell against the dealer. The dealer caught him, but one of Cloth's hands smashed into his face. He cursed, then threw Cloth back. The small man rocked on his heels.

"Watch what you're fucking doing," the dealer barked, but Salty's rage had already grown. His hips hit the table as he launched himself past Cloth toward the dealer.

Dick picked up his bottle of Blue Moon and took a long swig. He busied himself collecting the chips, the clay composite discs clattering against each other. Behind him, Doug announced, "Dick, let's get out of here."

Why does every game of poker I play turn into a goddamn Western saloon fight? Dick thought as Salty turned his way.

Dick scooped the chips into a pouch, his sights set on reaching the barman and cashing in his coin. As he made his way around the table, Salty stopped him. The big man's body was like a boulder in his way. "You cheated us."

"Bullshit. I played fairer than I ever have. This is my day off, remember?"

Dick put a hand on his shoulder.

Salty shoved him hard in the chest. His hands were the size of slabs, and the impact left Dick winded. Doug caught him and helped to steady him on his feet.

"You really don't want to do that," Dick warned Salty.

The man shoved him again as he stepped closer. Dick took a cautious step back, now inches from Doug.

A whisper came into his ear. "Go low."

Dick shook his head. How had it come to this?

"Give me my money," Salty demanded. "Then you're free to go."

Dick reached into the pouch. Salty's guard dropped, and at that moment, Dick jerked his knee up into Salty's crotch.

Air wheezed from Salty's mouth. He doubled over with his face inches from Dick's.

Dick said, "I asked you nicely," before punching him square in the cheek.

The blow threw Salty sideways toward Cloth, who'd now risen from his stupor and attempted to catch Salty. Dick and Doug sidestepped past them, freedom in their sights as they made their way to the bar. The door was only a few meters away.

A table of nearby gentlemen rose, creating a final barricade to the exit.

"This is what you do to relax?" Doug asked.

Dick pinched between his eyes. "Gentlemen, we don't want any trouble."

From behind, Salty announced, "Then you chose the wrong posse to fuck with."

Dick sighed. He leaned closer to Doug. "Four, one, three, two."

Doug nodded. "Gotcha."

The four ahead of them looked confused. The one on the left cracked his knuckles.

"Let's do this." Dick ran at the one on the right.

They fell into a flurry of fists and beaten flesh. Dick and Doug split up, dividing the attention of the four as they worked seamlessly around each other. Dick's knuckles grew raw from punches, his knee embedding into the two he faced until they were down and out on the floor.

Doug had one remaining as Salty realized the direness of their situation. He launched himself back into the fray, only to be dragged back by Cloth. They fell into a scuffle as the silver-haired woman watched silently from the sidelines. The table flipped, and cards fell everywhere as the dealer slipped out a back door.

Dick helped Doug with the final man, pinning his arms behind him as Doug launched a volley of blows to his chest. The man wheezed, then slipped to his knees and joined his comrades on the floor.

Breathless and walking to the soundtrack of Cloth and Salt scrapping on the floor, Dick placed the bag of chips on the bar's countertop. The barman lazily looked up as though Dick was disturbing his evening slumber, then disappeared into the back.

Dick and Doug watched the fight between Salty and Cloth. Despite his smaller stature, Cloth was pressing the win, his arms wrapped around Salty's throat as the large man bucked like a bound hog. Dick tapped his fingers on the bar. A door opened and closed.

He turned, expecting to find the barman, but instead found two figures standing in the doorway.

"Oh, fuck…" he muttered. A guilty grin spread across his lips.

Backlit by the hazy daylight filtering from the outside world, the man would've been difficult to recognize. The woman he could pick out of a lineup anywhere.

"Sokolov." Dick doffed an imaginary cap.

Santana had one hand on her hip with a bullwhip coiled at her side. She wore cargo trousers and a tank top that hugged her supple frame perfectly. Beside her, Gyles shifted on his feet.

She stepped forward, her features lit by the artificial chandeliers fixed to the ceiling. "Should I be surprised?"

"I didn't…" Dick started to protest, but before he could, the barman emerged from the back with a stack of blue Atlantican bills. Dick sighed. "Couldn't do this digitally?"

The barman shrugged and placed the cash on the counter. He turned his attention to the mess in the corner, looking at Cloth sitting triumphantly on Salty with a cigarette clamped between his lips.

"Shall we?" Doug motioned to the door.

Dick nodded. "Let's."

"So, to what do I owe this pleasure?" Dick absently tapped his thumbs against the table.

The diner was moderately busy with a gentle hum of chatter buzzing in the air. When he'd asked what Santana wanted after they'd left the bar, she'd pointed at the nearest place with seats and taken them there. Although he'd tried to create some small talk along the way, casting furtive glances at Doug, Santana had been silent as the grave.

Santana's eyes bored into him. He could read that she was deep in thought, her mind working a thousand miles per minute. Beside him, Doug sat back, menu resting in his hands as he tried to zero in on his food of choice.

Dick didn't know if they'd be staying that long.

"It's gone," Santana announced at last, leaving the two words to hang in the air.

Doug and Dick exchanged a look. Gyles looked clueless about the whole situation.

"I'm sorry… What's…" Dick started.

Santana interjected, "The pendant, John. It's gone."

Dick's eyes widened. He sat back in his chair, fingers running through his hair. "Wow…I didn't see that one coming. Can't you take care of your things? Do you know how hard I worked to reclaim that piece of nostalgia?"

Santana shook her head, and her lip curled. "There was no sign of a break-in. There was no forced entry. No one should've known where it was even hiding. Gyles didn't even..."

"Gyles is still living with you?" Dick asked a little too quickly.

Doug smirked as he glanced up from the menu. "Do I detect a hint of jealousy, Chambers?"

Dick snarled.

"Yes, he is," Santana replied. "He's looking for a new place though, aren't you."

Gyles nodded.

"It's not about that," Santana stated. "Someone has it, and if it's in the wrong hands, it could—"

"Could what?" Dick interrupted. "We still have no idea what that pendant does, nor any clue of what the codes and maps mean. It's a piece of garbage, nothing more than a trinket of your mother's. So what if it's gone? I'd say good riddance."

He leveled his gaze on Santana with a satisfied feeling in his stomach. After all he'd gone through to return the jewelry, she should've been more careful than to hide it under her closet floorboards.

"You can't mean that," Santana snapped as her ears reddened. "John, you *know* what that pendant means to me."

Gyles shrank back. Doug set down his menu. "Why don't we all calm down a little? Maybe grab some food. A milkshake, perhaps. We can get to the bottom of this. We only need to think and lay out the events as they happened."

Santana's gaze remained on Dick. "He sounds more like you than you do."

Dick shrugged. "Maybe I'm tired of finding things only for them to get lost again. Maybe I don't want to work another job for a woman who helped me rescue an artifact for my client, only to steal it the moment I turned my back."

"You what?" Doug shifted his attention to Santana. "That's pretty impressive."

"It was only a dagger," Santana replied.

"A dagger that unlocked an entire fucking temple," Dick shot back. "It wasn't only a trinket."

A waitress came to the side of the table with her digital tablet ready to take their orders. Doug ordered a round of milkshakes without asking if anyone wanted one, then sent the woman away.

The entire time Dick felt the heat of Santana's gaze on him.

Quiet fell over the table. Doug looked awkwardly between them all, figuring out how to break the tension. "So, Santana… When did you last *see* the pendant…"

"You took it," Santana stated flatly.

Dick's ears pricked up. "Excuse me?"

"You son of a bitch," Santana growled, disbelief written on her face. "You stole the pendant."

Dick raised his hands in defense. "I'd be very careful of what you're accusing me of—"

"Since when did John Chambers ever turn down a mission?" Santana pressed. "Since when did John Chambers turn down a chance to impress a woman and try to get in her pants? Since when did John ever back down in the face of a challenge?"

Doug's eyebrows raised. "Did you two…"

"No," Santana snapped.

"Not for lack of trying," Dick offered.

"Not even if you were the last man on Earth," Santana continued. "Don't change the subject. You stole it, didn't you?"

Dick broke into a satisfied smile.

"Say it," Santana growled.

"I did."

Gyles had to hold Santana back from almost throwing herself across the table. "You son of a!"

Doug drew Dick away from Santana's reaching arms. The waitress returned with a tray full of shakes. She stood cautiously by the table, waiting for the chaos to subside before setting the drinks down. She worked quickly as the drinks foamed above the tops of the metal containers, then dashed off without waiting to ask if they required anything else.

Santana drew a long breath, composing herself, although the heat remained in her eyes. "Where is it?"

"It's safe," Dick replied.

Doug took several swallows of his drink, then let out a satisfied gasp. "What have you taken?"

"Her pendant," Dick answered.

"What's a pendant?" Doug asked.

Gyles answered. "Isn't it a piece of jewelry? Like, a thing that hangs around your neck?"

"Where is it?" Santana repeated.

"Safe," Dick returned.

Santana snarled. "I'm not playing games, John. Either you tell me where the pendant is, or I loop this whip so tightly around your balls that the blood flow stops and they drop to the floor."

"Ouch." Doug winced.

Dick sat back. "I can get it back for you, after food."

"Dick…" Santana warned again.

"You owe me. Fair is fair. Tit for tat."

"Tit for tat," Doug parroted, losing himself in his shake.

"You stole something that belonged to my client," Dick continued, "so I stole something that belonged to you." When he saw the rage building in her eyes, he quickly added. "I was never going to keep it.

"I have to say; I was surprised that I was able to get it given your reputation for your security. However, given the number of deactivated traps scattered around your place, it was surprisingly easy." He nodded at Gyles. "Even lover boy was out cold and didn't move a muscle as I crept through your place and found where you hid it."

"How did you know where to find it?" Santana asked.

"You're not as smart as you think you are in that regard. Remember, my line of work is in the city. There are few satisfying hiding places in apartment buildings. You're probably not all that clued on the best ones since you spend most of your life out in the jungle, but in the future, consider air conditioning units or inside the plumbing. I'll admit, I was almost thrown off by that safe—which, I'll add, might've been a safer location for you—but in the end it was easy."

Santana sat back and allowed her anger to subside a touch.

"Come now." Dick clapped once and smiled. "The locket is safe, and we're all in good company. Let's make the most of it and fill our stomachs, shall we?"

Doug raised his empty milkshake glass. "Hear, hear!"

Even Gyles guiltily looked at the menu as his stomach rumbled.

Santana remained tight-lipped. Dick took that as a sign of consent.

"Good." He scanned the menu. "Now, what do they have in the way of steak and bourbon?"

CHAPTER SIX

Santana grew impatient long before they left the diner.

It wasn't only that Dick seemed to be taking achingly long to eat his steak, but it was clear that Gyles was enjoying his food as well. His plate was the size of his head and piled high with mashed potatoes and some variation of German sausage splattered with gravy. Santana felt guilty for dragging the poor guy out into the jungle. When would be the next time he'd enjoy the luxuries of a warm, cooked meal served on good crockery?

Doug was the first to clean his plate and sit back with his hands folded on his stomach in satisfaction. Dick sipped his bourbon, enjoying Gyles' company again and prodding him with questions between mouthfuls.

For the most part, Santana was silent.

It was hitting late afternoon by the time they finally crossed the city to Dick's latest apartment. Santana hadn't known that he'd moved—why would she? It wasn't like she kept up-to-date with the detective. She had other fish to fry. She had to admit that the apartment was nice. Business must be treating Dick well, even if he was unable to keep the place tidy.

"Take a seat," he instructed as he crossed the wooden floor into his bedroom.

Santana softened a little as the musk of his place filled her nostrils. He wasn't tidy, but he wasn't unclean. She supposed she could respect that.

"Nice place." Gyles echoed the thoughts in Santana's head. He plopped down on the couch as Doug made himself at home, crossing to an old vinyl record player and placing the needle on the disc.

Soft, scratchy music filled the apartment. An electric guitar played its melody as a warbling British voice rang out. Doug smirked and looked between the two. "Any idea who this is?"

They listened for a moment. In the far reaches of her mind, Santana could see the man's face and hear his music as she rode in the back of her father's renovated El Camino with the windows rolled down and a steady stream of heat pouring down from the summer sun. Her mother sat in the passenger seat, poring over ancient pages on her lap.

Gyles shook his head. "No idea. Elton John? He was British, wasn't he?"

"Rocket man?" Doug returned with a scoff. "Close, but no cigar."

The music continued, the man's singing rising with the pace of the music.

"Bowie?" Santana replied softly.

Doug snapped his fingers. "There it is. David motherfucking Bowie. Legend of an artist, God rest his soul. Can't believe you didn't know that one." His gaze turned to Gyles.

Gyles shrugged. "There are a million artists on Atlantica alone."

"These are the *legends*." Doug closed his eyes as the guitar solo kicked in and filled the room.

"Here." Dick emerged from the bedroom, the chain of the pendant spilling from the gaps in his fingers.

Santana took the pendant, noting the metal's warmth from Dick's hands. For a fraction of a moment, their hands froze. Santana caught Dick's gaze. He held hers.

"This is the best part!" Doug declared. He waved as though he was conducting an orchestra.

Dick retracted his hand.

"Thank you," Santana offered.

"You're welcome."

"I mean... Not thank you for stealing it, but... You know."

"Yeah." Dick dug his hands into his pockets.

"Although..." Santana started.

Dick raised an eyebrow.

Santana grinned. "I'm wondering. Did you hide the pendant beneath the floorboards?"

Dick shrugged. "That's my secret to hold."

Santana chuckled.

Doug busied himself near the vinyl player, pouring some liquor from a crystal container. He tipped his head back and downed the contents in one before smacking his lips.

"You going to offer any of that to anyone else?" Dick called. "Or are you going to abuse my things without permission?"

Doug waved. "You're salty because it's in front of company. You never minded before. In fact, you're often quite liberal with your sharing. I find that strange for a detective."

"Only around friends," Dick shot back before accepting a glass from Doug. He held it out to the others, silently asking if they wanted one.

Gyles looked at Santana as if for permission.

"We really should go," Santana answered. "There's...something that requires our attention."

"Oh, I know that look," Doug crooned.

Dick recognized it too. That was clear on his face. "What's the mission?"

"You know that confidentiality is of utmost import," Santana replied.

Dick smiled. "Yeah. I know."

"Seriously, where are you going?" Doug returned. "Dressed like that I'm going to assume that you're off tomb-raiding somewhere. Got a little Lara vibe to you, don't you? Although, even I have to add that it's much nicer to view in the flesh."

Dick flashed him a look.

"My business is my own," Santana returned before correcting, "*our* business is our own."

"You're taking company?" Dick asked. "Intriguing."

"Why's that intriguing?" Santana shot back.

"I've never known you to take a mission in company purposefully," Dick answered. "Well, besides with me."

"I smell jealousy," Doug stated.

"Who's the client?" Dick took his chance.

Before Santana could open her mouth to reply, a sultry and commanding voice answered from the bedroom door. "I am."

Santana glanced over her shoulder with an expression that said, "Why am I not surprised?"

"Val?" Dick commented.

Gyles cast him a strange look.

Doug scanned her up and down, eyes lingering on her curves in her red and black clothing. She wore a sunhat that shadowed her brow. A cloud of sweet perfume filled the air.

"Doug," Valentina stated.

Doug nodded.

"*You're* her client?" Dick was unable to mask the surprise on his face. "*You?*"

Valentina bowed her head. "I am."

Santana turned to face Valentina. "What are you doing here? I thought I'd tell you when we were meeting."

"My eyes are always on you." There was a hint of a threat in

Valentina's words. "Time is pressing, and you're off gallivanting across the city with your boy-toy."

Dick raised an eyebrow as his cheeks flushed.

"*My* boy-toy?" Santana replied. "I wouldn't touch any part of John if he was the last—"

"Yes, yes," Dick interrupted, placating with palms up. "We've been over this already. Val, what are you doing here? What's wrong?"

Valentina's lips pressed into a thin line.

Gyles shrank back into the couch, trying to make himself invisible. The air was pregnant with tension.

Dick took a step closer, his voice softening. "Val, it's me. If there's a problem, you can tell me. God knows you've helped me enough in the past. I'm happy to return the favor."

Valentina's eyes flashed beneath the brim's shadow. "It doesn't concern you."

"Now, hold on a minute," Santana stated. "You two know each other?"

"We've been acquainted," Dick replied.

Santana sensed the subtext in his words and rolled her eyes. "Of course you have."

Dick shrugged her comment away. "Val?"

Doug stood to the side and refilled his glass. His smile stretched from ear to ear. "Man, this is fun. The island's greatest mercenary shrinking under the withering glare of jungle girl."

"Who's withering?" Valentina's words were like blades. In a heartbeat, she swept over to Doug and stood an inch from him with cold steel at his throat. "You want to try that again, boy?"

Doug showed no sign of fear. Instead, he shook his head. "I'm good."

"Cool it," Dick instructed flatly.

Valentina stepped back while holstering her blade in an inner pocket. Her eyes remained on Doug's as she spoke to the room. "I've found myself in a predicament that happens to revolve outside of my orbit of expertise. "'Jungle girl,' as your friend is so kind to name her, has been hired to act as my chaperone as we attempt to retrieve something stolen from me. Precious cargo that I would very much like to see returned."

Dick frowned. "You can't do this alone? I thought you thrived off running solo?"

Something passed between the pair that Santana couldn't read, some history that would, for now, remain behind closed doors.

"Everyone has their limits."

Dick looked between Santana and Valentina. "Then I want in."

Doug scoffed.

Dick glared at him.

"Of course you do," Doug muttered. "Two pretty ladies and Dick wants to be the filling in the sandwich."

"What about me?" Gyles quickly regretted speaking up as all eyes turned on him.

"Sorry, correction," Doug commented. "A double dick-stuffed sandwich. Sounds delicious."

"You want in?" Santana asked. "Why? Don't you have your shit to deal with?"

Dick's expression turned sober. "Because, if it's important enough that Valentina has to hire *you* to help her—or anyone for that matter—then it's important enough for me. I know Val. I know her limits. I know her boundaries. We go back…"

There it was again, that subtext that remained unspoken but shouted at Santana and made her stomach curdle.

"…And Val doesn't work or play with others—for the most part," Dick continued. "I've taken plenty of coin to deal with petty squabbles and domestic disputes that barely make a difference to this shit-stain of a city, so yeah…I want in. I want to help make a real difference to…" He bit back his last words.

"Go on," Valentina invited.

To their surprise, Gyles finished his sentence. "To those he cares about."

Santana and Valentina fixed their gaze on Dick. He lifted his chin and drew a deep breath but didn't speak.

Santana turned to Valentina. "I say he joins us."

Val's head raised. "Excuse me?"

"Think about it," Santana replied. "John has a lot to offer. He has some skills that round out our own. If you're taking both Gyles and me along the way, why not add a third?"

"You're taking him?" Valentina nodded at Gyles.

"Oh, right." Santana chuckled. "I forgot to tell you."

Valentina met Dick's gaze. "Fine. I don't see why not if it means we'll pack up our shit and get this show on the road."

Doug dropped a couple of ice cubes into his glass.

"What about you?" Valentina asked. "Fancy coming along as well? Apparently, it's a party now."

Doug shook his head and frowned. "Not for me, thanks. Unlike Dick, I like my job, and I have clients waiting."

"You're serious?" Dick asked.

Doug nodded. "Of course. Don't get me wrong, but running blindly into the Atlantica wilds with two gorgeous women and whatever part this guy has to play to recover something that's still unspecified sounds…real fun. Unfortunately, I remain in possession of something that Dick doesn't. It grounds me to Atlantica and protects my…I don't know…life."

"What's that?" Gyles asked.

"An ability to resist the temptations of the female form," Doug declared, leaving the sentence to hang in the air.

Dick smirked before crossing to Doug and pouring a drink. After he downed the contents, he gave Doug a weak punch in the arm. "Always a class act, aren't you?"

"I learned from the best." Doug rubbed his arm.

"Enough chatter," Valentina commanded. "We leave now."

Santana clasped the pendant around her neck. She tucked it

beneath her top so only the gold chain links remained. "Very well. You ready, Gyles?"

Gyles rose to his feet. "As I'll ever be."

"You ready, John?" Santana asked.

"It's Dick," Doug declared.

Santana remained tight-lipped.

"Let me get my things." Dick slid past Valentina and closed the door behind him. After a quick minute, he returned. "Okay. Let's do...whatever this thing is."

CHAPTER SEVEN

"Last stop," Santana announced as Dick's gleaming sedan rolled along the dirt track toward the large building that sat beside the forest border.

"Make it quick," Valentina commanded. Despite Dick's lines of questioning, Valentina had remained quiet for the most part. She appeared uncomfortable, not used to riding like a civilian when her usual form of transportation had her traveling solo and leaping across the rooftops.

Santana exited the vehicle with a pang of guilt at leaving Gyles with those two. She had no idea what she would return to, so she decided to heed Valentina's commands.

She entered the building through the large front doors and followed the usual process. The guards stripped her of her effects before she climbed the building in the glass elevator, emerging a moment later into the impressive library. The smell overwhelmed her—ancient pages, knowledge, and history, all stuffed into the shelves of this room.

She quickly crossed the area, resisting the temptation to linger as she sought the one person who held the key to her functional entry into the forest.

The doors stretched to a towering height. Muffled voices chattered beyond them. She didn't bother knocking, instead choosing to open the doors confidently and step inside.

She needed her answers.

"Santana, nice of you to waltz on in," Taylor announced with a mirthful expression as he sat by the window, backlit by the setting sun. Beyond the glass, the rolling landscape of the Atlantica wilds stretched to the horizon where the fog ate it.

"I'm sorry to interrupt," Santana began.

"No you're not," Taylor interjected with no hint of annoyance in his voice.

"Well," Santana continued. "We need to talk. It's a matter of urgency."

Taylor clasped long fingers together. His thinning hairline shone silver in the sun. "It appears that's a theme that connects you two. Sorry, officer, for the intrusion."

The chair facing Taylor spun. Santana let out a soft chuckle, not quite able to accept the person facing her.

"Hey, Sokolov," Terra Kris announced. She wore her form-fitting blue AJS uniform with a black chest plate wrapped around her and a utility belt heavy with tools and firearms. Resting beside the chair was her custom assault rifle, the scope painted in the same blacks and hexagonal patterns as her chest plate. In the center of the plate was a digital display showcasing a neon blue diamond. "Fancy meeting you here."

Santana smiled and shook her head in disbelief. "What the hell are you doing here?"

"Miss Kris was visiting to follow up on my case profile," Taylor answered for her. "When we reported the missing dagger to the AJS, they sent several officers that were of little use to the case. According to Miss Kris, she wanted to file an aftercare report to ensure that I was okay and out of further harm's reach."

Terra met Santana's stare with a measure of mischief behind

those eyes. Judging by Taylor's smile, she could tell that he didn't believe what he was saying either.

"So you're doing well, is what you're saying?" Terra asked Taylor. "No issues, no additional break-ins? Everything is as it should be?"

"All is fine," Taylor replied. "I appreciate the concern of the AJS. If only it could be a much more official capacity, and if the laws were different, perhaps we wouldn't have been in that mess to begin with."

"You don't have to tell me that." Terra smiled. She saluted Santana as she rose from the chair. "See you around, Sokolov."

Terra exited the room, leaving Santana flummoxed. Her steps retreated from them. Santana jerked her thumb in the direction of the door. "*You* called the AJS after the break-in?"

Taylor shook his head and reached down into the bottom drawer of his desk. "No. A member of my staff did. Claimed it was an intention of concern, but they no longer work for this establishment. I can't have whistle blowers sniffing around my work."

"So what was she doing here?" Santana took the chair that Terra had occupied.

"What she said." Taylor smirked as he placed a pile of papers on the desk. "Or so she wants me to believe."

"What do you think it was then?" Santana asked.

"Yet to be determined. But that's not why you're here, is it?" He tapped a finger on the papers. "This is why you're here."

Santana's heart fluttered with excitement.

Dick left the engine rumbling, creating a soundtrack that would drown out the silence filling the car.

Gyles shuffled uncomfortably in the back, his seatbelt still fastened. He doggedly stared out the window, doing his best to ignore the casual glances from Dick or the snatches of stares from Valentina in the side mirror.

Dick took a pack of cigarettes from his pocket and tore off the clear wrapping. He tapped a single stick out before clamping it between his lips. He reached for his lighter, then froze when Valentina dealt him a warning glance. She nodded at the back seat.

Dick rolled his eyes. He cut the ignition and stepped out of the car. Moving over to the nearby line of trees, he stood in their shade, cupping his hand around the lighter to encourage the flame to hold. Hundreds of years of technological advancements from humans, and he still struggled to light a cigarette in the wind.

The flame took. He inhaled a large lungful of smoke. When he raised his head, Valentina stood beside him, leaning against the bough of a tree.

"You know those things will kill you?" she warned.

Dick nodded. "Out of the thousands of things that have *tried* to kill me, and the thousands of things yet ahead to try to kill me, I feel pretty safe about this one." He side-eyed Valentina, then turned back to the car, noticing the shift in Gyles as he relaxed in the absence of their company.

"You don't have to be here." Valentina didn't meet his gaze.

"I know."

"Why are you?"

Dick considered this. "Same reasons as before. I like you. Whether you choose to accept it or not, you're good people. Good people deserve help."

"If you decided to abandon the mission, I'd still fuck you," Valentina replied.

"I know." Dick's smirk took on a cocky angle.

For the first time, Valentina looked his way. "If you're after the girl, you know that she's not interested."

"I know. Unless you died and never came back."

Valentina blew out a breath. "You like her."

"Who? Santana?"

Valentina held his gaze.

Dick nodded. "I do."

"As more than a friend." Valentina held his gaze.

Dick scoffed. "Please. She's far from my typical type. Besides." He pointed his cigarette at the car. "I'm pretty sure Gyles has the hots for his mistress. Wouldn't want to get involved in that triangle."

"I'm sure that's never stopped you before." Valentina had a knowing look in her eye.

Dick smirked. "How often do you spy on me?"

"When the occasion strikes. You get around the city, don't you?"

"Part of my job."

Valentina rolled her eyes.

Dick breathed in another lungful of smoke. "So are you going to tell me what we're doing here? The great Valentina Winters, mercenary, rogue, assassin, calling for the aid of jungle girl... seems most outside your character. The media would have a field day if they caught you."

Valentina's lips thinned. Dick wondered what nerve he'd struck.

"My brother has been taken captive," Valentina offered, shoulders softening as her eyes fixed on the jungle. She explained as much as she was happy to, detailing a previous showdown with Santana in which a billionaire by the name of Archie Fontana managed to slip through their grasp and lose himself in the dense tropics.

They'd been trying to hunt him down for a few weeks, knowing that her brother was in danger. He was being kept alive by complex and innovative technology, and in those final moments when Valentina had last seen him, he'd been making progress.

"Now I have no idea of his status," Valentina continued, fists tightening. "If that motherfucker harms one hair on his head...or worse... Well..."

"I know what you're capable of," Dick soothed and rested a hand on her shoulder.

Their eyes met. Behind hers was a depth of emotion he hadn't seen before in Valentina. How much did he know about the woman he'd had an on-off affair with over the years? At one point, he'd wondered if he was falling for her. Then she'd disappeared for two years, and he learned that carnal urges weren't the same as the emotional hooks of romance.

He cared for Valentina, but he didn't love her. That much he was sure of. How could you love someone you didn't know? How could you fall for an idea instead of a person?

Love, now that was an emotion for friends and TV characters. Dick valued being alone, liked the time he had for himself. He'd slept with many women through the years, but had he *loved* any of them? No. No, he hadn't. To love someone you had to know them, to see them fully. They had to be open and honest with who they were and what was important, to wear their hearts on their sleeves. There was no one that Dick could think of who he could somehow love in this city...

A flash of movement caught his eyes. A woman in a striking blue uniform emerged from the front of the large estate building. Dick instantly recognized the dark hair and confident stride. Not a moment later, Santana stepped through the doors and ran down the stairs toward her.

Dick's heart fluttered in his chest.

"Terra, wait!" Santana caught up with the woman walking off ahead toward a carefully concealed AJS motorbike.

Terra spun with a grin, still walking backward. "Santana! Always nice to catch up."

"You want to tell me what's going on?" Santana asked. "I don't see you in weeks, and suddenly you're chilling at my benefactor's place?"

Terra shrugged with a knowing look. "It is what it is. Follow-up call. Courtesy care. Part of the job."

Santana grinned, slid past Terra, and blocked her way ahead. Terra stopped.

"Maybe for other AJS lackeys. Not for Terra Kris. This hardly seems like the right kind of use for your particular…" She examined the green light at the back of Terra's eye. "…talents."

"That's what you're going to call my animatronics?" Terra replied. She turned her gaze toward the sedan, then a little farther, her stare lingering on the man in the dark black jacket and the woman in tones of striking red. "Interesting…"

Santana pulled her attention back. "Kris… Seriously. What are you doing here? This seems like too much of a coincidence."

Terra relaxed a little and nodded at the others. "Them. That's what."

"John and Valentina?" Santana asked.

Terra chuckled. "Didn't realize you kept company with one of the city's most notorious mercenaries." Her eyes glazed as she read something that Santana couldn't see.

"I can't even begin to describe the numerous warrants and charges I have listed here to bring in the Red Countess. Murder, breaking and entering, the list goes on and on…" She focused on Santana. "And you, hanging out with Red, doesn't that make you an accessory to criminal activity?"

Santana's stare hardened. "I hope you're not suggesting what I think you're suggesting…"

"Kris!" Dick's voice rang out as he closed the gap toward the two women. Valentina had disappeared from view, and Santana could only wonder where she was hiding. "How come whenever

I'm about to get myself in trouble you appear at my doorstep? What brings you to our fine side of the jungle?"

Terra's hand dropped to her side, her grip resting on the butt of her gun. "Dick Chambers…"

"John," Santana corrected.

Terra ignored her. "Strangely enough, there I was at the AJS precinct this morning, running my routine scan through the security footage of the city with APRIL. I was trying to apprehend a criminal who caused something of a disturbance in Bon Vivant Valley last night."

She turned to Santana and spoke behind the back of her hand. "When are people going to realize that trying to rob a cashier in a high-profile location is never going to end well for them?" She turned back to Dick. "When I spotted a flash of red darting across the rooftops, making their way to the residence of one Mr. Dick Chambers."

"John," Santana repeated.

"Moreover," Terra continued, undeterred, "When I examined more closely, I found this unlikely gathering of friends and acquaintances in Dick's apartment."

"And that's a problem…how?" Dick asked.

Terra smirked. "Well, it's bad enough knowing that Valentina is on the loose, but putting you two together in the same room gave me a very bad feeling. So I thought I'd do my due diligence and try to figure out exactly what was going on."

Without another word, she walked over to the tree line. The others followed, curious about what was going on. Terra looked up into the boughs of a nearby tree and cupped her hands. "Really, Val? You know APRIL's capabilities better than anyone here. Did you think you could hide out of sight?"

Valentina dropped gracefully to the ground, cell phone in hand. She tapped on the screen and frowned. "You've unhooked me from your programming."

"Wait, what?" Santana stepped closer.

Terra replied, "It's thanks to Valentina that I was able to make this AI work *with* me instead of against me." She waved. "Long story, but let's just say that there were some bad guys in my head, and Valentina helped to kick them out."

"Always the genius with tech," Dick offered quietly.

Valentina smirked.

Santana flashed a glare his way.

"How did you do it?" Valentina asked, walking closer to Terra. She reached out as if to grab Terra's head, but Terra stepped back. "My program was sophisticated. It would've taken something special to remove my anchors from your software."

"Like an artificial intelligence?" Terra replied. "APRIL did a great job scanning through its programming to reset itself. Not you, not the AJS, not anyone can hack into this brain now." She grinned at Valentina. "Does that scare you?"

"Honestly?" Valentina folded her arms. "No."

Terra tapped the panel on her chest. The digital diamond on the display rotated as a voice stated, "Lie detected."

Terra smirked.

Valentina frowned.

"So how about we say enough horseplay?" Terra stated. "I'll ask you guys again: what exactly is going on here?"

The three exchanged glances. In the back of Dick's sedan, Gyles watched nervously.

Santana was the one to announce it at last, after throwing a surly glance Valentina's way. "Fine. If you won't own up, I will."

She squared herself to Terra and detailed their journey into the forest to recover something of value. She chose to avoid specifics, knowing that one of the last people she wanted to piss off in Atlantica was Valentina Winters. "We're not breaking any laws. We're not stirring up any trouble. We're only recovering something we need to get back."

Terra's shoulders softened. She looked between the three of them. "This requires all three of you?"

"Yes." Dick didn't expand further.

Terra narrowed her eyes. "Must be some valuable shit." She turned her gaze to Valentina. "What is it?"

For a moment, quiet hung between them. When it seemed as though Valentina wasn't going to answer, she finally spoke. "My brother."

Terra tapped her chest plate.

APRIL announced, "Truth."

Terra cocked her head, weighing up this new information. Santana's heart beat a little faster, but she wasn't sure why. After another beat of silence, Terra gave a firm nod. "I'm in."

CHAPTER EIGHT

"You're in?" Valentina asked. "Excuse me?"

"You heard," Terra shot back.

Santana smiled, but her brow creased in puzzlement. "But...why?"

Terra glanced over her shoulder toward the city's hazy skyline. "What's the use in me being able to harness all this technology if I can't use it where it matters? It's clear that the Countess hates companionship—hell, look at her records over the last ten years—so if it's big enough that it warrants a team, then you're damn certain I'm in." She met Valentina's gaze. "This *is* big, isn't it?"

Valentina nodded. "Huge. Archie Fontana has stolen artificial intelligence technology specifically designed to work with the human body's electrical circuitry. It works *with* the neurons and synapses, molding with the gray matter of the brain to fill in gaps and deficiencies caused by medical trauma."

She pointed at Terra's head. "Some of that technology lives within you. It's the same kit that helped you survive your car explosion."

"Then what's so special about this stuff? If it's already in my head, what's Archie doing that's so new?"

"It's more than that. Yours was a trial to experiment on exterior technologies put into your head to fill the gaps. This is *regeneration*. It's helping the body heal *itself*. Small pieces of hardware are the conduit. Then it encourages the body to regrow, repair, and to heal."

Valentina's eyes went dark as memory brewed. "What's more, it's stolen technology, taken from Tynamo Inc. The city's heavy hitters are hunting for Archie, each mogul eager to find him so they can claim the riches that come with the program. Pretty soon, the city is going to fall into a war of the billionaires, each one desperate to gain what lies inside my brother."

"Holy shit…" Santana breathed.

Dick stamped out his cigarette.

Valentina nodded. "There was a reason I didn't tell you this much before. But since we're here, there it is. That's what's at stake."

She took a step toward Terra. "I don't give a shit about the games of those who hoard money in their dens and abuse minions to deliver their blows. I don't care for twats who have played political games and choose immoral behavior over sticking to their guns and holding true to their integrity.

"I don't waste my time worrying about the future of humankind or what we're doing to this godforsaken planet because we're too far gone now. No amount of Atlanticore is going to change that. No sudden discovery of a Garden of Eden is going to protect us from what's to come.

"What I *do* care about is getting my brother away from that fucking psychopath so we can permanently disappear into the void. So that's where I'm going. That's what I'm here for. Join us if you want. Your knowledge will no doubt be useful. But can we get a fucking move on, please?"

They all looked at Terra. The AJS officer stood unblinking as she held Valentina's gaze. "Let's."

"Good." Valentina swept past them all, making her way to the sedan.

Santana drew her cell phone from her pocket and tapped the screen, revealing a series of photos she'd taken of documentation in Taylor's office. Terra followed Valentina, but Dick hung back.

"This is going to be an intense party," he commented.

Santana nodded. "Intense, yes. Hopefully not explosive."

"You know what you're getting yourself into, don't you?" Dick asked.

Santana sighed. "No. Not really."

Without another word, she made her way to the car.

Santana sat in the passenger seat with her cell phone nestled in her lap.

Behind her, Gyles was wedged between Terra and Valentina, his face a ghostly shade of white as he kept his arms to himself and tried to avoid eye contact with either woman.

"You know, you hardly dressed for the occasion," Dick offered, raising his gaze to the rearview mirror. "Blood red and electric blue offer little in the way of camouflage in the Atlantica jungle."

"Or in any jungle, for that matter," Santana added.

"Well, someone was eager for us to move." Terra glanced at Valentina, who continued looking out the window. "Still, I'd rather this than anything else. The nano-tech lends itself well to avoiding perforation from bullets. That's the kind of armor I need."

"Or you could be fast and silent enough not to get shot at," Valentina stated.

"Don't tell me you don't have scars," Terra commented. "We all have bullet wounds, don't we, Dickie-boy?"

Dick glared in the mirror. Santana recalled her conversation with Terra. He'd gotten in the way of her gunfire, and a bullet found a home in his ass. She wondered how uncomfortable it would've been to not sit for weeks on end.

Trees blurred past them. The suspension groaned against the uneven road. Ahead of them, the dirt track was becoming increasingly unmanageable. Santana knew that all too soon they would be on foot and the real journey would begin. She studied the small arrow on her navigation app, noting that the signal was already decreasing, and the movements of the digital marker were lagging more.

"Scars show weakness," Valentina replied. "Scars show that you're human."

"There's nothing wrong with being human," Terra shot back.

"Look who's talking," Dick quipped. "The only woman in the car who's half-android."

Gyles couldn't hold back. He turned to Terra, then quickly looked away when she met his stare.

"Even more reason to hold on to what makes me human," Terra returned.

"I know what makes us human," Dick commented.

Santana rolled her eyes. "All animals do that. It's not exclusive to humans."

"Not the way Dick does it," Valentina announced with a slight grin as she stared at the jungle.

Santana flushed. She side-eyed Dick, lingering on the uneven nature of his stubble, the deep grooves of wrinkles around his eyes and forehead. They hit a bump, and she looked at the jungle again.

They parked the sedan in the shadows of the brush, a short distance off the dirt track. The trees towered above them, their leafy canopies blocking out much of the light. The calls of jungle creatures already filled the air. Birds cried, insects chirped, and in the distance came the furious yowls of a big cat taking down its prey.

Gyles and Santana exchanged a glance, her mind filled with the sharp canines of the marsupial lion mother they'd released into the wilds. The cries didn't sound the same, but there was no way to be sure from this distance.

"Time for food?" Dick asked.

Santana raised an eyebrow. "I have a few power bars in my bag, but we need to hold off on stopping until we've made some headway. There's a rope bridge up ahead that takes us across the ravine that borders this side of the jungle.

"Another few clicks ahead is an old outpost where we can settle up and sate our hunger. For now..." She tossed out several silver snack bars to the others. "...fill yourselves with these. They should get you through to the next stop."

Without waiting for the others to protest, she walked ahead. The trail thinned into a sliver of what it once was, and rainwater filled the holes that pocked the uneven ground. She strode confidently along the path until she found what she was looking for—a tree whose trunk was so large it appeared as though four trees had grown and melded together.

She waited for the others to catch up. A small smile quirked her lips at the unlikely band of misfits who walked in tow. Terra was the first one behind her, with Dick and Valentina talking to each other under their breath as they followed. Gyles remained a wary distance behind the pair, bringing up the back.

She waved them on into the undergrowth. The greenery closed around them. Leaves as wide as paddles and as long as cars crossed their path. The ground grew softer, with small furry creatures running across their way and disappearing as quickly as they'd come. The land rose steadily uphill, the only break in the greenery the occasional interspersing of moss-covered boulders.

A little way into their journey, Santana paused. Her ears twitched as something rustled in the brush ahead. She held up a fist to alert the others, then uncoiled her bullwhip slowly. She held the handle, poised to strike, and waited.

Another rustle. Something grunted. Santana flicked her wrist, and the whip's coils flipped ahead of her.

The grunting evolved into a squeal. Santana's muscles corded as she tried to hold herself still. Whatever she had, it dragged her forward.

Her foot found a nearby rock. She braced against it. The creature struggled madly but was unable to gain distance. Santana got Terra's attention and motioned for her to move forward. Terra crouched, ready to leap.

The creature ran at her, and Terra jumped on its back. The wild hog was frantic in its movements. It bucked under Terra's hold, but she held on. Santana launched herself after them both, and her blade found its mark in the feral pig's side.

The animal slowed. Gyles looked on with disgust. Santana and Terra held the hog still until it was motionless, then rose to their feet.

"What was that for?" Gyles was unimpressed.

Santana shrugged. "Dinner."

Santana had field-dressed her kill and given everyone portions of it to carry. She continued leading the way, walking in a relatively straight line until the trees parted and a clearing opened before them.

A small valley unfolded below with a blue ribbon of water trailing through the path. The distance across the ravine was an easy fifty meters, and a swinging rope bridge was the only way to get to the other side. In the distance, Santana made out the rising towers of mountains as the jungle flexed its prowess and warned them away.

"Looks real safe." Dick stared at the bridge. "How long's that thing been there?"

"No idea," Santana replied. "Could be from the first occupation of the island in the 1940s, could be from the most recent occupation in the 1970s. All I know is that's our way across."

"Are you sure?" Gyles asked.

Santana considered this. "Unless you fancy climbing down this steep and crumbling bank toward the river, then crossing through waters filled with...well...who knows what lives in this river? Then of course you have the steep climb up the other side."

"What's that?" Valentina asked, pointing over to a thin ribbon of smoke in the distance.

Santana narrowed her eyes. "Another expedition party, by the look of things." She didn't add that the smoke came from the exact direction they were heading.

Getting closer to the bridge gave the party no additional confidence in its integrity. Santana was the first to step onto the wooden boards, their edges rotten and breaking. The rope seemed sturdy, but as Santana began her walk, she learned she had to time her movements with the rocking to reduce the additional sway.

Creaks and groans sounded from the suspended span. She looked over her shoulder. "Take it easy, okay? This isn't the time to rush."

Valentina rolled her eyes.

Santana was halfway across when she felt the bridge lurch. For a heart-stopping moment, she wondered if it was finally collapsing until she turned back to find Terra taking her first steps onto the planks.

Step by step, they worked their way across. Santana reached the far end and let out the breath she'd been holding. Terra was now halfway, with Gyles taking his first steps across.

Dick and Valentina waited behind, exchanging more words Santana couldn't hear.

Her ears warmed.

Why was this bothering her so much?

Terra closed the remaining distance without issue. The winds kicked up, the bridge gently swaying as Valentina took her place, ushered forward with a gentlemanly hand by Dick.

"You okay, Gyles?" Santana called between cupped hands.

Gyles stared at the wooden planks. His focus was set as he took each measured step. He offered a weak thumbs-up, hand momentarily leaving the rope. Another few steps and Santana's heart jumped into her throat.

One of the boards crumbled beneath Gyles' feet. His body sagged as his grasp tightened on the ropes. The sudden lurch took out the next board, and suddenly he was hanging from a white-knuckled grip. He kicked as the splintered board floated down into the ravine.

Santana stepped onto the bridge. A hand gripped her shoulder. Terra dragged her back, holding her in an unexpectedly strong grip. The light glinted off her metal thumb. "Hold on. Look."

Santana couldn't understand how Valentina did it. She was sprinting across the bridge, dancing with the boards as she made her way across to Gyles. Her footwork was nimble and light, the bridge barely reacting to her movements. It was as though she'd become part of the structure, her body and its frame working as one. In seconds, she closed the gap and had Gyles beneath the crooks of his arms.

She pulled him to his feet. His face was ashen. He took an unsteady step, and the board groaned beneath his weight, but his pace picked up, eager to close the remaining distance.

Santana extended her hand, which Gyles gladly accepted. He reached firm ground and fell to his knees, letting out a sigh of relief. Santana crouched by his side. "I thought you were a goner."

"So did I," Gyles replied softly, not wanting to state his truth to the others. He craned his neck to look at Valentina. "Thank you."

Valentina gave a curt nod, then turned her attention to the bridge.

Dick was halfway across, one hand in his jacket pocket, the other holding the rope rail. He took his time, casually strolling to reduce the sway. He smoothly hopped over the gap where the boards had fallen and continued toward the group.

He offered Gyles a weak grin and a pat on the shoulder on his arrival. "It happens to the best of us. Don't take it personally."

Gyles turned his gaze to the ground.

"All present and accounted for?" Dick clapped once. A smattering of birds in the nearby trees took wing.

Santana offered Gyles some water, then turned to the forest. The sky was already darkening, the foggy blues turning to shades of orange and pink with the setting sun. Clouds of insects were emerging from their hiding places, and she knew that she had to find shelter soon if they were to feast in peace.

Santana led the group on, grim determination on her face. She hoped that the worst for that day was over.

CHAPTER NINE

"You haven't seen *Robocop?*" Dick asked Valentina loudly as they strolled through a particularly dense patch of forest.

They'd removed their jackets. Although night was crowning and the temperature was dropping, the humidity in the greenery lingered. Dark patches stained the pits of Dick's shirt, Gyles ran fingers through his damp hair, and even Valentina had doffed her signature jacket.

"No," Valentina replied curtly.

Terra flashed a warning stare at Dick.

Dick continued, undeterred. "It's about a guy who gets taken in from the cops and becomes a robot. Or... No. That's not it, exactly. He works *for* the police, and they test some AI tech shit on him. Turns him half-android. It's pretty badass."

"Why are you telling me this?" Valentina replied.

Dick nodded at Terra.

"I'm not Robocop." Terra focused her attention on the path ahead.

"You're totally Robocop," Dick returned. "You've got the metal thumb and the thing in your head."

"APRIL," Terra corrected.

"Exactly. APRIL. That Automatic...Police, Really, Intelligent...Lackey."

Terra sighed and swatted at the cloud of bugs surrounding her head. "Advanced Police Relationship Intelligence Liaison."

"Yeah...that."

Gyles, who had been walking a touch behind Terra, looked at her with interest. She caught his gaze and offered a weak smile. "Ask your questions."

Gyles' cheeks flushed, but he collected himself. "Did it hurt?"

Terra offered a nostalgic smile. "Did it hurt to be caught in an explosion and nearly lose my vital functions, only to wake with artificial intelligence and a load of hardware fitted to my body?"

Gyles nodded.

Terra considered this. "At first. I don't know if you've ever been in an explosion, but it does something to your memory. Things get a little hazy. I remember a white light littered with bits of shrapnel. I remember my body feeling as though it was on fire and more pain than I could ever imagine swallowing every part of me until I blacked out."

She drew a long breath, her eyes narrowing as the memory took over. "I remember the fuzzy haze of being operated on and..."

"And?" Gyles pressed.

"I woke up." Terra stepped across a marshy patch of the forest floor. "The pain only lasted so long before APRIL's technologies began to kick in. Imagine having a button on your chest that you can press to activate your adrenaline response. Imagine having a lever you can crank to flood your body with the correct chemicals to numb pain and bring your heart rate down in even the most intense situations."

She gave a weak laugh. "APRIL has saved my life on more occasions than I can count. It's like having an assistant for your body, watching your back, doing all that it can to ensure that you're at your optimum and remain alive."

"Sounds like a dream," Gyles mused.

Terra nodded. "It has its advantages. It also has its disadvantages."

She didn't elaborate further.

"See? *Robocop*," Dick declared.

Valentina's glare matched Terra's. Santana was intent on the way ahead, the only one of them truly paying attention to their journey through the darkening wilds. She spun and laid a finger over her lips.

They halted. When their footsteps faded, only the jungle remained until they heard voices ahead.

Terra drew up beside Santana, eyes narrowing.

"How many?" Santana asked.

Terra concentrated, utilizing APRIL's heat detection to track the bodies. "Seven. What would you like us to do?"

"Hostiles?" Santana nudged.

"Hard to say."

Santana frowned. Her stomach rumbled. Other than this particular set of ruins, there was nothing around for miles that would provide any useful shelter.

"Worth the risk?" Terra asked.

Santana drew a deep breath, then walked ahead.

She reached the edge of the trees. The others remained a few steps behind. From behind the broad shelter of a nearby tree trunk, she watched the group already in the ruins.

A fire roared in the center of the clearing with seven strangers settled on various chunks of broken rock that had crumbled from the outpost tower. The building was wide with a set of stairs leading to the upper platform, but it was impossible from here to tell how safe the ascension would be. The group in question had set up camp for the night with several tents pitched around the fire. The flames cast dancing shadows into the surrounding foliage.

Laughter rang out as a woman tipped her head back and

drained her can. She crushed the aluminum in her fist with a triumphant squeeze, then tossed it to the ground. Cheers rang out from her nearby comrades. Only one person on the edge of camp threw a judgmental look their way.

Santana scouted for any particular symbol to identify the group. Often she would come across explorers in the jungle with bold ambitions. Many times she'd crossed paths with groups on the way in, only to find on the way back out that their campsites were tattered shreds or their bodies scattered in the trees.

There was nothing dangerous that she could see, so Santana took her first bold step out of hiding.

At first, no one paid attention to her. After a few more steps, the more observant camper pointed her way and rose to her feet. "Company."

They turned as one, their laughter fading as they spotted Santana and all reached for their weapons. Santana felt her people shift in the darkness behind them and could almost imagine Dick, Valentina, and Terra readying their weapons.

Santana raised her arms placatingly. "Evening, folks."

Quiet settled over the clearing. Santana waited patiently, listening to the gentle buzz of insects and the fire crackling.

A tent unzipped. From inside emerged a surly man with snow-white hair. Time and the mutations of years of scarring had warped his face. His lip peeled up at one corner into a permanent smile. As he rose to his full height—only around as tall as Santana—he cracked his neck. The bones *popped* so loudly that it made the person nearest to him twitch.

"It's a dangerous game to sneak up on strangers in the middle of the wilds," he croaked, his voice hissing like a broken pressurized pipe. "Especially these days. Out here in the wild, no one can hear you scream."

Santana cocked her head and kept her hands where they were. "Not necessarily true. Sound carries pretty far in these regions. I might also add that I never snuck up on you. I announced myself quite clearly upon arrival. How else would you have heard me?"

The man studied her. Santana estimated him to be in his late fifties, maybe early sixties. He wore a khaki tank top and long black combat trousers, and in the flickering firelight, she caught the glimmer of a knife blade.

"What's your name?" he asked.

"Santana Sokolov."

The woman standing nearest to Santana shifted at the sound of her name.

He considered this information. "What's your purpose?"

"Same as yours, I imagine," she stated coolly.

The whisper of a smile appeared on his lips as his eyes narrowed. "If that's the case, we're in competition."

"That depends what you're implying," Santana returned. "I'm a treasure hunter. If you've come across something of value, maybe we're competing. I figure there's enough in this jungle to go around, don't you?"

The woman who'd twitched at Santana's name moved across to the man. She whispered behind her hand into his ear. He nodded, and she returned to her original position.

"The *infamous* Santana Sokolov?" He rested a hand on his knife hilt.

"I prefer *famous*. Depends which stories you've been listening to."

"The ones where you leave a trail of victims in your wake," he stated. "That was you, wasn't it? The woman who single-handedly took down the Order of the Scythe and discovered the lost Temple of the Sun?"

Santana grinned. "It was." She knew that Dick would be seething behind her, desperate to have some credit acknowledged for his part in it all. "Though I believe you've likely fallen victim to propaganda from your employers. I'm no different than you. I only want what I can find. If you keep your secrets, I can keep mine. No one gets hurt."

The man took a step forward with a glint in his eye. "Or you can tell us what you've found and save us days of hunting in this godforsaken place."

Santana lowered her hands. The gunmen tightened their grip. "I don't think you want to do that. The treasure I'm hunting isn't the type that will bring you coin."

"What other treasure is there?" a man blurted nearby.

Santana turned to face him. "None of your business."

The surly man took another step forward, his toned muscles lit by the firelight. "If you want to survive the night, it *is* our business."

Thunder cracked through the forest, the sound enough to make the group flinch. They looked wildly around, their leader drawing his knife as they searched nearby for the source of the monstrous noise.

Santana turned to find Terra had stepped out of the shadows. "Sorry, friends, but it had to happen. You realize that we could've killed you all ages ago, don't you? It's by our choice that you're still alive. Now, lower your weapons so we can talk unless you want to turn this situation into a real blood bath."

Santana took the moment of distraction to draw her pistol. The others looked uneasily at each other before the man announced, "Two versus seven? We'd like to see you try."

Valentina dropped out of the tree behind Terra. Her crimson jacket flashed in the moonlight. The mere sight of her caused a few of the others to take a step back, each one looking at their leader for instruction.

"Three," Valentina announced.

Dick stepped out of the shadows. "Four."

Finally, Gyles showed himself. He didn't need to announce his number. Instead, he trained his pistol on the surly man.

"The Red Countess," someone whispered nearby.

Santana smirked.

Even the older man showed a little surprise at the arrival of Valentina Winters. He holstered his blade and held out a hand to his group. "Lower your weapons."

They hesitated.

"I said *lower them.*" The man kept his gaze trained on Valentina as the surrounding group lowered their firearms. He raised his head a little higher. "Your turn."

Santana looked at each of her group in turn. They all slowly lowered their weapons—all except Valentina.

"Val…" Santana warned. After a moment, she lowered her weapon but didn't relax her grip.

The man stood before the fire, flames licking up and stretching to try and reach him. His gaze remained fixed on Valentina. "You've brought the Red Countess into our circle…" There was awe in his voice and wonder in his eyes. "The fabled Red Countess? Or a mimicry of she who has dominated Atlantica for years?"

Dick grinned.

Valentina took a step closer. In a flash, she shot at the man. The others in the circle all reacted and took up their weapons. The man remained still, his grimace spreading to a grin. At his side, the bullet had sliced through the thin fabric of his shirt.

He glanced down and peeled the fabric apart. There was no mark on his skin, no blemish or wound from the bullet's passing.

"You want to ask me that again?" Valentina asked.

The man beamed, then clapped. "Now it's a feast. Gentlemen, ladies, get out our finest food for our guests. Tonight we dine with royalty."

It all happened so quickly that Santana couldn't keep track. Several people ushered them into the camp as the group busied themselves with finding places for the others to sit. The older man sat on a wooden crate, inviting Valentina to sit beside him. The fire was warm, and soon the clearing was filled with the scent of cooked meats as chunks of the pig they'd hunted cooked on a makeshift spit suspended over the fire. Pairs of people took turns rotating it periodically.

Santana took her seat near the fire and allowed the others to make a fuss of them, trying to understand the situation better. Dick sat beside her.

"They must love Val's work." He accepted a wooden goblet of something that smelled like mead.

Santana declined hers, watching the scarred man and Valentina closely. "It seems so." She drew a long breath. "So why don't I trust it?"

Dick chuckled. "Because you're smart."

CHAPTER TEN

The pig tasted delicious.

They sat around the fire under the general murmur of chatter. Santana remained beside Dick as the pair tucked into their food. Gyles and Terra took a crate nearby, and the other campers scattered around the old outpost. Although merriment grew with each glass of mead, Santana stayed sober, ensuring that she could keep an eye on what was happening around her. One lesson she learned very early on in life was never to trust anyone she met out in the wild.

"Loosen up a little," Dick muttered after swallowing the last of his pork. "You're so tense I could snap you with a poke."

Santana shook her head. "You can get merry all you like. I know you've made a career off remaining permanently tipsy, but I'm happy as I am."

"You might learn something from these guys." He looked around at the smiling faces and basked in the laughter. "When was the last time you truly relaxed?"

"2015," Santana replied dryly.

Dick chuckled.

"You said it yourself," Santana continued. "We can't trust them."

"Doesn't mean we have to be so tense. We can have some fun before the shooting starts." He closed his mouth as another explorer passed close by. When they were gone, he added, "*If* the shooting starts. For all we know, they might be okay. We'll only know when we know."

Santana swallowed her mouthful. "Is that how you've always lived your life? So lackadaisical like this? Isn't there anything that means anything to you?"

"Not since my parents passed."

Santana dropped her gaze. "I'm sorry."

"Don't be." Dick gently waved it off. "Couldn't be helped. Just the way life goes sometimes, don't you think?"

Santana nodded thoughtfully. "Sometimes it feels as though both my parents have died." She met Dick's gaze. "My mother... she was the driver of the marriage. She was my rock. My role model. My everything.

"When she passed... It was like something died within my father, too. He was never the same without her—isn't the same. He spends his days either working or sitting on the back porch and watching the stars. If there's a fire to light in him again, I can't find it. I don't know that anything ever will."

Dick watched Valentina. The woman's posture remained prim, her interest in the older man's conversation minimal despite his best efforts. "I'm sorry to hear that. It can't be easy for you."

"It hasn't been," Santana admitted, surprised by her confession. "I suppose that's why this mission matters so much to me. It's nice to know that although we can't bring back our own, we can help another retrieve someone they love. If there's even a tiny chance that Valentina can get her brother back, it's all worth it."

"What if we can't?" Dick played Devil's advocate.

"Then we continue with life," Santana replied. "What else is there?"

Dick sat back, leaning on his hands for support. When another camper offered him more drink, he declined. "What *are* you doing it all for, Sokolov? Why the risk and the adventure and the endless battling with death?"

Santana considered this. Although the question often danced in her head, she never fully let an answer form. Now, though, under the heady heat of the fire and the canopy of stars attempting to break through the overhead fog, she allowed herself the time.

"Because I want to make a discovery that *matters*." She gave a shy grin. "I want to change the world for the better. To find the thing that can leave a legacy and improve people's lives forever. That's what Mom would've wanted." She turned to Dick, her eyes lingering on a soft pink scar on his cheek. "What about you?"

Dick shrugged. "No idea. For coin and glory, isn't that what the pirates used to say?" He laughed at his joke, then looked down at his knees, oddly bashful. "As you say, what else is there? I want to make a difference, and I do that the only way I know how. By trying to scrub the stains off the back of the toilet while Atlantica repeatedly keeps topping them up."

Santana's face curdled. "Eww." She playfully hit Dick's arm.

Dick chuckled. "It's gross, but it's the truth." He frowned. "You're a good kid, Santana. You deserve good things, and I fear for you. I really do. This life..." He motioned a hand to the forest. "...Out on the road forever, living alone, forever facing danger...I just want you to be okay. That's all I'll say on the matter."

Santana felt a mixture of irritation and bashfulness as she turned away from Dick and looked into the fire. When had he ever shown a truly sweet side? When had Dick shown that he cared about someone other than Doug? It was no secret that Dick appreciated the female form—hell, he'd tried with Santana during their first meet, eyeballing her derrière—but she'd never seen anything that transcended lust.

But tonight… It was clear that Dick and Valentina had *something* going on, though she wasn't sure what. Images of the pair of them frolicking in clean sheets filled her mind, visions created by the whites of the dancing flames, and she closed her eyes to shake her head. She couldn't think about that—*wouldn't* think about that, and why it bothered her so much.

Their hosts offered them more drinks, which they both declined. The night progressed with animated chatter. A man and a woman drew Gyles into a conversation. Both seemed very interested in what he had to say.

At some point, Dick rose and wedged between Valentina and the older man, interrupting whatever the man's motives had been and causing Valentina to smirk. Santana sat mostly by herself, listening to snippets of chatter, most of the explorers talking about highlights of Valentina's career and headlines they'd seen in the paper.

A while into the night, the chatter slowly died. The group of seven handed drinks around the campfire at the scarred man's insistence—Santana overhead the name "Malcolm"—and when silence fell, he stood and raised a toast. "To our esteemed guests. Who would've ever imagined that a night out in the beautiful tropics would yield us such royalty in our presence?" He turned to Valentina and rested a hand on her shoulder. "To the Red Countess and her associates."

Dick and Santana exchanged a look, both smirking. Terra rolled her eyes. Gyles was pretty merry by this point and giggled behind his hand.

The group drained their drink in one go. There was only a little of the liquid that tasted something like a mix between *sake* and tequila.

Activity died down shortly after that. Santana overheard Valentina decline to sleep in the same tent with Malcolm, choosing to rest on top of the outpost. Santana gathered her things to join her, and soon the five of them were aloft.

Santana set up her bedroll, then stood by the wall and looked out at the jungle. Tiredness was overcoming her, and the tops of the trees soon fuzzed in her vision. She felt Dick standing behind her with a hand on her shoulder. She cast a goofy grin, closed her eyes, then all went black before her body hit the floor.

Santana's body awoke before her mind did.

She coughed, spluttering into the open air, then groaned, her throat raw and painful. Her eyes flickered, her mind expecting to see the open sky, but reams of thick, black smoke swallowed her instead.

She sat up sharply, her head swimming. An acute pain flared on the back of her head and as she touched the pain source, she felt the tacky blood in her hair. Her alarm rose as the sounds of gunshots rang out around her.

She stood, wobbling slightly on her feet. She couldn't make out anyone else around her, only the shouts and shots from down below.

She drew her whip, heading for the place she knew the stairs to be, but there was no use going down. She couldn't see anything, and overwhelming heat rose to meet her.

"Santana!" Gyles called.

Santana tried to blink away the dizziness as she rushed toward the sound. One hand held her head, the other the whip, waving its coils in front of her as she searched for him.

She found him leaning awkwardly against the wall, looking as though he was about to drop the long distance to his doom. She pulled him straight and hooked an arm around his neck—partly to support him, partly for her support.

"What's going on?" Santana asked.

"Fire," was all he could manage.

Santana leaned over the wall and dimly made out the campfire's dying embers. Malcolm's group had packed, and all that remained was the disturbed mud and a couple of stray bones from the pig. There was movement, though. A flash of electric blue stalked across the clearing, leading the way with her rifle in her hands.

"Terra!" Santana called.

Terra either didn't hear her or chose to ignore her. Something *pinged* off the wall, and then Santana spotted a few of the campers who'd kept them company that night scattered through the trees.

"Fuck." Santana's head pounded as she crouched. "Gyles, are you okay?"

Gyles nodded. "They blocked us in with fire," he gasped, speaking so slowly it was almost painful. "Terra...she tried to wake you, but..."

"They drugged us," Santana replied. "Why didn't that affect Terra?"

Gyles continued as if she hadn't asked. "Terra and Val...they... they jumped. Gave chase..."

Santana tried to imagine it, a flash of red and blue, the colors of the AJS, as the two women leaped boldly down and pursued the group on foot. Between them, they could handle the situation...couldn't they?

"What about John?" Santana suddenly noticed the missing member of their party.

Gyles didn't reply, only looked into the billowing smoke where a pair of legs were sticking out from someone lying down.

"Shit..." Santana muttered, easing Gyles out of her hold as she ran for the figure.

She waved off the endless fountain of smoke, but it did nothing to help her see. She grabbed the legs and pulled them away from the streaming black and found Dick unconscious.

"Shit." She coughed into her fist as she dropped to her knees. She placed her head on his chest, searching for a heartbeat.

There was nothing.

"Oh, God…" she moaned as she leaned toward his face. She pursed her lips and pressed them to his, breathing lungfuls of tainted air into him.

Dick's chest inflated. She pumped his ribcage, using the technique her mother had taught her years ago, only hoping that she remembered how to do it properly. After a few presses, she returned to his lips and blew again.

Gyles stood helplessly behind as gunshots rang out from below them.

"Come on…" Santana encouraged. She closed her eyes and placed her lips on his, cheeks puffing as she prepared to blow.

Dick's lips moved against hers, his tongue seeking her mouth. His hand cupped the back of her head and brought her closer to him. Caught in the shock of it all, Santana froze. Dick's tongue found hers.

"Get off me!" She declared at last, shoving herself away from Dick and resting with her back to the wall. She wiped her lips with the back of her sleeve as Dick coughed and raised himself to a seated position.

"You're not too bad, actually…" Dick mused, blinking the sting away from his eyes as he took in the surrounding smoke. "What the hell is going on?"

He clutched his chest, wheezing as he moved toward Santana. They both rose to their feet, the three of them now looking out at the jungle.

Santana scoured the area for the enemy but found none. Instead, she saw the flashes of red and blue as two figures hovered around the outpost's entrance, dragging sodden canvases with them.

Santana coughed. Her eyes stung. Her cheeks were warm, and

her lips were sore from the smoke, though the ghost of Dick's kiss hovered in her memory.

She glanced at him. He turned to her. Neither said a word as Santana vaulted over the outpost wall and scaled down the tower. She wanted to help the others quell the flames faster and to put as much distance between herself and Dick Chambers as she could.

For a short while, anyway.

CHAPTER ELEVEN

With the last flames extinguished, the three women turned their attention to helping the two men down from the outpost.

The majority of the staircase was intact, the stone scorched but holding its integrity. Although a few wooden support structures had perished, they were able to ease to the ground with little bother.

Both Dick and Gyles looked the worse for wear as they joined the others. Ash smudged grayness on their faces and covered their clothes. Dick's cough sounded awful, and Gyles struggled to keep his eyes open.

"Thank you," Dick offered to the women, eyes lingering on Santana's.

She looked away.

"What the hell was all that?" Gyles asked. "I thought they'd taken us in? I thought they were friendly."

"Lesson number one of the jungle," Santana stated. "There are no friends in the jungle."

Valentina adjusted her belt and double-checked her weapons were in place. "Those fuckers tried to drug us. Get us into a false sense of security before leaving us to burn." She shook her head.

"I read it in Malcolm from the start. Didn't trust that mother-fucker as far as I could throw him."

"Sure seemed that way last night," Dick commented.

Valentina glared at him. "We play the games we need to. Clearly, I've upset someone in his past, and he was trying to exact some kind of revenge."

"Oh yeah, make it all about you," Terra replied.

"How come you two weren't out for the count?" Gyles asked.

Santana turned to face them both, her attention caught. How *had* they not been put under the influence?

Terra shrugged. "I can't speak for Val, but APRIL took care of me. It detected the substance in my bloodstream the moment it started taking effect and altering my mental state. I passed out with the rest of you, albeit only briefly while APRIL worked with my biochemistry to fix the issue. When I woke up, the fires had already begun. I opened my eyes and found Val lying next to me, staring at me. I'm not sure how."

Val slid her arms into her jacket. "I didn't drink the toxin. Simple. I don't drink or eat anything given to me by strangers.

"When I saw what was happening with the rest of you, I emulated it. I trusted that Terra's circuitry would fix her condition and awaited my time. The moment she was activated, we leaped into action." She grinned. "It was easy, chasing them down and hunting them like the animals they are."

Santana's gaze flickered to a body half-in, half-out of the nearby foliage. Blood painted the ground.

"Well, thank you." Santana echoed Dick's sentiment. "I only wish we could've helped you more when it happened."

Terra replied, "We had it handled. You didn't need to worry."

"Still…" Santana added before glancing over her shoulder. The sky was still dark, though dawn was somewhere on the horizon. Her head was throbbing, but they had once again wasted more time than she liked. "We should probably get going again.

There's still at least another full day's hike before we get anywhere near our location."

"About that," Dick commented. "Where exactly *are* we going? Everything around here looks the damn same to me."

Santana adjusted her backpack. "The Giant's Heel. It's a bowl near the center of the jungle surrounded by the peaks of idle volcanoes. If Taylor's coordinates are correct, and I have no reason to believe they're not, we should find an indication of Archie and his operation there." She met Valentina's hard gaze.

"Beneath volcanoes? That's very Dr. Evil, don't you think?" Terra quipped.

"What can I say?" Santana replied. "There's little creativity among the morally corrupt and absurdly rich moguls of this land."

They left the outpost and its scorched earth behind. Santana steered the group toward a nearby lake hidden by the trees, but which had served as a valuable water source for Terra and Valentina when they needed to choke the flames. Dick, Gyles, and Santana washed the worst of the ash and dirt from their bodies. Dick went so far as to duck his head under the water as he aggressively scrubbed his face.

Satisfied, although not entirely "clean," they strode on, following Santana's direction as she guided them toward a steadily rising peak. The mountain rose into the fog, disappearing way up into the clouds. Occasionally Santana had to scale a tree to double-check they were on the right path, and the going was slow.

Conversation picked up as they walked. Gyles and Terra fell into deep discussion, Gyles quizzing Terra about her past and the APRIL technology and Terra gladly telling as much as she was able. Valentina and Dick once again stepped in line together, although their conversation was minimal.

Santana took the solo role ahead of the group.

By lunchtime, the heat had risen, and once again the group

removed their jackets. They occasionally swatted at bare skin, repelling the bugs until Santana handed around a spray that kept the worst of them at bay.

They climbed ever upward, passing rubble and debris that indicated activity from the Nazi occupation almost one hundred years prior. Santana offered tidbits of information to those who would listen, and when they reached one particular outpost, she took them inside for a short break from the trek and to enable them to cool down out of the growing heat.

The Nazis had constructed the outpost from large gray stone blocks. There were multiple rooms, although the wooden roofs had caved in long ago. Even now there were skeletal remains of former soldiers. Some had small pieces of armor and weaponry that had yet to be scavenged and taken back to the city.

"They never worked out what happened," Santana explained, meeting Gyles' eye as he stared at a nearby corpse with discomfort. "They were some of the first in modern times to stumble across the island of Atlantica—a legend of an island, lost at sea and forever shrouded in this mysterious fog.

"They took the land, explored the jungles, and made themselves at home, using Atlantica as an outpost to prepare for their invasion of America. They were spies, really. Hidden as they were from New York, they could eavesdrop on any signal they could pull in and pass intelligence back to their homeland."

Santana sipped her drink, recalling the details. "Until the US troops intercepted their signals. They sent their forces to the island, and in those years a great battle ensued for the occupation of Atlantica. One day, during a radio transmission picked up off the east coast of the US, something strange happened."

"What?" Gyles asked, enraptured. "What was it?"

Santana chewed on her power bar. Dick and Terra strolled around the room, examining the skeletons. Valentina sat brooding quietly in the corner.

"The radio frequencies picked up a battle." Santana's voice

lowered to a whisper. "Gunshots, cries of pain, shouts, and orders. Fighting had broken out between the US and the Nazis, then…it stopped."

"It stopped?" Gyles asked.

Santana nodded. "One minute the battle was taking place, the next everything went quiet. Reinforcements pulled into the dock on the shores, and they found everyone…well…"

"Dead," Gyles finished. He drew a long breath and pulled his eyes away from the corpse. "There was no sign of what happened?"

"None," Santana confirmed. "There are many theories, of course, but none grounded in hard evidence. The sudden defeat of both sides gave rise to several horror and ghost stories, and many of them put people off entering the jungle.

"Some believe the island is alive, that it harbors some great secret we have no access to. The island stayed hidden for so long, so why did it *want* to hide? Why would it let us occupy it now?" She chuckled. "Ghost stories and fables…"

Gyles, it seemed, remained unconvinced.

They merged into the jungle once more, following where Santana trod. There were no paths anymore, only unstable ground and walls of foliage and detritus. On a few occasions, Santana and Valentina worked together to hack through brambles and clear tangles of vines to make progress.

Animals showed their faces too, curious and drawn to the disturbance in their homes. Snakes uncoiled from the upper branches, mice and marsupials skittered around their feet. At one point, they stumbled upon a small clearing that held a lake turned green with algae. A dozen red-skinned elephants gathered around the hole, bathing each other and spraying the water into the air.

Progress was slower than Santana liked. The constant upward gradient sapped their energy, and by mid-afternoon, Santana lost a little of her internal navigation.

"Wait here," she commanded, already moving to a nearby tree. She scaled up to the canopy and stuck her head above the leaves.

All was green as far as the eye could see. Any trace of the city was gone, and only the jungle remained. Santana shaded her eyes with a flat hand and scanned the surroundings.

The mountain rose ahead of them. They were at least a third of the way up. From here, she could see what she was after, a break in the green where the gray rock jutted out and rose at a severe angle. They would have to scale this to skirt the narrower neck of the mountain and save themselves hours in the process. She wondered how the others might take the climb.

A little to the left of the wall was a break in the trees where Santana could make out the mist of a waterfall. She grinned, and as she slid back down to the ground, it was with a lighter foot and a brighter face.

"We still on track?" Dick asked.

"We are," Santana replied. "A little way up ahead, we'll find a river. Follow that, and it'll help us get around the other side of the mountain."

"You're sure we couldn't have flown all this distance?" Dick sounded antagonistic.

"Where would we have landed, dumbass?" Terra shot back. "The place is trees, cliffs, and pools as far as the eye can see."

Santana rolled her eyes.

Dick continued, glad to be pulled into the dispute. "You're telling me that in this, the year 2027, given the advances in technology on this island—the technology that exists in *your* head—we still haven't invented something that could've carried us into the jungle? No hoverbike or personal chopper that could've helped? We couldn't have chartered a flight over the jungle and parachuted out?"

Santana spun with a rebuttal. "John, you know as well as we do that wouldn't work. The island... Well, the jungle in particular, it distorts signals. Planes and helicopters can't map the damn space because of the Bermuda effect."

"The Bermuda effect?" Gyles nudged.

Valentina answered. "Takes its name from the Bermuda Triangle. We're in a technological dead-spot. There's a reason your phones aren't working." She raised her chin. "People have tried to fly and drop into the wilds. No one's ever seen them again."

"This is the only way," Santana reiterated. "It'll take even longer to get there if you're going to keep stopping and complaining."

Dick held up his hands. "If you say so, Lara."

Santana glared.

They climbed the mountain, the ground growing less and less stable as mud shifted and debris rolled beneath their soles. After another short distance, they arrived at a break in the trees. The roaring rush of the waterfall met their ears before their eyes. A large pool opened before them, rimmed with overhanging trees that cast the water in strange hues of green mixed with the distant misty blue.

"It's gorgeous," Terra offered. "You don't get this in the city."

"You don't," Santana agreed, stopping by the pool to cup her hand in the cool water. She brought it to her face and lapped greedily.

The others followed suit, taking a moment to refresh themselves. Gyles sat on the bank, tracking a group of lemurs on the far side who were jumping and playing near the trees.

They filled their canteens. While they sat and filled their stomachs on more power bars, as well as some fruit that Santana foraged from a nearby shrub, Santana sat with a length of wood between her legs and a coil of string she retrieved from her bag.

She whittled the ends of the stick, honing them into sharp points. Terra, Gyles, and Dick sat and admired the view while Valentina refused to sit and patrolled the bank around the trees instead. Santana made a notch in the upper part of the stick, then began weaving the string around its edge.

"That's an impressive skill to have," Terra offered. "The bow. You're making a bow, right?"

Santana nodded, her face creasing as she pulled the string tight. "Mom taught me how when I was only seven. We sat near a pool in Northern India, not too dissimilar to this one. She was hunting for a long-lost totem of the Indian gods."

A wry smile crossed her lips. "My first few shots were dire. She asked me to shoot fish in the pool, and every shot missed. When she demonstrated, it was a bullseye every time."

"Your mom sounds like an amazing woman," Dick stated.

"She was," Santana agreed. Her face hardened as she worked on the lower part of the stick.

"Couldn't you make something like that?" Dick asked Terra.

Terra considered this. "Give me some time to practice and maybe."

"You telling me that robo-brain doesn't give you instructions?" he probed. "You can't close your eyes and let the system take over?"

Terra frowned. "I'm not a robot. I'm mostly human, only part machine. That's different. I still have everything human about me."

"Except the heart, eh?" Dick teased.

Terra shoved him. He rocked onto his side and fell into Gyles' lap.

"Hey," Gyles protested.

Santana finished the bow and stood. She plucked the string a few times to test its strength.

"Great," Dick commended. "Now you have a bow and no arrows. That'll be very useful when a predator comes."

A *crack* sounded around the waterfall. The lemurs on the far bank froze, eyes all turning to them. Sand and dirt kicked into the air as Santana's whip left a deep line behind in its wake.

Dick rubbed his knees, his gaze fixed to the groove where Santana had hit. "That was pretty close, Lara."

Another whipcrack sounded. This time Dick recoiled, his hand moving to his knee. There was a tiny tear in his pants around where the knee bent, although no graze marked his skin.

"Less Lara," Santana warned. "Stop dicking around. The arrows will come. I'm getting us ready."

Dick grinned.

"What?" Terra asked. "What about this is funny?"

Dick shrugged. "She almost said my name properly."

Santana raised an eyebrow.

"Stop 'dicking,'" Dick replied. "Come on, Sokolov. Just surrender it. I want to hear my name on your lips."

Santana rolled her eyes and stormed into the forest.

Terra slapped Dick's arm. "You just can't do it, can you?"

"Do what?" Dick asked.

Valentina appeared behind him. "Leave the poor girl alone."

Dick laughed but said no more, choosing to sit quietly and pick up a rock by his feet. He leaned back and skimmed the stone across the water. The lemurs finally retired into the boughs.

Gyles turned and tracked where Santana had gone. A moment later, he quietly rose to his feet and followed her into the brush.

CHAPTER TWELVE

Santana sensed Gyles before he arrived.

She was testing sticks, searching for those that were the straightest to fashion into arrows. She would have a quick hunt around the shores for stones that were jagged and weighted in the right way to work into something deadly, but for now, she wanted space.

It wasn't the same in a group. By herself, Santana could go where she pleased, at her pace, and that would be fine. Out here, responsible for the welfare of four other people—people whose personalities were on supercharge—was a lot. She only hoped for a moment of quiet, a chance to clear her head and prepare herself if they encountered further trouble.

The twig *snaps* and gentle grunts alerted her to Gyles' presence. Although he'd visited the jungle before, he didn't seem to adjust to its obstacles. He swatted at flies, lifted his knees high to escape brambles, and finally stopped a short distance away.

Santana didn't turn to face him. "What do you want?"

"I wanted to check that you're okay." Gyles stood awkwardly, unsure what to do with his hands other than swat. "You seemed...upset."

"I'm fine," Santana replied curtly.

Gyles shifted uncomfortably. "Do you two…"

Santana whirled. Gyles froze.

"Go on," Santana encouraged.

"Do you two have a history?" Gyles asked nervously. "You and Dick?"

Santana scoffed, then returned to her hunt. "I hired him to help me recover my mother's pendant a while back. Our paths have crossed a couple of times, but no. There's no history. He's just a damn good PI with an ego to reflect that."

Gyles nodded, satisfied with her response. "He's a lot to take."

"You're telling me," Santana replied. "What are you doing here, Gyles? You could've waited with the others."

"I know." He moved closer and leaned against a nearby tree. "It's Valentina…she scares the crap out of me."

"Good." Santana had a dozen sticks in her arms that would be useful to craft with. "You'll do well to remain scared. She's intense, and she could kill you before you realized what was going on. That last flash of red you'd see…who could say if it's your blood or her jacket?"

Santana picked up a few more, then turned to Gyles. "Why are you looking at me like that?"

His stare melted away, but in that brief moment of connection, she sensed a feeling of something…romantic? Gyles looked at her the same way many boys had over the years, taking Santana's mind back to the awkward conversations she'd had to have with many guys she'd considered "friends," who, it turned out, only hung with her because they wanted more.

Her stomach twisted into a knot. She could almost swear in the darkness behind Gyles that she could make out the shape of Dick watching her with a mischievous grin.

"Like what?" Gyles protested innocently enough. Santana sidled past him. "Come on. We need to get moving."

Something dropped out of the trees. Gyles gasped in alarm. Santana spun, her whip uncoiled and ready to strike.

Valentina unfolded and stood straight. She was inches from Gyles, staring into his eyes. "She's right. You'll do well to watch your back around me." Without waiting for a reaction from Gyles, she turned to Santana. "How long?"

"You'll have to be more specific."

Valentina's impatience showed on her face. "Sokolov…"

"Another day's hike," Santana replied uncertainly. "If all goes well." She nodded due north. "Once we round this mountain we'll be able to see the bowl. Well, provided the fog is clear enough for that kind of view."

Valentina's lip curled. "Then we march."

Santana indicated the sticks in her grasp.

Valentina added, "You can whittle while we sleep."

"Isn't it 'whistle while you work,'" Gyles commented, instantly regretting it as Valentina snapped her head toward him.

Dick weighed the stone in his hand, thumb rubbing against the flat top. He pulled his arm back, then whipped the rock across the water. It skipped across the surface for eight bounces before losing itself at the base of the falls.

"Why do you do that?" Terra asked softly. She was resting back on her hands, her gaze fixed to the water.

"It relaxes me," Dick replied. "There's something therapeutic about tossing the stones—"

"You know what I mean," Terra interrupted. "She's a sweet girl. She's leading us through this hellscape. You'd do well to cut her some slack."

Dick chewed his lip, then selected another stone. "She's a big girl. She can take it."

"Dick…" Terra turned to face him.

"What?" he shot back.

Terra drew a long breath. "Leave her alone."

Dick met her gaze, finding an intensity in Terra that gave him goosebumps. He wasn't sure if it was simply her look or the blinking light behind her eye, but at that moment, he knew to stop playing around.

Dick sighed. "Don't worry. She's made it very clear that she's not in my league. We're working professionally, promise."

Terra raised her eyebrows.

"Double promise?" he added.

Terra turned back to the shore. "Good. We already have enough shit lying ahead of us without me needing to castrate you in the heart of the jungle."

"You hardly know me," Dick stated.

"I know you better than you think," Terra replied. "I know your sort. I've met plenty of you in my lifetime."

"Yet you won't sleep with me." Dick grinned.

Terra leveled her gaze at Dick. "Precisely." She shifted and narrowed her eyes on the far shore.

"What aren't you telling me?" Dick followed her gaze. The black and white lemurs that had been monitoring the shore were gone. Something silver leaped out of the water and splashed. "What do you see?"

"Something's tracking us," Terra replied. "A pack of...something. It's hard to make out through the trees. Maybe wolves. Maybe something more...feral."

"Great," Dick replied. "Just what we need. Rabies."

"Maybe that's how we'll end up castrating you," Terra teased. "Leave your cock to the dogs."

Dick was about to reply when they heard the others approach through the brush behind them. "Break time's over," Valentina announced. "Let's move."

Santana emerged with the bow strapped over her shoulder. A bundle of sticks poked from the top of her bag. Dick and Terra rose to their feet, Dick's gaze meeting Gyles as he stepped out of the tree line.

There was a warning glare in Gyles' eyes, one that Dick brushed away as he glanced over his shoulder toward where Terra had focused before following the others away from the pool.

A steep path led around the edge of the trees and up toward the top of the falls. It was a narrow track with gray, jagged stone on either side. Spray from the falls had created a thin layer of moss on the top, and the higher they climbed the ragged spine, the more they relied on all four limbs to guide them.

Santana took the lead, confidently striding up the pass and gripping chunks of stone. She'd demanded that Terra take second place so Dick wouldn't spend the whole time staring at her ass and would focus on the task at hand instead. Behind Terra came Valentina, with Gyles and Dick taking the rear.

The climb took them ever higher. Soon they came to a small stone shelf that sat twenty feet from the top. Several brightly colored birds littered the rocky face, but they only paused a moment to take in the breathtaking scenery.

"We should tell Santana," Dick muttered to Terra as she stared below, gaze fixed on one particular spot in the brush.

"She already knows," Terra replied.

Santana inspected the sheer rocky face before them, placing a hand on the holds and testing their integrity. There were many gaps and chunks to place their feet and hands, but that wouldn't make the fall any less treacherous if things went awry.

Santana took her first steps up. She kept her body close to the wall, moving with expert grace. She reached the top, gripped with her fingers, then pulled herself the last distance.

She looked down at the others. Gyles was closest to the wall, looking uncertainly up at her.

"You can do this," Santana replied. "Just be confident."

"Easier said than done," Dick replied, looking as worried as

Gyles.

Gyles placed his hand on a jutting rock, then brought his weight to his climbing foot. The rock crumbled beneath his feet. He fell back, teetering into Terra, who caught him and offered him support.

Valentina waited patiently with her hands in her pockets. Gyles tried again.

This time, he made it a few feet up before he fell. Dick and Terra were ready, moving to catch him while Valentina simply rolled her eyes. She drew her hand from her pocket to reveal a small gun. She aimed up at Santana, who quickly ducked.

A rope trailed from the weapon with a small grappling hook on the end. It reached the top of the trees above and coiled itself around the trunk. Valentina tested the rope with a few tugs, then handed the gun to Gyles. "Grip tightly. Both hands. Press this button."

Gyles did, gasping as the gun pulled toward the grapple, swiftly reeling itself in. He had no choice but to ride the wave as it launched him into the air and cleared the way past Santana until he reached the branches above. He hung for a moment, swaying in the boughs. When he recovered his sensibilities, he found his footing and managed to uncoil the grappling gun.

He tossed it down to Santana. She caught it, then tossed it to Valentina. The Red Countess offered the gun to Dick, who accepted gracefully before quickly rising into the air. While Gyles overshot his mark, Dick released the trigger and landed smoothly beside Santana. By the time he turned to look down, Valentina and Terra were already nearing the top.

"Great to see who the athletes are," Santana offered.

Dick smiled, then handed the gun to Valentina. She put it back in her pocket as Gyles climbed down from the tree.

"You got any more of those?" Dick asked. "If we all had one, we could swing like Tarzan through this place."

Valentina ignored him and walked ahead.

CHAPTER THIRTEEN

Night fell, and with it came an impending sense of dread.

They'd set up camp on the far side of the mountain after finding an outpost that offered an unmatched view of the way ahead. A large stone platform held towers and seats that looked like giants had crafted them. Santana got a fire going and worked on cooking the tapir she'd brought down for their dinner.

Gyles sat dutifully beside her, hugging his knees to his chest. Dick was a short distance away, sitting on a chunk of rock and staring out across the forest. Valentina had disappeared some time ago, though no one knew where—they knew better than to ask.

Terra stood on the edge of the stone platform, studying the horizon. "They look like dragon's teeth," she offered.

Santana nodded. The mountains were dark in the distance, jutting up in large spikes. The way ahead was dense with trees, and once they started the final stretch of their trek, they wouldn't have a better view than this until they were up the mountain and heading for the bowl inside.

"It's worse inside," Santana offered.

"You've been there?" Terra asked.

"Once." Santana prodded the tapir before resuming her grip on the handle and turning it. "It's a desolate place. The volcanoes ringing the area are known to spill and dribble semi-regularly. The lava intermittently trails down the mountainside and kills any foliage that tries to grow in there. The result is black rock, ash, and rubble."

"Shit..." Dick muttered. "Couldn't have warned us about this before we set sail? That we're heading to a fiery bowl that might spell death for us all?"

"Does it matter?" Santana offered. "Our goal is the same."

"Yes, it matters," Dick replied. The cherry of his cigarette glowed red as he inhaled deeply. "We're fucking with fire and smoke. That's different from trees and water."

Gyles looked up at Dick. "You're inhaling smoke right now. You'll be okay. You should be used to it by now."

Dick examined his cigarette with a smile. "Can't argue with that logic."

He glanced back at Santana, then turned his attention to Terra. Something rustled in the nearby brush. She met his gaze, then looked away.

"Anyone know where Val has gone?" Dick asked the group.

"You can't keep quiet, can you?" Terra chuckled.

"Just trying to make conversation," he replied.

Gyles scanned the surrounding darkness. "No idea. Figured it's best not to ask."

"You're right there," Santana replied. "Her business is her own."

"But it's all our business," Dick shot back. "I bet she hates that, too. A person as private as Winters having everyone else involved in her business. Jesus, can you imagine if, after all this, we discover that her brother is...well..."

"Don't say it," Terra shot back.

There was another rustle from the bushes. Santana looked into the shadows, finding the glint of dark eyes watching them.

She glanced at her arrows, then returned her attention to the tapir. The juices from the meat dripped and *hissed* in the fire.

The ground rumbled and shook. A low growl emitted around them as they fought to hold their positions. Their drinks fell over and rolled across the stone platform.

The rumbling lasted a minute before it stopped. The world stilled once more.

"The hell was that?" Dick asked.

Gyles' eyes were wide.

Terra narrowed her eyes. "The volcanoes. Santana, is this something we should worry about?"

Santana shrugged. "Whatever will be, will be."

The others exchanged glances in silence, not comforted by her answer.

They filled their stomachs around the fire, then laid out their bedrolls. There was still no sign of Valentina as Dick took the first lookout and sat by the fire.

Santana closed her eyes and fell into an uneasy sleep. In the darkness, she saw the hungry eyes of a thousand salivating creatures narrowing in on her position. A hundred volcanoes burst into life, spewing ash and lava and rocks into the sky. She was surrounded by black fog, unable to breathe as ash clouds flooded and choked her airways.

Somewhere in the midst of it all, a familiar and maternal voice called her name. She rose and ran toward her mother as the beasts snapped at her heels. Her arms spread before her as she stumbled blindly through the dark. Her arms closed around someone and she embraced them tightly, tears rolling down her cheeks and leaving clean tracks on her grimy face. She eased back, expecting to see her mother...

Dick's eyes bored into hers. Only, they weren't Dick's eyes at all. They glowed a brilliant blue, seemingly made more of rock than water. She gasped, fell back, and the ground opened. She tumbled down into nothingness, the blue glow of those eyes tracking her until they, too, were gone.

Santana woke with a gasp before she hit the ground. Sweat peppered her forehead, and as she peeled herself from the comfort of her bedroll, she heard them, the low growls of closing predators.

The fire was down to its final embers. Dick had handed over lookout responsibility to Gyles, who had fallen asleep and was lying at a strange angle. Gentle snores came from Dick's bedroll, and the only other person awake was Terra.

She knelt with her pistol ready. Santana followed where she was pointing and spotted five shaggy wolves inching toward the group. In the faint moonlight, it was difficult to tell their color. Santana had only seen the Atlantican wolves a few times on her travels. They were smaller than those she'd encountered in Siberia, but she knew they were inclined to be a little more aggressive.

"Easy now..." Santana crooned. "Terra, lower your weapon."

"No," Terra replied.

Santana's jaw clenched. "If we shoot at them, we not only scatter them into a frenzy, we draw the attention of anyone who might be nearby. We're getting too close now to ruin the element of surprise."

The lead wolf, an alpha with a dark silver scar running across its flank, snapped its jaws. It let out a small growl, and Gyles stirred.

"Shit..." he cried, retreating toward the embers and putting his hand near the dying fire. His sudden movements sparked the wolves to stir.

"Hold," Santana ordered, one arm held out toward Gyles. "Keep calm."

"Calm?" Gyles hissed. "They're rabid." He carefully reached for a stick of firewood and nudged it into the embers.

"No, they're not." Santana slowly moved to her feet. The alpha tracked her motions, shifting on his haunches. Santana carefully lowered her hand to her whip and allowed it to unspool on the stone. "Now, now, pooches... Let's not make this difficult."

Meanwhile, Terra had moved over to Dick and was gently rousing him from his sleep. He grunted before rolling over and opening his eyes. While not as dramatic as Gyles, he quickly rose to a sitting position and fumbled for his gun.

"No weapons," Terra hissed.

One of the wolves broke rank and moved toward Dick, its gaze set on the man. The other wolves slowly fanned out, working into a formation Santana hadn't witnessed before.

"Enough." She cracked the whip at the alpha's foot. The wolf yelped, jumped back, and gnashed its fangs. The rest of the pack bristled.

Another *crack* sounded from Santana's whip. "Back!" The wolf recoiled, and the group inched back toward the tree line. She cracked the whip two, then three more times. The wolves almost disappeared into the trees.

"There," Santana announced without turning. "You just need to show them who's boss."

She moved back into the center of the area, closer to the others. Her gaze stayed fixed on the wolves who were already padding back toward them and more spread out than before.

Are there more of them now?

A blood-curdling howl from behind answered her question. They spun, only to find another group of wolves had crept up on them—or was it the same group?

A shaggy shape sprinted out of the trees and darted for Dick. It leaped at him, paws landing on his chest, jaw dripping with saliva as it aimed for his neck.

Thunder *cracked* from Santana's whip. The wolf squealed as the lash knocked it off course.

Dick, Terra, and Gyles were on their feet, back-to-back and aiming their weapons out at the gathering mongrels.

"How set are you on that 'no shooting' rule?" Terra asked.

Santana retreated toward them, working her bow off her shoulder. Another wolf broke rank and ran for them. Terra brought her rifle up and cracked the beast on the skull. The creature skittered into the remaining embers and howled as the heat sizzled its skin.

Dick kicked the next wolf. It spun off-course but soon regained its footing. It sprinted toward the private investigator who kicked again and cracked his firearm down on it.

Santana let rip with her bow, shooting her hand-crafted arrows at the alpha. The beast reared back and darted around the projectiles. She put an arrow in its flank, but it still sprang at her, accompanied by three of its brethren.

She jumped to the side and paused long enough when she landed to nock an arrow and fire at the beasts. She was vaguely aware of her team fighting, but her focus was on the wolves closing in and intelligently separating her from the group so she was alone on the camp's fringes.

Teeth clamped around her boot. Tough jaws broke through the thick material of her shoe. She shook the wolf off, then fired an arrow down its throat.

Enough of this shit.

She reached into her pocket and took out a small glass vial of clear liquid, then swiftly smashed it on the ground between the cluster of disheveled wolves. She grabbed a Zippo lighter, ignited it, then tossed it down into the liquid.

The cries and howls of the wolves were instant and magnified. Fire exploded around them, catching on tufts of fur and spreading rapidly among their kin. Santana stayed near the flames, watching the shaggy beasts sprinting into the forest, taking their trail of embers with them. She hoped the woods were wet enough to withstand the flames. The pack began to thin.

"Oh, sure!" Dick's voice called over the top of the din. "We can't use our firearms, but you can make the wolves howl and squeal as much as you like!"

"I had no choice," Santana retorted. She aimed her bow and arrow at the cluster near the others and fired. She moved closer. Terra resorted to using her rifle and unleashed a spray of shots into the pack. Howls, yowls, and yaps joined in a bitter chorus before their number began to diminish.

Something pulled at Santana's heels. She tried to spin only to find a wolf, almost double the size of the others, with its teeth sunk into her pants. She twisted but couldn't free herself from its grasp as it dragged her back toward the shadows.

An explosion of sound bounced around the clearing. Dick's pistol smoked. The wolf's head vanished in a spray of flesh, its grip releasing. Santana shook herself and ran the remaining distance to the group.

As she passed the rekindled campfire, she took a blazing stick and held it before her. The wolves were thinning, but they still seemed determined to be rewarded with flesh for their efforts. She swung the stick back and forth before her, the after trail leaving blazing auras in her eyes.

"They're not relenting," Gyles stated.

"What the hell are they?" Dick asked.

Santana didn't answer. With her spare hand, she cracked her whip, driving the creatures back once more although they were hesitant to move.

Terra aimed her rifle and unleashed a spray of bullets. The sound was immense. Santana's ears rang when the gunfire stopped.

Only a few wolves remained now. They clung to the shadows, their beetle-black eyes winking in the firelight. Santana stood to her full height and strode toward them, raising her arms high and roaring at the creatures. The technique worked on bears, but she'd never attempted it with wolves. She figured it couldn't hurt to try.

The wolves slinked back. Santana held her flaming torch before her, eyes pinned on the darkness until they'd finally melted away.

A hand rested on her shoulder. Santana flinched, almost burning Dick's face off with the fire on the end of her stick.

"It's okay," Dick offered, hands raised. "They're gone."

"Not entirely," Terra replied. "They're lingering, but they're no longer advancing. That's something."

"Fuck…" Gyles rubbed his shoulder.

"Are you okay?" Santana crossed to investigate.

"Yeah, I'm fine. Just pulled a muscle somewhere."

Fire crackled on the ground where Santana had smashed her bottle. The flames twisted into hues of green and orange, slowly dwindling as they ate up what remained of the concoction.

"You ever encountered them before?" Terra asked.

"No," Santana replied. "Well, not as up close as that. They always keep themselves to themselves."

"What are they?" Dick asked.

"Atlantican wolves," Santana replied. "I don't have another name for them."

"Original," Dick commented.

"Hopefully we can keep them at bay until the morning." Terra glanced around the clearing. "Or, since we're all up, we could move on. Where's Val?"

They all looked around at the jungle, the bags beneath their eyes oddly shadowed in the firelight.

"Who saw her last?" Gyles asked.

They all turned to Dick.

"Why me?" Dick asked. "It could've been any one of us. The minute we got to this place and set up camp she was gone." He shook his head. "I don't know how she does it. She's like a specter. Here one second, gone the next. Like catching water with your bare hands."

"What if she's gone ahead without us?" Gyles offered.

They all went quiet.

"It's a possibility," Dick confirmed. "I mean, she knows where she's heading now. Over toward those volcanoes. She doesn't need us anymore to find them."

Santana had been thinking the same thing, but saying it out loud made her uneasy. "She doesn't know the jungle. She wouldn't just...Would she?"

"It's Val," Dick replied. "You've read about her, right? You've *met* her. She won't stay tied down to anyone or anything. She's in it for her. Gets what she wants then fades into the mist. If she's tired of us and our stop-starting, I don't doubt she's out there by herself alone."

Santana drew a long breath. "That's not a great place to be for a city-bred mercenary."

"Fuck," Terra grunted. "What's the point in us all coming out here with her if she's only going to go off by herself?"

Santana ran her fingers through her hair. The scent of smoke and ash and burned wolf hung in the air. She looked out across the moonlit canopy toward the dark rises in the distance. She could almost swear that she caught a flicker of light on the edge of the mountainside.

A wolf howled in the trees. Their skin involuntarily prickled to gooseflesh.

"Let's move," Santana stated. "We can rest up somewhere safer if we need to."

"What if she comes back?" Gyles asked. "What if we're making a huge assumption?"

"It's Val," Dick replied. "She'll find us if she needs us. Although..." He chuckled. "The day I see that is the day Santana and I hop into bed with each other."

CHAPTER FOURTEEN

Advancing through the jungle at night wasn't ideal, but Santana had to admit that it was beautiful.

Fireflies tracked them, hovering around the group, inspired by the warmth of their sticky flesh. They gathered in mystical clouds in the air, the jungle seeming to guide them on their way toward the volcanoes. On the ground around their feet, they stumbled across fungi that boasted forms of bioluminescence, large domes of fragile mushrooms shining in dim rays of pinks and greens and whites.

Creatures scuttled around them in the dark, some alerted by their presence, others encouraged. Santana knew that visitors to these depths of the jungle were rare, and the creatures who lived here would be bolder than on the fringes of the wilds. Several small shrews crept toward them, taking investigative nibbles at the toes of their shoes.

Snakes lowered themselves toward Santana's flaming torch, though Terra detected them and Santana quickly avoided them. At one point in the thick of it all, they came across a stream trickling through the green, its bank littered with sleeping capybara.

The wolves still followed them, skulking along behind. Terra turned intermittently to check and report the update, much to Dick's chagrin.

"Why are they so determined to eat us?" Gyles asked, casting a glance over his shoulder. "There's plenty of other food sleeping around here."

Santana swept a hand before her, clearing a spider's web from their path. It was larger than a shield, stretching from bough to bough, but there was no spider in sight. "Could be several things. Could be that they haven't tasted human before and they're curious to try. Could be that they *have* tried human before, and they've got a taste for it."

She drew a long breath after spotting several tracks in the mud below her that made her chest drop. "Could be there's a larger predator in this territory that's driving them away from their catch, and their fear and desperation are forcing them to leave familiar ground."

"I don't like that last one," Dick stated. "What kind of creature are we talking here?"

Terra and Santana exchanged a glance.

Dick scoffed. "Fine, keep your secrets. Just know that if whatever it is you're thinking of finds us, they'll be staring into the barrel of my trusty gun. I wonder how they'd like being animal pate, splattered across the jungle."

The ground slowly declined, which Santana was thankful for after all that climbing the previous day. Their pace increased. Every half an hour or so, Santana would scale a nearby tree to check their trajectory toward the volcanoes. Excitement prickled her flesh, despite the dangers that surrounded them.

Although she'd gone deep into the wilds before, this area was new to her, and adrenaline heightened her senses. While the others trudged along behind, her eyes were wide, drinking in the creatures and foliage as the sun rose, covering the fog and the canopy in a blanket of glittering gold.

When they stumbled across another outpost, Santana ran

ahead, keen to be the first to investigate it. Surprisingly this building was almost whole. The outposts around the jungle's edges had been tampered with and explored to within an inch of their lives, but this one appeared fresh—maintained.

There were a few shelters made from stone, the only signs of degradation in tiny rotten holes in the boards in the ceiling. Santana examined each building in turn while the others sat on surrounding rocks, quenched their thirst, and rested their weary legs.

Santana saved the largest shelter until last. A wooden door swung open easily to her touch. Inside was dark but with less dust and moss than she'd witnessed in other outposts. Most surprising was the passage at the back leading to a set of stairs down into the ground.

She made her way to the entrance and waved the others inside. Her torch had died some time ago, so now she flashed her cell phone's flashlight ahead of her.

"A random staircase leading down into the ground?" Dick stated. "Seems safe."

Terra smirked.

Gyles stepped to Santana's side and peered into the dark. "What do you think's down there?"

"Only one way to find out," Santana replied.

"Shouldn't we stay focused on...y'know...heading toward the place we want to get to?" Dick asked.

Santana knew that Dick was right, but she couldn't help herself. Curiosity pulled her forward as excitement broiled in her gut. What if they were to discover something that changed the course of history? What if they found a secret passage toward some unknown treasure trove? What if *this* was the way down to Archie and the others?

She knew the last one was highly unlikely, but the voices still called her forward.

She started down the stairs, once again surprised by how

well-maintained this area was. The bricks in the stairway were mostly free from grime and dirt, absent even of spiders and insects. As they made their way down, a faint smell of something familiar met her nose—the scent of cooked meat.

A room opened before them. It was modest, around the size of Santana's apartment, though colder and bare to the bone. The temperature dropped several degrees now that they were away from the jungle's humidity. In the center of the room was an abandoned makeshift fire and spit, the floor blackened and charred from its recent use.

Santana knelt and examined the remnants of the fire. She slid a finger across the ash, brought it to her nose, and sniffed.

"It's pretty fresh," Santana stated.

Dick took a step closer and ran his finger through the black ash. He rubbed his fingers together, mimicking Santana's moves. "Yeah. Pretty fresh," he confirmed.

"What does that mean?" Gyles replied. "How fresh are we talking?"

Santana stood straight, looking back toward the staircase. Light filtered down from the top. "I'd say whoever was here must have left here about two days ago," Santana stated. "They seem to be pretty nimble with their fingers and handy with the craft. This isn't a shoddy fire for someone who's surviving in the jungle alone."

Terra scratched the back of her neck. "Maybe it was Valentina."

Dick looked up at Terra. "Sokolov says this was from two days ago. Valentina only went missing last night."

Terra shrugged. "Maybe she keeps going ahead and coming back. Maybe *she's* the one leading the pack, doing Santana's job for her."

Santana smirked. She examined the walls around her, looking for other signs of disturbance or clues about who might've been here. When nothing presented itself, she added, "We might've gotten lucky here and found a safe place to hunker down. Grab some shut-eye. We can barricade the door and keep the wolves out. It will be dark enough down here that sleep shouldn't be any trouble. Hopefully, we catch a few hours before we carry on."

"What about the journey?" Gyles asked. "What about Valentina?"

"We need to recharge," Santana replied. "The worst is ahead of us."

Santana and Dick headed to the doorway to find a way to hold it closed. It was wooden and not all that strong, but Santana had other methods to keep them safe.

Taking a small series of objects from her bag, she placed them in front of the door. "If anyone opens the door, it'll knock them down the stairs," she explained to Dick. "I'm a light sleeper, so this will act as a perfect alarm system for us."

The others climbed into their bedrolls on the hard ground. While Dick set himself up to sleep, Santana sat at the bottom of the stairs, lost in her thoughts.

By the time Dick was situated, the others were snoozing softly. "You okay?" Dick questioned softly.

Santana didn't reply. She felt wired. Her skin still smelled of smoke. Her mind whirled with a thousand thoughts. She wondered about Valentina and whether she was okay out there in the jungle. Although many of Atlantica's residents compared the metropolis to a concrete jungle, it was a city with buildings, walls, and structure.

Out here in the jungle, they were at the mercy of nature. Anything could happen. Santana was no stranger to quicksand, marshy bogs, and the thousands of predatory animals that crawled through its environs. Valentina was self-assured and confident in her abilities. She would no doubt be okay walking through the night in the city, but the jungle was a whole different story.

Not only that, but Santana was holding back the truth about who might've been here. The fire was fresher than the two days she stated. It had been less than twenty-four hours. Although she didn't think it was Valentina, she wondered who else could be lurking around the forest.

Who could survive alone in the jungle out here, living and foraging off fruits and berries and killing for their meat? Who could survive the constant humidity, the parasites, and the insects with their disease-ridden bites?

At the same time, a tiny niggle held her. A glimmer of hope that had never quite extinguished in her heart. They'd never recovered her mother's body, nor the others who'd fallen during the cave-in. Although it had been years since her mother's passing, back when she'd stood in the rain next to her father at her mother's funeral, she never fully had that closure.

Eventually, Dick's snores joined the chorus. Santana glanced back at the doorway, light leaking through the gaps in the wood, then took her place in the farthest corner from the others. She closed her eyes and fell into an uneasy sleep.

When Santana woke, it was to the sound of something rolling down the stairs.

She sat quickly, turning her attention toward the staircase. Terra was already sitting, her gaze fixed to a place that Santana couldn't see. Santana wondered whether she was using APRIL's alternate visions to see who was waiting for them.

Because someone was there.

"Who is it?" Santana asked.

Terra hesitated. "A man, by the looks of his shape."

"Is he by himself?" Santana asked.

Terra nodded. "I believe so. The wolves are out there, too. Holding back in a cluster in the trees. For some reason, they're giving him a wide berth."

Santana gently eased to her feet. Metal *clinked* down the stairs as the door opened another fraction. The light grew up at the top of the chamber.

"Get ready…" Terra stated as another object came down the stairs, this time louder and larger than the others.

Smoke hissed from the chamber of the object, dense smog pluming into the small, cramped space.

"Get up!" Santana shouted, her voice magnified in the small space.

Dick and Gyles woke blearily, pawing at their eyes.

"What the…" Gyles managed before he began spluttering into his fist. The smoke tasted sour, disappearing down their throats. Terra tore ahead, racing up the stairs. She fired several warning shots around the door frame, then burst into the clearing. Santana chased after her, but her legs grew progressively weaker as she climbed. Her chest was tight, and her eyes narrowed as they began to sting.

Behind her, Gyles and Dick fumbled in the smoke. Santana tripped and crashed her knee against the stone steps. She looked up toward the hazy rectangle of light, the door torturously far away before all went dark, and all fell silent.

CHAPTER FIFTEEN

The first thing Santana noted was that her throat was dry, and she was lying on a cloud.

She couldn't shake the grogginess. Her eyelids fluttered as her lips smacked dryly together. Someone spoke to her, their voices lost and muddled as cool liquid trickled onto her lips. Her tongue came out, lapping the water greedily, its chill soothing in her throat.

Blurry shapes moved in the darkness overhead as though they were on the other side of a foggy lake. She tried to lift her head but found that she couldn't. Somewhere nearby she could swear she heard a monkey chatter.

She rested, allowing her mind to race with colors and visions, waiting for the worst of it to pass.

She didn't know how long she lay there. She came to in fits and starts, sometimes for seconds, sometimes for minutes. Metal pots clattered together, and at one point she thought she heard laughter. Rain pattered outside, and though the temperature dropped on her left side, her right side was kept warm by a crackling fire.

One eye opened. She could only see brown and then the large dome of a black, featureless face. "Here…" More water trickled down Santana's lips. Strings of cold snaked down her cheek to the back of her neck. A weight pressed on her stomach then was soon dismissed by a quick "Shoo" from the voice's owner.

"It won't be long now," the voice soothed. "I promise."

Santana asked what was going on, but the words stayed in her head. She became aware of a shifting beside her. Dick's cologne reached her, mingled with sweat. Was he here with her? Were they together? Where was Gyles?

She opened her mouth to ask her burning questions, but soon all that came were snores.

"You cannot go there," the voice warned.

A familiar voice replied. "We don't have a choice. It's our destination. We haven't come this far only to come this far."

"It is folly," the voice replied. "You don't know what you face. The ground, it is unstable. The spaces beneath the earth, they are volatile. The mountains are quick to anger, and there's no telling whether you'll live to see the end of your journey. You cannot do this."

"We must," the second voice replied. "To turn back now would mean failure, and that is something we don't do."

Santana's eyelids fluttered. She let out an involuntary cough.

"Santana," the second voice stated.

Santana opened her eyes a crack. Dark hair fell across her face. Terra chuckled and pulled her hair back into its neat pony-tail. For a moment her features were blurred, but after a few more blinks they sharpened. "Terra?"

"In the flesh," Terra stated. "How you feeling?"

"Like someone hit me with a dump truck." Santana struggled to sit up. Terra placed a hand behind her back to lever her into position. "Where the hell are we?"

They were in a log cabin constructed from dark wood. The space was large, with animal skin rugs and throws scattered around the room. Windows were set in three walls with no glass to keep out the winds, but in the center of the room, a fire burned merrily, kicking out waves of heat. Santana had never seen something so rustic, so homely, so...

Natural.

Terra sat by Santana's bedside. She laid a hand on her knee. "It's okay, Santana. We're safe. We're out of harm's reach."

"The smoke." Santana's memories flooded back. Pain prickled in her knee as her mind reminded her of her fall. "We were...he was..." She scanned the room and found the man hunched by the fire. A leg of some creature roasted on a stick. A long white and gray beard coiled down to his stomach. "You..."

"Hardly the merriest of introductions, was it?" the man offered.

Santana pulsed with rage. She wanted to climb off the bed, run over to him, and sock him in the jaw. She wanted to pound her fists against him until he passed out and make him feel the pain he'd caused her, the confusion and anguish.

Instead, she teetered off the bed and fell toward the floor. Terra caught her smoothly and helped her back. "Santana, this is Connor Hardymont. He's on our side."

"Funny way of showing it." Santana scowled.

Connor lowered his head. "I admit it wasn't the brightest of welcomes, but you have to understand that...living in these parts of the forest...you have to prepare for the worst. Adventurers come through here, sometimes bad people with guns and bands around their arms. You have to shoot first and ask questions later." He glared at Terra. "Unlike your friend here."

Terra smirked. "We've been over this. You forgave me."

"Forgiveness is earned."

Santana looked between the pair, utterly perplexed. Terra was talking to this man as though they'd known each other their whole life. Santana was the third wheel, eavesdropping on the banter between the pair.

"Terra…" Santana grumbled. "Mind explaining what the fuck is going on?"

Terra helped Santana to her feet. Her knees were weak, and her legs buckled several times before she managed to sit on a spare stump around the fire. Outside the windows, all was green.

"Connor found us," Terra started. "He attacked us because he was under the impression that we were looking for him, wanting to bring him back to the city."

"Not quite," Connor interjected, taking over. "Once more, I'm terribly sorry about our introduction, but I couldn't have it any other way." He drew a long breath.

"Living in these parts of the forest, danger looms around every corner. Initially, I was tracking the movements of the wolves, trying to work out if the appearance of a new predator had driven them out of their territorial zones. It seemed that they'd taken an interest in a group traveling our way, so I came to investigate."

"He watched us heading into the shelter," Terra reported. "I didn't pick him up because I was concentrating on the wolves and—admittedly—I was fascinated by the outpost we found."

"So why the hell did you gas us?" Santana pressed.

"I thought it was better to be safe than sorry." Connor's dark eyes glittered. He scratched his beard with his free hand. "You didn't seem like the other types to come through here, and once I caught sight of your friend in the AJS uniform, I figured I had to find out more. I never wanted to scare or hurt you. I only wanted to disarm you so you couldn't do any damage to me when I introduced myself."

"How were you going to do that?" Santana asked. "Set up

traps, loop us by the legs, then interrogate us when we were hanging upside down?"

"If that's what it took." Connor's answer held no hint of sarcasm or irony.

"Fuck," Santana whispered.

"He's a good guy," Terra stated. "When he threw the smoke grenade down the stairs, I activated APRIL immediately and got to work fixing my biochemistry. I stormed out into the open, shooting around his feet, and spooked him so much that he dropped his firearms."

"She pinned me," Connor stated, as fondly as though he recalled a practical joke from high school. "She held me to the ground and pointed the rifle in my face. I screamed...I hate to admit it. I screamed like a little girl and begged for mercy."

"I've spent a lot of time around people," Terra replied. "I've pinned criminals, trapped convicts, and I know fear from malice. I got him to talk, to tell me what the fuck was going on. For a short while, my body battled with the toxins from the gas, but I managed to keep alert."

"Tell her about the wolves," Connor nudged proudly.

Terra shook her head. "He's trained the wolves."

"Only to my command," Connor added. "They're feral with everyone else. I spent a few months back feeding them and getting them familiar with my scent. I sent them away when they wouldn't leave you alone."

"I thought you wanted me to tell it?" Terra smirked.

"Sorry, go on."

"All of that to say that we're safe right now," Terra repeated. "We have a warm bed and a stock of new provisions. Dick and Gyles were affected the most by the gas—well, they were in it for the longest—but Connor reckons they'll come around in a couple of hours at least." She flashed a warning glare to Connor. "Right?"

"Absolutely." He chomped into his meat and chewed greedily.

Santana looked between the pair, her tired mind struggling to grasp the situation. "Can we rewind a bit?"

"Sure," Connor mumbled through his food.

"Who the fuck *are* you?" Santana asked.

Connor laughed, almost choking as his food slipped down his throat. There was a grunt from behind, and Terra rose quickly, moving to Dick's bedside. Santana looked behind her, finding Dick coughing and attempting to sit up. Gyles stirred beside him.

"Maybe we can hold this one until your friends are more with it," Connor suggested. "That way I only have to tell the tale once more."

Terra provided Dick with some water. He drank greedily, and Terra soon disappeared out the only other door in the place to get more. She returned with two glasses, gave one to Dick who could sit up by himself now, and the other to Gyles.

They roused slowly. Connor offered Santana food, which she reluctantly accepted. Despite herself, she enjoyed the meat immensely. It wasn't something that she'd tasted before, the strips melting on her tongue and sliding easily down her throat.

Her eyelids were heavy, and a dreamy haze took over her mind as the fire kicked out heat. Connor prodded the flames, keeping them going as the others slowly gathered around. Although Dick was a man of many words, he kept them to himself now, eyeing Connor uneasily as he accepted a seat on a leopard-skin rug on the floor. He rested back against hand-stitched cushions, then ate his share of the food.

When Terra finally guided Gyles to the fire, she returned to her seat and relaxed. She cupped a clay pot in her hands and drank from the steaming contents. "Over to you, Connor."

Connor acknowledged Terra with a nod. "I'm sorry that we met under such negative circumstances," he announced, sweeping his gaze across the room. "Truly. Had I known your mission or your character, things would've been vastly different." He drew a long breath.

"I've been living in the jungle for many years now. Surviving and thriving off what nature has to offer. For the last...six years, perhaps...I've rooted myself in this position, within observation distance of the Covenrane Peaks—the series of volcanoes in which you four were heading—using them as my primary marker. Over the years, they've been a source of mystery, murder, and woe, and for good reason. Although mostly inactive, their sporadic eruptions have taken down large chunks of the surrounding jungle and left ash in their wake."

Connor cast his gaze into the flames, memory swimming in his eyes.

"What brought you out here?" Santana asked. "What were you looking for?"

"In the beginning, it was only cartography," Connor explained. "My employer sent our expedition team out here to chart the wilds and create some semblance of a working map so the big-wigs in the inner cities could work out how to loot, pillage, and rape the jungle for its resources. My employer was specifically interested in Atlanticore fragments, more so when she heard of the shortage of the energy source and its rising prices for buyers.

"We made great progress, charting a wide swath from here to the city," Connor continued. "There were issues, of course, dealing with the Atlantican wildlife and on more than one occasion, as much as we tried to stay on track, we got lost."

"How many of you were there?" Dick asked.

"Twelve, at the start." A wry smile appeared. "We were a merry band of adventures, a real cauldron of personalities. It was exciting—brilliant at the start—but as the months wore on, patience waned and the jungle took its toll." He prodded the fire, avoiding the gaze of the others. "We lost two only three months in. Animal attack. A cat of some kind that we hadn't encountered before, nor were we prepared. By the time we put bullets in its head, they were beyond medical help." He nodded to Dick. "That very same cat you're now sitting on."

Dick glanced down at the animal skin.

"A month later, greed took another four of our number," Connor informed them. "We stumbled across a pocket of Atlanti-core, and before the night was through, they'd taken off as a group and left us out here to perish. They tried to block us into the mine, but we managed to carve our way out—though it took us days and in that final stretch of tunneling, another one of us died from malnourishment."

"Sounds awful," Gyles stated.

Connor nodded sadly. "It was." He rose from his seat, then grabbed a large bottle from across the room. Again it appeared to be made of some kind of clay with little decoration. He filled a cup with something that smelled both sweet and sour before draining it in one gulp.

"Suffice to say that we tried to work our way back home. There were five of us left, and as hunger and desperation took us, we turned on each other. Things grew tense. Nights passed, and anger rose. Before long, Denny and Francine darted off into the night. A few days later, Harvey brushed against some toxic plant for which we had no remedy."

"Then there were two," Terra muttered. Santana wasn't sure if she'd spoken with Connor about this, but the tale enthralled her.

"Then there were two." Connor sighed. "Samuel Rathborne was his name. He was my closest pal going into this ordeal and the one I was thankful to be stuck with in the jungle.

"The others had taken the maps with them, and other than guiding ourselves with the sun's hazy orb, we were lost. We'd depleted our resources. We spent days trawling through the jungle, keeping predators at bay with nothing but a hunting knife. We found ways to clean water to drink and learned the berries that we could rely on for safe consumption."

Connor chuckled. "They were the roughest days of my life,

but they were some of the fondest. For days we wandered in circles, the jungle leading us ever farther into its belly. At first, I thought we were making progress back home, until one night when we consumed the last of our mead, and in a dizzying headspace Samuel confessed something that I couldn't believe."

Gyles sat forward, his interest piqued, although he had to fight to keep his eyes open.

"He told me of a rumor he'd heard in the city," Connor informed them. "Of the island's discovery and a secret power beneath the earth. He spoke of finding the Atlanticore fragments and the lost source of the treasure." A nostalgic smile curved his lips. "He spoke of a secret cave, bedecked in Atlanticore and containing the remnants of a lost civilization, more advanced than any to have walked the Earth..."

"Atlantis," Santana finished for him, unable to hold back.

She'd heard of the lost city of Atlantis before, on many occasions. Not simply because of the movies and books produced that showcased athletic protagonists discovering the lost city beneath the ocean and resurfacing its secrets. In her line of work, Atlantis was a kind of Mecca, a hidden jewel that all explorers who graced Atlantica's shores hunted.

"Nothing more than a myth," her father had stated, dismissively waving as they camped around the fire one night in Siberia, the sky a canvas of glitter and ink above. "Bullshit, the lot of it."

"Enough of that language," Santana's mother had admonished. "You know better than I do that myth is born from truth. In every story, there's a grain of something real that began it all, even if hyperbole took over." Her mother looked beautiful that night, illuminated by the flames, eyes glazed with wonder.

"Imagine it... Imagine discovering something *that* big. An entire lost civilization beneath the ocean, a culture so advanced that we look as though we're living in the Stone Age."

She turned her gaze to her husband. "They've found energy

sources, y'know? Fragments of an unexplained power in Atlantica. Hunters and adventurers are seeking more, the island over. There's money to be had."

Santana remembered the memory through a glossy haze, too young to appreciate the words fully at the time. That wasn't the last time her mother had brought up the lost city, either. It became something of a mantra before she disappeared on one of her expeditions. Santana would wave her off with a, "Go find something amazing." To which her mother would reply, "I will bring you the lost city."

"Atlantis," Connor confirmed. "It sounded ludicrous at first, and I wondered about his mental state, whether he'd perhaps been worn to the end of his tether, maybe eaten a berry that affected his mental state. Then he produced documents, yellowed, cracked papers from his pockets. He showed me paragraphs penned about the lost city, diagrams, and ancient maps he'd procured from old archives. Take me for a fool, but the evidence was convincing."

He reached across to a woven box and removed the lid. Inside were several papers, which he handed around the group.

Santana relished the feel of the ancient papers in her fingers. The sketchings were faded, but she'd seen many like these in her day. "These aren't forgeries or fakes."

"They're originals from the island's discovery, the first *real* occupation before the Nazi invasion," Connor declared. The others lost themselves in reading the papers before passing them to the next in the circle.

Santana held the map. She recognized the mountain ranges sketched on the borders and some of the key lakes and hillsides nearby. "You've been looking for the lost city?"

Connor nodded. "At first it was Samuel and me. We started work on this cabin, creating a place that could keep us aloft and as safe as possible in a place like this. We had nothing to return to, no real family, and no need for money when we could live off the earth like this. It was exciting. A fresh start. We spent days roaming and hunting for paths and caves and entryways that might take us to the city."

"But you never found it," Terra commented.

Connor shook his head. "We searched. Dear God, we searched." Sadness shadowed his face. "I still search, to this very day. It's around here somewhere. I know it must be. I feel the others must know, too."

Santana finally passed the map on to Dick. "What happened to Samuel?"

A sad smile played on Connor's lips. "I don't know."

"What do you mean you don't know?" Terra asked.

"He vanished," Connor replied. "One night I woke to find him missing. I searched for him in the morning, looking for any evidence of where he might've gone. I thought perhaps he was seeking food or needed to stretch his legs. He'd been having nightmares, and perhaps a walk had helped soothe them away. But he never returned. That was two years ago, now."

"Fuck..." Dick grunted. "All that effort, only to end up here alone."

Connor's eyes glazed over as he stared into the flames.

Santana straightened. The throbbing in her head had increased its intensity. She would need sleep again soon, but there were so many questions unanswered. "You mentioned the others," she commented. "People with bands. Murder, mystery... Who are they?"

Connor looked up at her. "Bad people. They showed up a few weeks ago, causing havoc and drilling and digging and making more noise than I'd heard in some time. I fringed on their activity to investigate, and they almost caught me several times.

"Then they went silent, seeking some hole in the ground. Occasionally I find bodies thrown out into the wild, bullet-riddled and bloody, but I daren't go nearer. I've already almost lost my life more occasions than I care to admit."

Santana and Terra exchanged a glance.

Connor didn't miss this. "You know them, don't you?"

"Maybe," Terra replied.

"Connor, can you take us to them?" Santana asked. "Wherever you saw them last. We need to know where they are."

Connor eyed them curiously. "You've heard my story. Now it's time to tell me yours."

Santana drew in a long breath, her pounding head making her vision blurry. "Soon," she replied softly. "First, I think we could all benefit from another sleep."

Terra offered a smile, but there was an intensity in her eyes that matched the fire growing in Santana's gut as she pictured herself finding Valentina's brother and bringing Archie Fontana to justice.

CHAPTER SIXTEEN

Valentina hated to admit it, but she was a little breathless.

That's what you get for trekking out on your own. You knew this would happen eventually. You just didn't know it would happen so quickly.

She sat in the boughs of the tree, high above the ground. The tree she found was one of the tallest in the surrounding area. Large fruits the size of footballs clustered around her, and the chattering of hornbills filled the air.

She looked out across the jungle, the entire landscape alien to her. A proud woman, she hated to admit the uncomfortable feeling settling in her stomach, but there it was. *This isn't the city anymore.*

Nor was this anywhere near her comfort zone. For the first time since she'd left the others, she began to doubt her decision—a feeling that didn't come often.

At the time, rage had consumed her. She already hated relying on others to complete a task, used to running solo for so long in the city and getting the job done with ease. That was how she built her reputation, as someone who Got. The. Job. Done.

There she was, waiting for weeks for Santana—jungle girl—to

discover the location of Archie Fontana. She still had nightmares of the day he'd slipped her grasp and shot off into the tunnels beneath the jungle. Flashes of visions haunted her as gunshots fired and the flickering eyelids of her brother almost rousing from his coma for the first time in years plagued her mind.

She wanted to—no, *needed* to find him. She understood that the logistics of finding someone in a mostly unexplored jungle were complex, and no one was better suited than Santana and her guys on the ground levels, but things were taking too long. Things needed to get moving.

The stop-start of their trek burned inside her, boiling in her gut. How many times did Dick and Terra and Gyles and Santana *need* to stop? How many times would they get waylaid? Didn't they understand that every second counted? Someone's life was at stake.

*He's fine...*she reassured herself. *They need him alive. They need Kit to survive to show that the AI works. He's patient zero...*

No. Not patient zero...

She shook her head, clearing her thoughts. Her breath was recovering, though judging by the sameness of the landscape ahead she would once more be breathless as she attempted to track through the jungle.

That night, while they took up camp around the fire, had been her last straw. She stood on the fringes of the campfire, watching them mill around and eat and sleep. Wolves had been hunting them all day, and still, that didn't keep them moving forward. Valentina grew impatient, and the only part of her that she was thankful for was, although Terra could see her through the trees —of that she was sure—Terra remained quiet. She *allowed* her to carry on without them.

Great. Look where that got you.

She sought her next landmark, then slipped down the tree. She'd already left several brave creatures in her wake, taking them out with steady dexterity and exploiting the fragility of the creature's necks. As she closed in on the volcano, she found her hands increasingly straying to her pockets where the concoctions rested.

Two small glass vials were her only source of strength and resilience against the second personality that lived inside her.

The closest she'd come to giving into the formula had come after crossing a shallow river. Valentina had taken a moment to rest her legs, closed her eyes, and before she knew it, found the vials in her palm. She hadn't remembered putting them there, but the second voice inside her head justified their reasoning.

Just take one, Isabella Harris commented. *You need it. I need it. I don't want to wake up inside your consciousness in the middle of a jungle. Please. Just do what you need to do to get Kit back, then bring me around...*

Valentina pinched the bridge of her nose and screwed her eyes shut. "No. Not yet. I only have limited stocks of the formula, and I need it for when we finally encounter the others."

You can't risk it, Isabella replied. *What if it's only me out here alone? If I wake up in this body, I'll die within hours. This isn't safe.*

Valentina shook her head, then closed in on the volcano range.

The journey was hard, and each step questioned her decision not to drink the formula. A few hours later she stumbled, passing from trunk to trunk, using them for support. Her brow was slick with sweat, but her dogged determination remained.

She was on the cusp of yielding, feeling Isabella rising in her consciousness as she shrank ever deeper when she heard voices up ahead.

A small distance farther, keeping to the shadows, and she found them in the gloaming forest. Two people—one held a flaming torch, the other cradled a rifle steady across her chest.

Valentina moved as close as she dared, eavesdropping on the pair as they slowly strolled through the jungle.

"...really think they're going to come?" the woman with the

rifle asked. She wore long-sleeved black fatigues with her hair pulled back into a severe bun. "I thought animals were smart. Why would they encroach on territory where we slaughtered their kin?"

"Nature?" The man shrugged. "I don't make the rules. We patrol, scare the fuckers away, then return."

"Did it have to be with you?" The woman scowled.

The man sighed. "I wouldn't have made the pairing, given a choice."

"Assholes," the woman hissed. "They knew what they were doing. Set Audrey up with the man who went off and shagged another woman. Great idea, guys."

The man looked her way. "I'm sorry. How many more times do I have to—"

"Enough to unfuck her, perhaps?" Audrey retorted.

They fell into an uneasy silence. Audrey glanced Valentina's way, but the Red Countess was confident they couldn't see her.

They walked through the forest, following a narrow trail on the ground. Valentina skulked along behind them, not concerned about losing them given the amount of light coming from the torch. The pair started talking again, but Valentina was beyond caring about their domestic dispute. She wanted to know where they were heading.

A short while into her stalking, Valentina felt Isabella resurfacing. She stopped and gritted her teeth, mentally pushing her back down. It was a strange sensation, as though she were being dragged from a pool's shallow end into the deep end, while Isabella did the opposite. She grunted and forced her down, finally managing to clear her head again—for a short while, at least.

She opened her eyes. The light had shrunk. Valentina increased her pace, growing breathless as she closed on the pair.

She stopped at the edge of the trees. They were heading toward a large cave in the side of a rocky cliff. Vines and foliage draped down, covering much of the gray stone with dirt and roots.

The torch lit the inside of the cave. Valentina waited until the light was all but gone. The footsteps, magnified by the stone tunnel's acoustics, echoed long after they were gone from sight.

Now? Isabella asked, surprising Valentina—the only one who could.

Valentina narrowed her eyes as she raised the formula to her lips. She drank the cool, sour liquid. Within seconds, strength coursed through her veins, revitalizing her energy and sharpening her mind.

Isabella shrank from conscious thought.

Valentina stalked ahead.

CHAPTER SEVENTEEN

Santana wasn't sure how long they slept for, but it was still sunny when they awoke.

Terra was stalking around the place, making herself at home. Connor was nowhere to be found, only the remaining bones of his meal indicating that he'd been here and that this was all real.

"How are you feeling?" Terra asked.

"Better," Santana replied. "I feel less like someone has swung a wrecking ball at my head and more like I've had a few too many goes on the merry-go-round."

Terra laughed.

"Where's Connor?" Santana asked.

"He had to jump out," Terra replied. "His daily ritual. He's checking the traps and bringing in provisions. He'll probably climb up soon—or so he tells me."

"Climb up?" Santana asked.

Terra smirked. "See for yourself."

Santana went through the doorway toward the curtain of green. She took one step outside and couldn't believe her eyes.

The house was suspended meters off the ground, high in the trees. Thick boughs formed the foundations, connected by rafts of logs, with lengthy coils of vines binding the whole construction together. The roof was a thatch of twigs and mud, and a few small colonies of birds had made it their home as they stared down curiously at her.

"Hard to believe they made all this themselves," Terra stated.

Santana couldn't agree more. This was a lot of work for two people to accomplish. "You two seem like you're getting along pretty well. Something you want to tell me? Didn't know you had a thing for guys with beards."

Terra rolled her eyes. "I don't fancy him. I'm being friendly until you guys are good enough to trek out again." She leaned closer, speaking in a low whisper. "We need him to find our targets."

"We don't *need* him," Santana retorted, then reconsidered. "Although, it would be nice to have some certainty before diving into the snake's pit. Have you seen anything of Valentina yet?"

Terra frowned. "Nothing. Nothing at all. I figured that if she were still with us, she'd at least have graced our presence by now, but nothing. Not so much as a flash of red."

Santana wobbled gently on her heels. The floor shifted slightly. In the distance came a low rumble.

"She's up early," Santana offered, looking out through the leaves toward the volcanoes—what Connor had called the Covenrane Peaks. A knot formed in her stomach as she wondered how close they'd have to get to the volcano. A little rumble could mean nothing, but it could also mean terrible danger ahead.

Wasn't what they already had facing them a bad enough challenge to face?

Dick and Gyles soon roused from their slumber, strong and rested enough to explore the cabin and get familiar with their settings. Dick took an extra long time peering over the edge of the wooden balcony. "There's no ladder up or down."

Santana craned her head. "You're right."

Dick turned to Terra. "How the hell did you carry three unconscious bodies and lift them into the trees with you?"

Terra tapped her nose. "Secrets."

"Bullshit," Dick replied. "I want to know."

Something creaked below them. Someone started whistling.

Santana peered over the edge and found a rustling in the canopy below. A series of ropes rattled as something below coiled them up. A moment later, a head of hair appeared through the canopy, followed by a plank platform as Connor worked the ropes, hauling himself to the treehouse.

"Oh, I see." Santana gave Terra the side-eye.

"Good morning all," Connor announced cheerfully. He brought the platform in line with the balcony, then tied the rope into place. He stepped off, then dragged several woven baskets off the platform and into the house. Each one had a furry animal or lizard inside, eyes blank, heart still. "Catch of the day," he stated proudly. "Not a bad haul. Did you feel that rumble from the mistress volcano? Gentle one this morning. Must be snoozing."

They followed him inside. He laid out his catch, several shrews and voles, as well as a snake and something that seemed similar to a monitor lizard. In one of the baskets was a marsupial that was eerily similar to a wallaby but with jet-black fur rather than the grays and reds of Aus.

"Should keep us going for a while." Connor drew a keen blade and set to work on the food. "We'll dissect these into portions and take them on our travels. How are you all feeling? Good to go?"

They all exchanged a glance. Gyles seemed uncertain but not as much as Dick. Dick looked out at the trees, and Santana wondered if he was thinking of Valentina.

"We're ready," Santana replied for the group. "When are we setting off?"

"The moment this is done," Connor answered. "Your bags are

packed? Mine are over by the door. Let's stock up on these provisions, then set sail."

Santana crouched beside Connor and drew her blade. She maneuvered the wallaby into position.

Connor turned to her. "Do you know what you're doing?"

"Please," Santana returned.

The two prepared and packaged the food. Then all five took a bush-crafted bag and slung it over their shoulder. Soon they were on the platform, steadily being lowered to ground level.

The floor was damp and soft, and if Santana had any idea of direction before, she'd lost it now. Everything looked unfamiliar, each direction a mass of green and brown with the occasional explosion of flowers.

Faint paths littered the ground, branching out in all directions. Connor took point, leading them confidently into the bush.

It felt strange to be hiking again after being forced to rest. Santana became a little breathless from the walk and made a note to ask at some point what the toxin had been to knock them unconscious. If it was something useful, she could harness it herself in the future.

If there was a future for her.

The ground wound down toward a marsh grove. Progress was slow, and the group was quiet for the most part. Connor took a large stick and used it to support him as he walked. Out here in the open air, Santana couldn't help but note how much older he seemed. His back was beginning to hunch, his hair was wiry, and his face was a wrinkled map of his life.

Yet he still walked boldly, unencumbered, as though he were in a younger man's body.

As the day wore on, the cries of the jungle greeted them. Occasionally they heard the yowling of a large predator. Santana wondered what creatures lurked near here, whether it was a big cat or some kind of forgotten creature recently released into the wild.

Her mind strayed, encouraged and emboldened by their previous day's talk. As her boots sank in the mud and she wiped the sweat from her brow, she saw the map she'd held, the ancient coordinates that could take them all to Atlantis.

She chuckled. Atlantis…a pipe dream for explorers the world over. None of it made any sense. Why would a civilization that was so advanced just vanish? Why would a group of humans who'd uncovered limitless energy and resources, who had advanced vehicles and power and political structures disappear from the Earth without a trace?

Not without a trace…Atlanticore…

Santana shook her head. No. She couldn't allow herself to follow that line of thinking. Sure, when the second main occupation of Atlantica had commenced, the excitement and buzz around Atlanticore and the energy source's possibilities were the topics of all conversations worldwide.

Many had tried to steal Atlanticore fragments, the mysterious pulsing blue energy source that never seemed to die, only to find that a few miles out of the island and into open waters, the elements inside would become unstable and explode.

Only Atlantica could benefit from the fuel source.

But why?

What was here?

Why could one island benefit while no others could?

These are questions for which others have searched for the answers for years, Santana reminded herself. Almost sixty years after the second occupation took place, in the year 2027, there were still no advancements. Atlanticore was drying up. Explorers and scientists had searched for more, for answers, and they'd turned up blank. This island had revealed all that it had to hide. Only the trinkets and skeletons of faded explorers remained beneath the ground.

They passed a series of wide trunks, the roots spreading out into deep murky pools like tentacles.

Santana sighed. Even she didn't believe it was over. How could an island this mysterious, this...sentient...not harbor more discoveries? Something was out there. She knew it.

But Atlantis? That was a pipe dream for her mother and this crazy jungle man.

The ground rose, and they climbed out of the marshes toward drier ground. Up here the air was warmer but less humid. They reached a rise and through the breaks in the trees could see the Covenrane Peaks ahead.

"I first sighted them around here." Connor continued to walk ahead. "A group of people, around a dozen, perhaps. They looked lost and hungry. I offered them food, but before I could finish my sentence, they shot at me. I darted into the trees, slipping away before they could do mortal harm."

They approached a series of large boulders blocking their path. Santana wondered if these were old fragments of former eruptions, rocks spat into the sky by the mighty volcanoes, landing where they may.

Connor began the unsteady climb. Dick moved to help him, but Terra blocked him with her arm.

"Allow him his dignity."

Dick nodded.

Connor still spoke, a little more breathless as he climbed. "For a few weeks, the path ahead was littered with them. I don't know if they were scoping out the area or lost, but soon they all disappeared. I made a point of—oh, hold on..."

He clambered over the largest boulder and took a moment to sit at the top. "I made a point of incorporating this area into my daily routes and found an entrance over that ridge there." He pointed to an area that none of them could yet see. When Santana made it to the top, she spotted a severe wall of dirt and rock some distance ahead. "You see it?"

"I do," Santana replied.

"There's an old cave system." Connor swung his legs around and began the descent. Behind them, Gyles accepted Terra's help as they neared the top. "Untouched in years, by its look. Nowadays it's mostly a den for bears to hibernate. When we get there, you'll spot the beaten track, the flattened ground where boots have trodden. At one point there were dozens of them loitering around that area, but lately it seems as though they've either vacated or gone missing."

"Great," Dick grumbled. "So we might be on a wild goose chase."

Connor's ears pricked up, his hearing more attuned than Dick gave him credit for. "No geese in this part of the wilds, my friend. Unfortunately for me. Love a good bit of roasted goose in the morning."

They worked their way over the boulders, Connor pausing as they waited for Gyles to complete his descent. At the bottom, they drank from their canteens then ate the last of Santana's power bars. Connor was overly thankful for his, admitting that it had been years since he'd been able to eat anything processed in the city.

"You forget how good sugar is," Connor stated before sucking his fingers in turn.

Dick cast him a judgmental glare, gaze lingering on the film of dirt that stained the pads of his fingers.

"There's a lot I can imagine you miss," Terra stated.

"There is," Connor admitted. "The biggest one is company. Even if this is for a short while, I'm glad I got to meet you guys."

They offered him a warm smile before continuing their trek.

An hour later, the jungle began to close around them. Connor and Santana drew their blades, working together to hack at the worst of the brambles and vines that blocked their way. Progress was slow, and Santana's arms were scratched and raw when they finally cleared enough to make the final distance toward the wall.

They lingered in the bushes within viewing distance. A cave mouth yawned open, the inside sucking in the light until all that remained was darkness. Connor was right. The area in front of the cave had clearly been disturbed by the determined trampling of many feet. Even now, a few bootprints lingered in the mud, the treads of the soles creating small puddles that held rainwater.

"No surprise, all is quiet," Connor offered.

Terra appeared at Santana's shoulder. "I can't detect anyone inside the entrance."

"How far can APRIL's vision see?" Santana asked.

"Far enough," Terra replied. "It'll be more difficult penetrating through thick rock. As far as I'm concerned, outside of night vision, we'll be blind in there."

Connor cast a curious glance at Terra. "Night vision? You brought goggles with you?"

"No." Terra didn't elaborate.

"Why would they be in a cave?" Dick asked. "If this guy is anything like Valentina described, wouldn't this be more state-of-the-art? Doorways and corridors and all that kind of stuff?"

"Weren't you paying attention?" Gyles earned a pointed stare from Dick. "They're in *hiding*. The last thing they'd want to do is make the entrance easier to find."

"Yeah, they're *hiding* in the middle of virgin fucking woods," Dick snapped. "What's the need for camouflage when you're the only ones out here?"

Santana felt the tensions rising between them. "Steady," she offered. "All we know is that this *could* be a way in. Terra, any sign of Val?"

Terra narrowed her eyes, allowing herself a moment to scan around the place. She took a few crouching steps forward, her attention caught by something the others couldn't see. A moment later, she turned, presenting something in the palm of her hand.

The small tear of fabric was blood red and leather. It had been clinging to an offset of brambles. Terra held it closer to her eye, the green light blinking. "That's not good."

"Is it Val's?" Dick asked.

"Hard to say for certain," Terra replied. "Though, how many other people out in the jungle have been known to wear a blood red jacket while on their merry adventures?"

"She's been here then," Santana mused. "I'm not sure if that's a good or bad sign."

"Only one way to find out." Dick rose to his feet. He strode through the bush, stepping high over the foliage as he beelined for the cave.

Something *snapped*.

A branch *cracked*.

Dick cried out as something took his leg and swept him off the ground.

Santana looked for Dick. The man somehow disappeared into the sky. She ran forward and found him suspended twenty feet above her head, the folds of his jacket hanging down and covering his face. He wrestled with the fabric, face growing red as the blood rushed to his head.

From somewhere in the cave came the sounds of people running.

CHAPTER EIGHTEEN

"Shit," Santana grumbled, working quickly to climb the tree.

Dick swung above, staring toward the cave mouth where light began to glow inside.

Terra took a position kneeling out of sight with her rifle lined up toward the newcomer. Gyles waited behind her, his weapon ready in his hand. Connor waited beneath Dick.

"Quickly," Dick urged in a low hiss.

Santana shinnied up the tree, using the rough bark for her hand- and footholds. She ascended as fast as she could, but the steps were growing louder, and her heart beat fast.

The flames grew brighter. An orange glow flickered in the cave's mouth.

Santana reached Dick's height. She drew her blade and worked on the rope. She sawed the blade back and forth as the rope creaked.

The sudden realization of what was about to befall dawned on Dick's face. He shook his head. "Stop, Santana. No. You're gonna kill me."

"Hands out," Santana warned. "Land in a roll."

Before Dick could protest any further, the rope snapped. He

plummeted toward the ground, an involuntary moan escaping his lips. The tree sprang back. Dick had weighted down the tops of its branches.

Connor was ready for him. He held out his hands, able to scoop Dick into his arms and slow his fall. It wasn't elegant, and both men hit the ground with a loud *thud*, but it was enough. Connor was winded as he rolled on the ground, while Dick quickly rose to his feet.

The footsteps grew, and the first of their number came from the cave. Santana slid down the tree, then hopped back to the ground. Her whip was out and at the ready. "Hold steady…" she commanded.

They obeyed, each of them focused on the group that was heading their way. Now they'd done it. Now they'd kicked the hornet's nest, and an army would spill out and take them down with ease. Perhaps they should run. Maybe they should turn and hide before they were captured and tortured until…

A single figure appeared from the cave, torch held aloft. It jogged toward them with a terrified expression.

"Hide," Santana hissed.

The figure broke from the cave at full sprint, arms wildly pumping as it tore from the opening. It raced toward the others, then took a sharp turn before the trees. The group relaxed a touch as she sprinted off into the darkness.

"What got her so spooked?" Dick asked.

More footsteps approached, rapidly growing in volume as two more spilled from the cave. One was limping, and the other one determined to break for the trees.

They ran straight at Santana's hiding place. She moved out of their way, but Gyles froze in place. They knocked into him, and the limping man sprawled. Without waiting for a reason or explanation, the other sprinted into the darkness. The man who'd fallen scrambled to his feet, fear painted clear in his eyes, then dashed off after him.

"What the hell was all that about?" Gyles brushed himself off.

Terra turned her attention back to the cave. "Only one way to find out."

They advanced slowly, each one ready with their weapons. As they crossed the threshold, a strange stench hit their nostrils. The temperature dropped several degrees, for which they were thankful.

"Tread lightly," Terra warned, the cave snatching the sound of their movements and magnifying them as they tiptoed ahead.

"Speak for yourself." Dick glanced down at his thick-soled boots, then over at Terra's with a lighter tread.

They gathered behind Terra, forming a line so they could follow her into the dark. Even Connor, who was confused about how this woman could see in the pitch-black, remained quiet as they journeyed forward. Snippets of sound rang around them, distorted and misleading. Lost in the various walkways and passages they came across were voices and whispers.

Terra saw the cave ahead in shades of green and black.

She still hadn't fully gotten used to the various lenses APRIL could impose on her ocular nerves. Before the accident, a journey through somewhere as dark as this would have her heart racing and her every sense on fire.

This was a breeze, not least because APRIL was equalizing her biochemistry, but because she knew she had the advantage. The AI highlighted every crevice in the walls, every bump and rock on the ground, every twist and turn of the passages, making them easy to view and access as she guided the others forward.

There were footprints on the ground, cold in temperature, but whoever's boots made the imprints were heavy and left their mark in stains of mud. Only once as they walked did they have to duck into a crevice to hide from another pair of fleeing feet, a skinny man who looked as if he was barely twenty years old flying past them and out the cave entrance.

The strangest part of it was that there was little sign of scuffle or reason for fear. Terra asked APRIL to increase the sensitivity of her hearing, but nothing was detected. All she could hear was the attempted light treads of those following behind her.

The cave sloped down before opening into a large chasm. Stalactites hung from the ceiling like rocky teeth, and small pools of water glowed silver from the hazy moonlight spilling down shafts and glittering on their surfaces.

Terra was about to return her vision to normal when she spotted something moving in the distance. *APRIL, home in and magnify.*

The AI obeyed, drawing Terra's vision toward the farthest reaches of the cave. A single figure slipped through a crevice. Only the faint heat signature she captured illuminated their shape.

Before she could get a solid read, the figure was gone.

The others detached from Terra, able now to make out the way ahead. As they neared the first large pool of water, Connor called their attention.

"I'm sorry, but...this is as far as I can take you," he stated softly.

Dick frowned. "Not got the jitters already, have you?"

"Who's taking who?" Terra teased, tearing her gaze from the far end of the cave.

Connor offered a warm smile. "This isn't my business to get involved in. You have your goals, and I have mine." He touched his head with two fingers then slung his backpack onto the ground. "Here. You can take my portion of the food. I hope you don't need it and that your journey is quick. But it's there for you."

Santana picked up the bag. "Thank you. For everything." She corrected herself, "Well, not everything. I mean, I didn't appreciate being fogged and knocked unconscious and waking up in a strange treehouse. What was that stuff, anyway?"

Connor tapped his nose. "Personal recipe. Home secret."

To Santana's surprise, he stepped forward and hugged her. She tensed, then relaxed into the embrace, his stale scent not unpleasant.

He smiled and held her at arm's length. "Make me one promise."

"Sure," Santana replied.

"If you find it, you'll share it with me."

Santana could see the wonderment in his eyes, the years of curiosity and passion and belief in the myth that he'd shared with them all. Santana wondered what held his conviction so strongly, if the maps and the papers were all he had, or if there was more. She was no stranger to runes and carvings of an ancient civilization and often allowed herself to dream of the place, but reality was a vastly different realm to imagination.

"You got it," she assured him. "Atlantis will be yours."

Connor bade his goodbyes to the others, then slipped back into the darkness behind them. He lit a torch, confident that the way back was now clear, and soon the last of its flickering flames vanished from sight.

"Then there were four," Dick offered. He reached into his jacket and drew out a cigarette.

"Really?" Terra chided. "Now?"

"When's better?" Dick asked. "We have a moment's pause in relative safety, and who knows what lies ahead? This could be the last good cigarette I have before my life ends and all fades to black."

"Cheery," Gyles muttered.

Dick turned on him, intense. "Cheery or not, the reality of our situation is bleak. We're not fucking around here, Gyles. You're no longer in the safety of the little cult you joined. It's four against…well, who knows?"

He scoffed, shook his head, and drew in a lungful of smoke. As he spoke, smoke filtered from his mouth in a gentle plume. "We might finally be nearing the doorstep of those we're hoping to track, but what then? What's the plan, Sokolov? Without Val, we've lost one of the greatest invisible mercenaries on the island.

"All we have is an AI built for the city in a human, a jungle girl, and whatever Gyles chooses to qualify himself as. Oh, and me, of course. A private investigator who works in the shadows and takes his time to piece the puzzle together."

He laughed a little louder than Santana was happy with. "This is going to be a fucking riot. So, excuse me for allowing myself a moment to enjoy one of life's simple pleasantries."

Terra looked out from under lowered eyebrows. "Are you done?"

"For now. What are you looking at me like that for?"

"I never had you down as someone who would get the jitters this close to the goal. I guess I was wrong."

"I don't have the jitters," Dick clarified. "I have a severe disdain for those who tell me not to do the things that bring me joy."

Terra chuckled.

"What?" Dick asked.

"I can see why you struggle so much around Santana, then," Terra shot back.

Dick glanced at Santana, then down at the ground. He soothed himself with his cigarette.

Gyles turned quietly to Santana. "What *is* the plan?"

Santana looked ahead in the cave. "We move closer. Find the entrance. Gather intelligence. Find Kit."

"Seems simple enough," Terra replied. "The way ahead still

seems quiet. I can follow the footprints through this cave, and hopefully, we'll find something soon. I can't seem to track down whatever had those guys so skittish that they ran out and away."

"Hopefully we will soon," Santana stated.

Gyles didn't share her enthusiasm.

CHAPTER NINETEEN

"Stay back," Terra ordered as they neared the far end of the cave.

A crevice opened before them, a zigzag in the wall that was dark on the other side. They pulled back together into a single file, allowing Terra to take point and see the things they couldn't.

"What is it?" Santana asked.

Terra hushed her with a wave, then tightened her grip on her rifle and eased ahead. She ducked to enter, encouraging the others to follow her.

The temperature dropped again. Terra walked torturously slow, which worked to keep them all quiet. Dick walked behind Santana, stinking of cigarette smoke.

They walked blindly into the darkness. Before they knew it, Terra had taken a turn, and the faint light from the caves behind was gone. The path descended even further, everything bringing them deeper and deeper into Atlantica's underground.

Terra stopped. No one spoke. Somewhere in the caves, water dripped gently, the sound grown gargantuan in the gloom. Santana's skin turned to gooseflesh as the cold began to set into her bones. Gyles shuffled uncomfortably behind them.

An explosion of light seared her eyes. Santana drew her whip and unfurled it by her side, prepared for use. She didn't need it. Terra held up a single match, illuminating the cave around them.

Santana gasped. Dead bodies. A whole group of them, choked and twisted and taken out by deft hands. Only one or two simmered in pools of blood. The rest were blue in the face, eyes wide, tongues lolling from their mouths.

All of them wore the same uniform as those who'd fled the cave.

Terra glanced around at them in turn. "I guess we're getting warmer."

"They're not, though." Dick smiled.

Santana couldn't tell if that was because of his joke or for something else.

"She was here." Terra picked up the shell of a smoke grenade, then crouched beside the nearest body—a man with a thick brown beard and part of a tattoo poking out of his collar. She tugged down his jacket to reveal a swastika on his skin. "I wonder what Archie's vetting process is for recruits."

"Probably the same as most of the assholes in this city," Santana replied. "Will you accept money for blind loyalty?"

"It's a massacre," Gyles commented. "They didn't stand a chance."

"Not against the Red Countess," Dick confirmed. "These assholes didn't know what was coming for them."

"Probably a good sign," Santana stated. "She'll lead the way for us, help thin out their number."

"She'll reduce their number to zero." Dick chuckled. "We're redundant here."

"No," Terra stated. "This is only the entrance. An outpost. Look." She pointed at where a store of supplies rested against the wall. Someone had looted the box. Clothes and ammunition and foodstuffs spilled over its edge and onto the ground. "They're stationed here for some time, swapping maybe every few days. We have farther to go."

"Great," Dick snarked. "I wanted this to be an extended holiday."

Santana rolled her head on her neck, coiled her whip, and hung it on her hip. "Sarcasm aside, let's keep moving. These bodies are still relatively fresh. That means she can't be too far ahead."

Terra realigned them in single file and extinguished the flame.

They marched into the dark.

Valentina watched with keen eyes.

The way ahead had been treacherous, her light sources only adequate to see the next step forward on her journey. In the darkness, even the slightest wink of light was enough to alert others of her presence. By the same token, it was enough to alert her to the presence of others.

They'd gathered around a campfire, the cavernous room glowing in flame. By the time she rounded the corner, her light—which, for the most part, had stayed pressed against the material covering her legs—was extinguished, and she could focus on what lay ahead.

The first scout group had been easy to terrify. Using a series of sound manipulations against the rocky walls and the explosion of her light sources, she'd manipulated their minds into believing that she was everywhere at once. She'd focused on extinguishing their lights, shooting with her silenced pistol to knock the flashlights out of their hands before jumping on each in turn and delivering a sharp blow to the face.

The outer guards were wimps. Without waiting for their brethren, they ran from the cave, choosing to save themselves rather than warn the other guard groups. To give them credit, they would likely fare better in the jungle than stuck in the cave system with Valentina.

Valentina was pissed. Her muscles throbbed, replenished by her formula. Her senses were sharp, and her mission was clear. There was no more fucking around. It was "kill or be killed," and Valentina was ready to destroy anyone who stood in her way.

The second group was tougher than the first. Their fire was large, as were their numbers. This time, Valentina covered them in smoke. She rolled the grenade gently into their midst. The group was already distracted and a little drunk. Keeping guard in this part of the jungle didn't see many enemy attacks, and the group had grown complacent.

She'd swept among them, keeping low and taking them in turn from behind. A quick snap of the neck or a choke-out from a firm stranglehold was enough to keep their guns quiet and their voices down. She worked quickly, oddly proud of her efficiency in clearing the path ahead.

When the smoke cleared, Valentina allowed herself a moment to breathe. She took some quick snacks from the chest, then laid a damp cloth over the fire.

Now she strode silently through the caves, the floors sloping ever down. A glow came from ahead so she turned off her flashlight.

The voices were merry, another group who perhaps didn't understand that danger could always creep up and surprise you.

She rounded the corner, the tunnel once again opening up into a huge hall. The sound of rushing water met her ears, and she wondered if they'd come across an underground river system.

Valentina crept a little closer and discerned a balcony ahead of her with a metallic guardrail. It was the first sign of artificial construction she'd come across, and it made her heart leap. Three men with riot gear and rifles stood by the rail, lost in conversation.

"...only so many times you can watch *M.A.S.H.* re-runs before you grow sick of it," one of the men groused. "That's what Archie needs, some live TV or something. What's the good in being out here and keeping guard if we can't entertain ourselves during our time off?"

The guard beside him playfully swiped his arm. Her ponytail waved out behind her helmet. "Because the signals would give away the location, dumbass. Do you not get what we're doing here? We don't get paid a mint to watch TV. We're changing the fucking future."

"Could still do with something on those days off," the man replied. "Aside from playing the 'Fuck Me' lottery with whatever bimbo free time is paired with, what is there to do?" He nudged her with his elbow. "When's your next break time?"

The woman raised an eyebrow at him as a second woman beside them laughed. "You'd have better luck using your dick as a fishing rod and trying to get sucked off."

Valentina crept closer, finding a nearby alcove that protected her from sight but gave her a good view of those ahead. She listened closely and detected the ringing of feet on metallic stairs.

What the hell is this place?

"Sounds like a great day out to me." The man chuckled. "You weren't so disappointed last time we shared a few days off together."

The woman shoved him, the man teetering dangerously close to the edge of the balcony. Beyond it, all was black.

Valentina fished in her pocket until she found the small ball bearings. The ground ahead was bumpy, but she calculated the throw before releasing them into the air.

A soft *tapping* accompanied their travel as the balls spread around the three guards' feet. The second woman caught the glint of silver and glanced down. "What the…"

Valentina triggered the bearings into motion. Crackling accompanied the appearance of blue sparks as the small spheres exploded with electricity and created a web around their feet. The guards stiffened as their arms clamped to their sides and their hair shot out to stand on end. They toppled one by one and came to a jittering stop on the floor.

Someone shouted. Valentina broke from cover and turned off the bearings to allow her to stand on the metal grate. She swung her pistol to her left, able to make out the platform stretching along the chasm's edge. More guards lined the span, and she shot at them. Her silencer muted the reports, but the guards' cries rang out in the cavern.

Flaming sconces lit the way ahead. Valentina picked off the sentries as she tore along the platform. A handful of guards began their descent down a long metal staircase. Someone shot back, forcing Valentina to slow and duck out of the shooter's sight.

A guard lying on his stomach and bleeding out from a gut shot raised his head and lifted his gun. Valentina shot faster. His hand turned to mush, and the pistol spun off the grating and dropped.

It took a long time before she heard the weapon hit the ground below.

She eased forward and leaned over the guardrail. Three guards neared the bottom, the stairs taking a sharp ninety-degree bend every fifty steps or so.

That's a loooong way down.

Valentina lined up the shot and caught one of them in the leg. They howled as they fell down the stairs, curling into a ball until they hit the next available bend.

Valentina sprinted for the top of the stairs. She skidded to a halt, about to jump down the first step when something exploded nearby.

She jumped back as the rock wall around the steps shattered. The metal anchors that held the staircase in place flew out in a spray of smoke and debris. The hidden explosives embedded along the structure triggered sequentially until the whole thing groaned and tilted away from the wall.

Valentina glared down. One of the guards kept their hand on

a button nearby, watching the devastation. The other sprinted past him, aiming toward a thin pathway that ran parallel to the gushing ravine below.

Valentina's lip curled. She switched to her rifle and aimed, then pulled the trigger twice. The running man fell flat on his face, still and bleeding. The man with his hand on the button flew back and slammed against a nearby stalagmite.

The stairs twisted and compacted, the metal bending with a series of declarative screeches. Valentina could only watch as the one visible path down toward her destination crashed and collapsed into a mass of metal and rock.

She waited a moment, listening for any other signs of action. Somewhere far away, a lone pair of footsteps sounded. Valentina closed her eyes and aimed with her ears. She shot once, then twice. After the third shot, the footsteps stilled.

She didn't know if it was because of her or because they were out of range. She only hoped it was the former.

"Fuck…" she grumbled while pacing back along the platform. She peered over the edge at the ravine, an easy sixty feet below her. Other than the water, little was visible. The oppressive darkness in the distance cloaked all else in the cave.

She stayed there for some time as she studied the situation. The water gushed, foaming white as it descended through a treacherous path of jagged rocks. Occasionally a fish's scales glinted as it leaped up the rapids.

Valentina took her grapple gun and fixed the anchor to the guardrail. She vaulted over the edge and swung down. With her feet placed firmly against the wall, she began her descent.

She worked slowly, careful of her footing as she neared the water. The spray slicked the rock and moistened her grip on the gun.

She planted her feet firmly on the uneven rocks, let go of the tool, then pivoted to face the water. She looked around for anything that might provide an easier way to cross. The river was fifteen feet wide, with only a few stones poking above the surface. She knew she could make it, but it would be dangerous, and she wanted to limit any chance of hurting herself.

Nothing presented itself. All was rock and water.

With a heavy sigh, Valentina turned to the grapple gun. She wanted to take it with her but knew that she couldn't, not least because she couldn't withdraw the metallic hooks from where she was.

Besides, she needed to leave herself an escape route…

Abandoning the line, she turned her attention to the rocks. She assessed the path, imagining her movements in her mind before executing them. After a three-count, she deftly leaped across, nimble and quick-footed.

She reached the reassuring firmness of the opposite shore. In the air came the smell of cooked food—not only meats, but roasted vegetables and something sweet, too.

I'm getting close. I'm finally getting close…

I pray to God there's an easier way out.

CHAPTER TWENTY

"She's on the warpath," Terra mused as they approached the metal balcony.

Santana pulled up behind her, taking in the sights. More dead. More scattered in their path. Surely this proved that they were on the right trail, but what about Val? How far ahead was she?

She took solace in the fact that they'd finally reached artificial structures. The platform was relatively new, the metal clean and unmarred by rust or time. They spread out, keeping their wits about them as they explored the area and tried to understand the way ahead.

"That'll do it," Dick announced. His hands gripped the guardrail as he leaned over the edge. He drew their attention to the staircase below, the whole construction on its side and twisted as though it had curled up and died of a debilitating illness. "There goes our way down."

"Hey, guys," Gyles called warily from the other end of the platform. They gathered around him and followed his line of sight down into a gushing ravine below. "Look."

Santana peered over the edge, barely able to make out a thin length of black coiled around the rocks, one end trailing into the river. "Is that…"

Terra nodded. "Valentina's grappling gun. Looks like she used it to descend, then…" She didn't have to say it. The others could read between the lines.

Dick frowned. "No. She wouldn't do that."

"Do what?" Gyles asked.

"Stop us from following," Dick finished. He looked around as if trying to find another route, another sign that she'd helped them. "Why would Val deliberately cut off a way down after her? It doesn't make any sense."

"Because she used us from the start," Terra replied. "She found what she was after. What else did she need us for? She's Valentina fucking Winters."

"Exactly," Dick retorted. "I know her. She wouldn't do this. She might come across severe and hard around the edges, but that's not who she is. This isn't her."

"Then who is it?" Santana shot back. "John, read the signs. She drew us into this mess, then when our use had expired, she fucked off and left us." She motioned at the gun. "See for yourself. Val has made it clear that this is *her* mission, and her mission alone."

Dick ran a hand through his hair. The evidence was compelling. Even Santana had to admit it, but she didn't like it one bit.

"So, what?" Dick asked, exasperated. "Are you saying we give up? Head back and let Val pick up all the pieces? Is this it? Are we done? Is the adventure over?"

Santana frowned. "No."

Gyles looked at her in surprise.

"Of course not," Santana continued. "I don't know about you, but I made a promise to Val, and I intend to keep it. She's going to need us in there. More than that, this whole operation needs to stop.

"She might think she doesn't need us, she might sever the ropes that connect us, but we're not stopping until we find her and her brother and bring them back to the city with us." She shook her head. "Stubborn bitch."

"Santana!" Terra grinned.

"It's the truth," Santana replied. "Now, shall we begin our descent?"

"How?" Gyles asked. "That fall is huge, and I'm not good at rock climbing."

Santana slung her pack off her shoulders and drew out a length of rope. "Good thing I always prepare, isn't it? We might not have Val's fancy gadgets, but we at least have methods."

Dick raised an eyebrow. "You didn't think to use this when we were struggling near the falls?"

"I didn't have it then," Santana clarified. "I took this from the guards' chest. Keep up, John. I know you're not as dumb as you look."

Santana was the first to test the descent on the rocky face. She secured the rope with a knot she'd devised, then slowly lowered herself toward the water. Gyles watched with trepidation, occasionally uttering encouragement and warnings as she swung to the side.

Her feet found firm ground. She encouraged Gyles to come next. Reluctantly, he accepted Terra's help and worked his way down, guided from below by Santana. Only once did he nearly fall, allowing his grip to slacken as fear took him. He quickly recovered, holding the rope with white knuckles and closing his eyes until his bravery returned.

He joined Santana on the rocks.

Terra slipped down easily, using the rope as one might use a fireman's pole. She was standing beside them before they knew it, leaving only Dick to descend.

Dick was a little slower but assured in his footing. A minute later, all four stood on the rocks, their next obstacle roaring before them.

"Now what?" Gyles asked.

"Fair question," Dick agreed.

Santana assessed the waters, her attention caught by the black trailing wire. She fished out the grappling gun, then examined the mechanism. With a touch of the button, the rope coiled back in, unaffected by the water. "Stroke of luck," she stated.

"Yeah...luck," Dick replied.

Santana looked up, hoping to find something on the ceiling that she could attach the grapple to, but from here, the roof was in darkness. She looked ahead, finding a large stalagmite on the other bank. She aimed, then fired. The rope uncoiled, wrapped once, then twice around the stalagmite before the grapple secured itself on the cord.

Santana took the other end of the gun and coiled it around a crevice in the rocky face, double-checking its security. "Okay, time to step over some stones."

Keeping hold of the line, she began her crossing, unknowingly following the same route Valentina had trodden. She slipped once but used the rope to hold her steady, preventing herself from washing away in the current.

Gyles followed once again, surprisingly not misstepping at all, and soon arrived on the opposite bank.

Terra moved quickly, joining the two, leaving only Dick remaining.

"Why am I always last?" Dick asked.

"How gentlemanly," Santana shot back.

Dick motioned to Gyles. "He gets to go first."

"Just get your ass across, Chambers," Terra replied.

Dick held the rope and began his crossing. His boots were larger than the others, the treads not built for this kind of environment. Santana watched his first footstep slip before he found his balance by clinging to the rope. Another step and he was away from the bank, the water rushing past below him.

Halfway across, his foot slipped again, his body toppling back. He grabbed the rope, fighting to regain footing as his pants and shoes dipped into the water. The rope lurched, small pebbles flying from the anchor where Santana had secured the gun.

"John!" Santana cried and reached toward him.

Dick fought to regain his footing, but the water worked against him. Every time he tried to pull his legs up, it felt as though thousands of tiny hands were pulling him back.

"Fuck!" he grumbled, looping his elbows around the rope. He blindly felt with his feet, hoping he could find a weakness in the slipstream that would allow him to pull himself back.

"Hold on," Santana called.

"What do you think I'm doing?" Dick replied, heart racing. Something *cracked* on the other bank, and he felt the rope slacken.

Using the rope to support her, Santana stepped onto the rocks, reaching out to try and help Dick. He grunted as the rope lurched again.

"Get off," Dick called. "It can't take us both."

"I won't let you go," Santana cried. "I'm almost there."

He turned to the side, Santana's hand a few feet from him. If he let go of the rope, he might make it, might be able to hold her for support. At the same time, he wasn't confident that the water wouldn't wash him—

The rock crumbled. The rope went slack. Dick was dragged along the current, clinging desperately to the now-sodden rope. He gripped with everything he had, barely able to grip the gun at the other end.

Water rushed him. He tried to open his eyes, but the spray

was too much. He gasped, swallowed water, and his body smacked around the rocks like a pinball. Somewhere above it all, he heard raised voices, Terra and Santana and Gyles as they ran along the bank and drew closer.

The current threw his body around. He gasped and spluttered, unable to take a proper breath. Something wet and slimy hit his face, and he gasped again as his grip on the gun loosened. It slipped from his hands as the water grabbed him with powerful arms and dragged him away. His head *cracked* against something hard and smooth. Sparks blossomed in his vision before all faded to black.

CHAPTER TWENTY-ONE

"John!" Santana cried as she sprinted along the bank and followed the river.

For a moment she could still see his body, a dark object intermittently appearing above the foaming waves of the water. The ground was uneven as she ran, and as much as she paid attention to her footing, she tripped.

When she picked herself up, Dick was gone. She aimed her flashlight, called for Terra to help, but the river was too fast. Dick was nowhere in sight.

She hurried along the edge of the bank, stopping when she met the cavern walls. The water slipped through a crevice and dropped into the darkness below. There was no space to follow unless Santana was willing to swim, and Terra warned her that she couldn't pick up a trace of his body anymore. No amount of night vision, thermal vision, or otherwise could detect him.

"Shit, shit, shit..." Santana muttered, fingers threaded in her hair. "He can't be... He can't..."

They stood awhile at the cave wall while Terra investigated, hunting for a way down to where Dick might've gone. The cave barred their progress, and after a few minutes, Terra confirmed that the slipstream was the only way through that she could see.

"Oh, man..." Gyles muttered.

"What do we do?" Santana asked, taken aback by the overwhelming ache that lingered in her stomach. Dick had sometimes been a little much, happy to flaunt his charm and do nothing to calm his cockiness, but he was a good guy. Good guys deserved a better end than this, didn't they?

Terra's eyes sparkled in the limited light. Her lips were thin, and dogged determination showed on her face. Santana could tell that she was equally affected, but neither of the women wanted to show it.

It all happened so quickly. One minute you're there, the next...

"John!" she cried, cupping her hands and yelling as closely as she dared to where the water dropped into oblivion. "John!"

"Dick!" Gyles yelled, adding to the din.

Their collective voices bounced around the cave, echoing back at them. Santana wasn't sure what she was hoping for. Something. Anything. Unsurprisingly, no sound returned.

"Fuck..." Terra grunted and turned back to the dark, open chasm behind them. "Our numbers are dwindling a little too quickly for my liking. We'll stand no chance getting anywhere near Archie and finding Valentina at this rate."

A rush of emotion surged through Santana. "You're kidding, aren't you?"

Terra frowned.

"He's been gone for two seconds, and you're already speaking about carrying on with the mission. This isn't a case of one of our crew running off ahead of us into the night, despite sending us into the forest. This is John Chambers we're talking about. *John.*"

Santana's vision grew foggy as tears came unbidden. "So give us a moment to mourn before we do anything else, would you? He was a good man. A *great* man. A vital asset to our team." She stared into the darkness, back the way they'd come. "I don't know how we can do this without both John and Val."

Gyles gingerly moved closer to Santana and laid an arm around her shoulder. She tensed, then eased into him, resting her head on his chest. He held her for a long moment while throwing occasional awkward glances at Terra.

She allowed herself a moment to let the tears fall. The heat of Gyles' chest warmed her cheek, the rush of the falls hushing all else around them. When she looked up, a thin, silvery trail ran down one of Terra's cheeks.

"Are you done?" Terra asked, not indelicately. Santana knew the reality of their situation and could see the concern in Terra's eyes. "We came to achieve a goal. Dick Chambers died for that. Let the loss of his life not be in vain."

Santana gave an affirmative nod. With a final glance back at the top of the falls, Terra led their way farther into the dragon's lair.

Every sound traveled in the cave as though the source of the noise was right beside her. Valentina stepped carefully, heightening her senses so she could tune into the troubles that lay ahead.

There were more of them now. Archie's army grew as she snuck farther into the cave system. The walls had begun to show more signs of human intrusion. She passed carved doorways, walked along stretches of floor covered in rubber mats to make passage quieter and smoother, and now she reached a door locked by a digital panel.

She heard people mumbling on the other side. She had no idea how deep underground she'd gone, but the air was oppressive and cloying.

Valentina whirled as a sound came from behind her. She

heard the whispers of words, voices that sounded like her former comrades. There was urgency in them, desperation, and Valentina wondered if it could be them—if they'd finally found their way into the cavernous labyrinth.

After a moment, the sounds faded. Valentina turned her attention back to the digital panel. She examined the system, then punched in a series of codes she'd learned long ago, a little-known base code installed in most Tynamo Inc. security systems to allow the user to access the administration panel.

The screen flickered green. Valentina played around with the options, exploring her possibilities.

After a few moments of toying with the machine, she sighed. She reached into her pocket and fished out a solitary finger. Its end was bloody, but at least the blood had dried now. She placed the finger's pad on the scanner and received the satisfying *beep* of confirmation.

The doors unlocked. Valentina tentatively eased through.

The voices grew in volume. She closed the door and tightened her grip on her gun.

She moved quickly, found a supply room to her left, slipped inside, and rooted around in her pockets until she found what she was looking for.

The drone was micro-sized, appearing more like a fly than a piece of machinery. She smirked, impressed by the capabilities of modern technology. The tiny black item rested in one palm as she activated its system with her cell phone. The drone's camera feed appeared on her phone screen, showing her a high-quality picture of herself.

She launched the drone, guiding it with controls on her screen. The device slipped out a gap in the supply door and flew along the hallways, giving Valentina a glimpse of the path that lay ahead.

She'd reached the motherlode, she was sure. The pathways were grated metal. The walls held wires and electric bulbs, allowing a clear view all around. They'd used the cave to their advantage, turning pockets of it into more rooms that contained things she could only guess at.

The drone hovered high above groups of Archie's men and women. They strolled around the space, little concerned about any invaders to their lair. Why would they be? They were in the middle of nowhere, miles beneath the Earth's surface, lost in the center of an area where few explorers dared to tread.

Valentina was patient in her exploration, taking the drone down a set of long, grated stairs. She couldn't believe this place went even deeper. In the few weeks since she'd last seen Archie, the man had accomplished so much. She wasn't sure whether or not parts of the space had been in the works before he'd fled or if it was all designed and built since he arrived, but it was impressive.

Wide corridors stretched on into infinity. It was a perfect mesh of nature and artificial construction. The rocky cave walls melded almost seamlessly with the metal elements, although there was still a lot of work to be done—pebbles littered the floors, and many of the walls were still works in progress.

To have achieved what he had so quickly was impressive.

The drone slipped farther down into the darkness, an annoying little buzzing sound accompanying its movements. There was the occasional glimmer of men and women swatting the drone as though it were a nuisance bug, not one of them questioning how a fly had made it this far into the caves.

She mapped out the system, her cell phone tracking its progress and creating a digital cartographic representation of what the drone saw as more turnings than she could imagine turned into more endless corridors.

At one point, she made the drone hover by a poster installed on the wall, a set of directions and instructions written on its surface

She read down, gleaning, as she suspected she would, that the farther down into the cave she went, the more senior the staff would be.

After a few more minutes of exploration, the footage on her screen went fuzzy. It happened in small glitches, eventually turning into a snowy white fuzz. Valentina knew that she'd reached the farthest reaches of her signal and worked to turn the drone around and bring it back within range, wondering whether she could map out more of the corridors along the way back and whether it was worth it.

Voices drew her attention to activity outside the room. She quietly made sure the door was closed.

"I'll go check," someone announced.

The echoing stamp of footsteps moved toward her.

She pocketed her cell phone and ducked behind the door, shrinking against the wall to remain free from sight. The door opened. A light flicked on. Valentina remained quiet.

The large woman who entered had her hair in pigtails and wore an ill-fitting uniform. She riffled through some boxes, unaware of the intruder who stood behind her.

An idea came to Valentina. Working swiftly and quietly, she hooked an arm around the woman's mouth, muffling her protestations. She held her tightly, located the pressure point in the sensitive tissue on her neck, and jammed her thumb down on it until the woman's eyes rolled back.

The guard went slack in her arms. She was heavy. It was all Valentina could do to guide her down gently without causing too much disturbance.

She pushed the door closed and worked quickly to undress the woman. As much as it pained her to, Valentina removed her distinctive outfit. She folded each item meticulously, then hid them in a half-full box.

She dressed in the woman's clothing. The tight, ill-fitting material that was too small for the large woman's frame swamped Valentina. With a few pinches, twists, and adjustments, she worked to make the garments fit her a little better. She only hoped this idea would work…

As she took a confident step out of the supply room, Valentina met a young man waiting expectedly.

"Who are you?" He had a strange look on his face.

"What do you mean, who am I? How's that a good way to greet someone?"

The man cocked his head, attempting to crane his neck and see over Valentina's shoulder.

"Where's Steph?"

Valentina shrugged. "Who are you talking about?"

The man looked uncertain, gaze darting back over her shoulder toward the closet. "I thought she went in there?"

Valentina shook her head. "I haven't seen anyone. Now, if you'll excuse me, I have to get these down to Matt on the lower levels." She strode confidently past the man, leaving him baffled behind her.

Her pace increased as she slipped away. She boldly strode ahead, following the mental map she'd created from her drone's mapping efforts. She took a right, her feet *clacking* on the metal grating. She tried not to meet the gazes of others she passed, knowing that confidence often worked better as a key than any kind of swipe card or key code.

She took a left and descended the stairs. When she reached the floor below, she continued to follow the map in her mind, moving toward her drone. After a few more turns, she heard the familiar buzzing.

The drone hovered near the ceiling. She brought it down as voices and the clatter of footsteps sounded behind her. She wasn't being as subtle as she would've liked, so she quickly descended the nearest stairs with the drone clutched in her hand.

She wound through the labyrinth, weaving and twisting to ensure that she'd lost the people she'd passed. Doorways lined the corridors. She strode past them until she found one that was slightly ajar.

She slipped inside and closed it behind her, finding herself in a rudimentary bedroom—one that looked far more comfortable than it should this far into the Atlantican wild.

A neatly made double bed occupied the corner. There was an en suite bathroom, but she didn't want to know where all the waste flushed out to. It was basic compared to any apartments or places she'd visited back in the city, but what else could she expect?

The drone vibrated in her palm, bringing her back to the job at hand.

She took a moment to collect herself and check that the drone was still in full working order. Then she cracked open the door and sent the drone back out into the world.

Her digital eyes once more hovered above the ground. This time she worked slower, trying to gather her bearings, knowing that she was now in the heart of the ant colony.

They were all around her now. She felt it in the air, people scurrying about their business like insects in the crevices and cracks of their nest. She sent the little drone buzzing down the corridor. Only a moment later, she stopped it.

A group of men and women wearing white lab coats advanced from farther down the corridor.

To the drone's right was a ventilation shaft. Valentina expertly guided it onto a perch. She aimed the camera toward the group and brought the volume up to hear what they were saying.

"...a medical miracle," one of the men stated, "to see such advancements so quickly. It's beyond understanding. We're playing in the territories of God."

A woman nodded eagerly. "We could be changing the entire fabric of medicine. Imagine it, cellular-level revival. To resuscitate the parts of the body that were once impossible to heal. Everything we ever understood about biology, synapses, the channels, pathways, and nerves within the body—it could all be reshaped now. It's…remarkable."

The third doctor agreed with a nod.

The fourth shook his head in disbelief. "We have to tell the others about this. We can't keep this to ourselves. This is too huge… Too valuable to hold underground—"

The first doctor whirled on him. He was larger than the fourth doctor with a muscular frame beneath his lab coat. His gaze held a harshness Valentina could see even from afar.

He pinned the doctor against the wall and wagged a finger in his face. "Do not utter those words out loud. We all know what's at stake here. We all know what this could mean to the wider world. As doctors, this is something we promised to deliver to help millions of people the world over. But we cannot say that here. We cannot do that right now.

"We play the game. We play well. We must first glean the full information. Then, once we're out of this godforsaken jungle, we work. Understood?" He looked over each shoulder to check the corridor and ensure no one was approaching or listening. "Understood?" he nudged.

The fourth man nodded. "It's exciting, is all. Can't blame a man for letting his thoughts run ahead of him."

The woman made his case. "You're not wrong there."

"Those are the thoughts that will get you killed," the first doctor scolded. "Keep them to yourself, and you might survive long enough to bring this information to the world. For now, stay silent and keep your head down. Once we've drained this maniac for all the coin he has, then we can unleash this information bomb to the public."

They continued on their way, silence falling thickly between them.

Valentina allowed the drone off its perch. She guided the machine the way the doctors had come. It didn't take long until she found what she thought she was looking for. Her heart beat fast in her chest at the idea of seeing Kit again.

A thick steel door barred her way. A small window allowed Valentina to see inside.

What she saw surprised and terrified her.

CHAPTER TWENTY-TWO

A finger.

Santana stared down at the lonely digit, confusion on her face mixed with a small assumption that she guessed wouldn't be too far off the mark.

Terra crouched and picked up the finger. After a quick examination, she confirmed Santana's thoughts.

"Valentina," she announced.

Santana exhaled. "Both my first guess and every guess thereafter."

Without waiting to discuss it, Terra set the finger on the digital scanner. The door unlocked. "Are you ready for this?" Terra's rifle was ready in one hand. Her determined expression gave Santana confidence.

Santana glanced over her shoulder at Gyles. He was a little paler in the face than the women, but he held his gun with conviction. "Ready when you are."

Santana drew a deep breath. "What's our plan of action here?"

Terra set her gaze on the door ahead. "To conquer. If we go in there with enough gusto, we might catch some of these motherfuckers off-guard. Who knows? Maybe a very generous chap will be able to guide us to the lair's inner workings."

Santana exchanged a look with Gyles. *Who knew? Stranger things had happened.*

She drew her weapons. A pistol filled one hand, her whip in the other. Although thoughts of Dick clouded her mind, she knew she had to continue.

They were close now. She could feel it, the tension pregnant in the air.

"Let's go," Terra announced.

She swept through the door, taking her first bold steps into the inner ring. No one was there to greet them, but they sensed activity and heard voices farther down the corridor.

Santana followed Terra as they briskly walked on, trying to drink in their surroundings as they passed. Rocks and metal fused in a modern dungeon created by one billionaire psychopath. They traversed the first stretch of corridors with ease and found the first group of hostiles to their left. Terra aimed at them, announcing, "Freeze! AJS!"

To their credit, the group obeyed. Their hands flew into the air.

Terra advanced on them swiftly and pulled out sets of magnetized handcuffs, which she quickly slapped on their wrists. With Gyles and Santana, she dragged them into a side room to keep them out of sight. Terra warned them about what might happen if they caused a fuss.

The trio continued until they found a solitary woman strolling down the corridor with a clipboard in her hand. She looked as though she'd never seen a gun in her life.

They swooped down, incapacitated her, and left her locked up in a nearby room.

They paused before they continued. Terra's hand rested on the door.

"Where are all the guards?" Santana asked.

Terra looked back the way they'd come. "Maybe they're all on the perimeter, and we skirted them to take out the worst of the enemy?"

Giles raised an eyebrow. "Do you really think that?"

Terra shrugged. "Impossible to tell. The only way to know is to carry on forward. Keep close. The worst is yet to come. I can feel it."

They moved on through the corridors, taking down another group of white lab coat-wearing doctors. As Gyles and Terra dragged the final one into a room off to the side, Santana looked at the wall and a list for what was on each level.

When Terra emerged from the room, Santana pointed at the sign. Her finger hovered near B4: Lab. "Sounds ominous, doesn't it?"

Terra nodded her agreement. "Well, I know where we need to head, then. If there's one place here where they'll keep a medical experiment, my money is on a lab."

"Agreed. Where are the stairs?" Gyles replied.

They looked in all directions.

Terra replied, "No idea. Let's keep moving forward. That's all we can do."

Gyles followed, adding, "How do we find our way back out?"

Santana and Terra exchanged a look. Both of them had the answer, but it wasn't worth saying out loud. They weren't thinking that far ahead.

Valentina was worried.

Things had been remarkably easy so far. Considering the value of the project they were hiding, Valentina had imagined platoons of shooters, automatic turret guns set into the walls, more security panels, the whole works. The outside area had been impressive at first, but the farther into the rabbit hole she went, the more she realized this was all they'd managed to do.

The one thing that changed her mind on that was when she finally stood outside the laboratory doors. She peered through the small glass window. Inside, all was blinding whites, steel tables, silver computers, dazzling lights, chemical paraphernalia, monitors, and a half-dozen or so scientists milling around the space.

That wasn't what drew her attention. She'd expected all of that and saw much of it the last time she'd encountered Archie.

Now, there were more of them. Dozens of cadavers rested on silver tables, some posed upright and bound by metal braces around the arms. Large metal braces around their necks secured their heads from flopping to the side or forward. Their bodies were pale with thin blue veins on stark display, contrasted against their skin. There were men and women of varying ages, each with tubes feeding into an arm and reddened marks on the skin where they'd been prodded and poked.

They're not cadavers. They're subjects. *They're very much alive.*

Valentina's lip curled. Monitors and machines pulsed with information on each subject. The doctors milled around, taking notes or sipping their coffees as if this was the most natural thing in the world. Valentina couldn't understand it.

Were these subjects linked to her brother? Were they somehow an extension of the AI program? How did Archie ferry them here while keeping the base a secret?

Unless...

Her blood ran cold. A question bounced around in her head, one she didn't particularly want the answer to. Were these people former employees of Archie's business?

Valentina looked over her shoulder, ensuring that no one followed or watched her. She set to work on the security panel.

This one was different from the others. Users could only enter with the swipe of a card. There would be no severed finger, no voice activation, merely good old-fashioned analog tech-nology—in Valentina's opinion.

She examined the panel, wondering if there was a way to short circuit or overwrite it. The techs had securely anchored it in the wall, but Valentina spotted a small crevice where she could gain access to the main panel.

She took a small silver instrument from her pocket and slipped it into the scant opening. The metal groaned and cracked, and the corner flew off and clattered on the floor as she worked to lever the panel free.

Footsteps came from behind her. She played inside the open-ing, gripped the jagged corner she'd created, and tore off the panel.

This time, she gently placed it on the floor.

When she stood, someone was watching her.

The man froze ten feet away from where Valentina stood. He was tall. His white lab coat only reached his thighs, showing that Archie's people hadn't thought of uniform sizes when they'd invited their staff to join the mission.

"Hello?" Valentina offered.

The man gingerly raised his hand and wiggled his fingers in hesitant welcome.

He was much larger than Valentina in both height and girth. Although he was a scientist, his shape and muscular definition suggested that his skills extended beyond the intellectual and into the physical.

She looked back at the panel, then at the man. "This is noth-ing." Her mind flashed back to a Jedi in a film she'd watched as a child.

The man cocked his head as his gaze drifted to the panel. His eyes slowly widened as he realized the intruder in their midst. He drew a deep lungful of air and was about to call out when Valentina rushed him.

Her knee found the pit of his stomach. He doubled over

wheezing, but he didn't go down. Valentina followed up with a right hook to his cheek, and the man's saliva turned pink as his head jerked to the right. Moving quickly, she twisted behind him and swept his legs out from underneath him.

He smacked down on the floor, his head close to crashing on the hard surface. She straddled him, trying to use the same incapacitation technique she'd used on the woman in the closet.

The man was down but not out.

He reached out, grabbed Valentina's throat, and squeezed tightly. His hands were warm and clammy. His reach kept Valentina at bay, and suddenly she was flailing, unable to execute the final takedown. His grip was tight as it compressed her windpipe.

Valentina's face turned the same shade as her hair. She kicked wildly, finding the soft flesh of his stomach. She hunted blindly, using her toes to feel the different areas of his body.

He brought his knees up to try and shield himself from her attack.

She soon found his delicate parts.

His grip weakened just enough. She used the opportunity to slip out of his hold and fell beside him. She sputtered, gasping for breath. She couldn't remember the last time someone had choked her so.

She pushed herself up for more leverage, only to find that the man was doing the same. She got to her feet and ran straight at him, striking him in the center of his stomach, attempting to bring him back down. He remained steadfast despite his visible pain, getting one foot under him, then the other.

Valentina launched a series of punches to his ribs before attempting to sweep his legs out from under him again. He stood firm and tall, like a stone giant.

The scientist gathered himself, looked down, and swung a meaty fist at her. It connected with her face, the blow like an anvil strike. She flew into the wall, and her head smacked against the rock.

A warm sensation met her forehead. Something trickled down the bridge of her nose.

She heard him coming before he arrived. The man cursed as he hurtled toward her with death in his eyes.

She spun away this time, and his blow met the rock.

He shook his fists wildly, but that didn't change the cracking of bone she'd heard a moment before. Then she was on him once more.

She scaled the man's body, secured a firm grip, hooked one elbow around his meaty throat, and locked the chokehold with her other arm.

The man's breath rasped, and though she squeezed tightly, he was a tough boa to constrict. He stepped back and slammed her against the wall. The air gushed from her lungs. She held on— what else was there to do? Her back ached, and she was sure more blood poured from the back of her head, yet slowly, surely, he weakened.

Valentina gritted her teeth as the man began to wobble. She felt his muscles soften as his eyes rolled back. He toppled forward with Valentina clinging to him like a desperate surfer attempting to survive the waves.

Then he was down.

Valentina paused a moment, gathering her breath. For a scientist, this guy had been a challenge. She only hoped there weren't more like him ahead. Or that she could get the advantage easier if it happened again.

She rose to her feet, brushed the dust and debris from her clothing, then turned her attention to hiding the body. She heard others farther down the tunnels, but this place was still surprisingly quiet.

She poked her head into the other corridor and located a nearby doorway. She dragged the man with some difficulty, his cheek scratching along the metal grates. When she opened the door, she found two staff members sitting on a couch, facing away from the door with headphones on. They sat cross-legged, one rolling a joint on his lap, the other happily smoking his.

Valentina moved slowly, dragging the man inside. The pair were in another world, clearly on some kind of break. There was an overflowing trash can in the corner, a shelf filled with dog-eared paperbacks, and several bean bags.

Valentina placed the man in the corner, then turned her attention to the other two. She debated leaving them but figured that wouldn't be in her best interest. She crept up behind them both and targeted the pressure points in their necks.

They struggled, but only for a moment. When they joined their mountainous comrade in slumber, she headed back out into the corridor.

She straightened her hair as she returned to the door. With the panel off, she pulled one of the wires and shut down the locking mechanism.

She wiped the blood from her head, then strolled inside.

CHAPTER TWENTY-THREE

Dick's head spun and throbbed.

He spluttered, and great waves of water sprayed from his mouth. He rolled onto his front, gasping for breath, his whole body aching and throbbing with pain.

Fuck...

It was dark—too dark to see anything at all. He blinked between grimaces, wondering if the world was dark or if he'd gone blind. His thoughts raced, his body dealing with the stress and physical pain while his mind attempted to understand his situation.

Where am I?

He tried to push himself off the ground, but blinding pain flared in his shoulder. Nearby something rushed loudly, echoing around his head until it was the only sound he knew.

He coughed.

He spluttered again. This time the water mixed with viscous bile. He lay there a moment, allowing himself to feel his body and understand his mind.

The ravine...the water...it dragged me away...

Snippets of memory came to him. The last he remembered

he'd been falling into blackness, hadn't he? Hadn't that been where he was? His grip on the gun had failed, and the rope had slipped from his hands…

Yes. That had been it. He remembered fighting the current, his head smacking the rocks, and total weightlessness coupled with the dragging force of gravity.

Dick tested one arm for mobility. He reached out until it was straight, then flexed his fingers. He was a little sore, but there was nothing broken.

He tried to move his other arm—

—the blinding pain returned, searing his shoulder. He gritted his teeth and bit into the damp collar of his shirt.

Yep. Broken. What to do? What to do?

Dick drew a couple of strengthening breaths, then used his good arm to lever his body upright. More pain flared around his ankle as he worked onto his side. He allowed the shouts and cries of pain to sound around him, echoing back even louder than they left his lips. He roared until he sat upright, his good arm scooting him back until his back met rough stone.

A cave. I'm in a cave…

Dick tried to see around him, but nothing came to light. There was no natural light source, no way to make out how far he'd fallen, or whether there was a path back to the surface—if he could climb that far.

He blinked away the hot tears and steeled himself. He gingerly brought his good hand to his painful shoulder. A surge of pain spiked as he felt the place where the bone shouldn't have been. He flexed his ankle, and though it hurt, he was thankful that it didn't feel broken.

A short, tender examination of his injuries gleaned multiple lumps on Dick's head, one which was still weeping, and more fleshy bruises than he could count. He thanked his lucky stars that it seemed only his shoulder had taken the brunt of the topple.

How did I escape the water?

Dick patted himself down, hunting for his effects. He felt their shape in his inner pocket, then hunted inside. He felt his cell phone, as well as a cold, square shape resting inside. He pulled them both out.

He placed his cell phone on his lap, then checked the second item. He fumbled to unscrew the top, then brought the spout to his lips. He raised the hip flask high, draining the contents without much fanfare. The liquor burned his throat, but it was the closest thing to an anesthetic he was likely to get.

The liquor warmed his stomach. After the final drops had poured, he slipped the flask back into his jacket and picked up his cell phone.

He found the power button. The screen lit up. The glass had cracked, but he could make out the company logo as the pixels flared to life. Although ordinarily dim, the screen cast a glow around him that was bright enough to see his immediate surroundings. He pointed it nearby, unsurprisingly finding uneven cave ground and the surrounding wall.

When the menu loaded, he checked the battery. There was less than twenty percent left.

Dick grumbled, then found the flashlight app. The cave burst into light.

He was in a grotto. The nearby entrance opened to a pool of water that rippled gently. The pool trailed onto either bank, the water growing shallower and shallower. Dick concluded that he must have drifted ashore and that possibly his body had done some of the work for him. Judging by the damp trail leading from the pool's edge, that confirmed it.

He rose to his feet and limped toward the water. He shone the flashlight to his right where white, foaming water gushed past about fifty yards from where he stood. It flooded into the pool, and in the cell phone light, he spotted colorful mushrooms dotted around the damp rocks, as well as bleach-white crabs and fish swimming in the crystal water.

"What the hell is this place?"

His voice echoed back, asking himself the same question.

A jolt of pain surged in his shoulder. He gasped, reaching for it with his good hand, before hesitating and deciding better than to touch it.

He knelt, grimacing as he tugged at the corner of his shirt, tearing a long strip of cloth and revealing his stomach beneath. Dark, damp hairs coiled on his flesh. Working carefully, he tied the ends together to create a makeshift sling, then maneuvered it around his body.

The cave filled with more cries of anguish as he fought against his instincts and moved his arm into place. When he finished, he was surprised to find himself cross-legged on the ground. The pain subsided in his shoulder but left a gentle pulse.

"You're in it now, Dickie-boy," he muttered and turned to look up at the waterfall. Even with the light shining, he couldn't see the top.

How far had he fallen? Where did he whack his shoulder?

More importantly, where were Santana, Terra, and Gyles, and how the hell was he going to get out of here?

He took his time examining his surroundings, not quite ready to leave the known land of the waterfall. Over the next half hour, he tested his strength. He grew breathless as he walked farther from the falls and explored the innumerable tunnels and off-shoots of the cave system.

Not too far from where he awoke, he found a black hole leading down into nothingness. The edges sloped inward as though the cave was trying to suck others inside. The light from his cell phone wasn't powerful enough to see the bottom, and even when he dropped a pebble into its center, he heard no collision.

By the water's edge, he found a series of stones he could walk across, their tops flat and wide and only a little slippery. He crossed to the other side and discovered a wall with a series of carvings and sketches on its surface.

"What the..." he marveled. There were pictures of people scratched into the stone, some with rudimentary colors staining the rock. He saw spears and creatures that had been long extinct, along with runes and strange shapes that made no sense to him. He'd viewed things like this before on the Internet, but to witness it in real life...

He wondered if anyone else had found these before.

Something *clattered*. The noise bounced toward Dick. It sounded as though someone had thrown a stone and it had landed nearby.

He turned in all directions, looking for the culprit before chuckling to himself. He was alone. Maybe a fragment of rock had fallen from the ceiling. Of course, there would be strange noises down here.

He walked along the water bank, following its winding path. Occasionally he took short rests to regain his breath, his tired legs protesting with each step. The pictures followed him, working like a primal zoetrope, telling stories of hunting and tribe culture and early celebrations of some humanoid race.

He rounded a corner and disturbed a small nest of bats. They rushed into a dark cloud and whizzed past him, their wings batting his cheeks. He threw his good arm up to block the barrage. The movement jerked his broken shoulder.

The flaps of their wings were audible for minutes after they were gone from sight. Dick shook his head, the pain in his shoulder beginning to make him nauseous. He turned back to face the way he'd been walking when something caught his eye.

A strange, dull, pulsing light came from up ahead. At first, Dick wasn't sure he could believe what he saw until he moved a little closer. The light throbbed steadily. The nearby walls glowed bright, then dull in its presence.

As Dick walked toward the light, he discovered that the pulsing glow and the ancient carvings on the wall beside him weren't the strangest things he could see.

As he glanced down at the rocky ground, he found the wet, fading prints of human feet.

CHAPTER TWENTY-FOUR

"Shit, group up ahead," Terra muttered and frowned.

"How many?" Santana asked.

"Eight."

Gyles gulped. "Can we take them?"

Santana offered Gyles a surprised smile. "Now we're getting into the fighting spirit."

Gyles gave an affirmative nod.

Terra pressed her back to the wall. Santana sensed her determination, but she worried about what they might've potentially dragged her into—which was more than could be said for Valentina. Santana's thoughts kept flickering between Valentina and Dick Chambers.

Santana's chest grew tight. Terra drew her attention back to the moment. "They're coming."

Footsteps sounded. After a silent count of three, Terra stepped out from their hiding place with her rifle pointed at the group's center. Santana accompanied her. Gyles flanked the other side. The group paused.

"Who are you?" The man wore a far more casual outfit than Santana had seen so far.

"It doesn't matter," Terra replied. "What matters is that you cooperate and make this easy. Otherwise, we'll have a real problem, won't we?"

The man's gaze flashed to Terra's uniform. Santana spotted a hint of silver by another's side.

"Terra," Santana warned.

"It's okay," Terra replied. "Two and six."

The woman on the left of their group frowned. "Two and six? What kind of code is that—"

Santana cracked the whip. The coil lashed out and struck the second on the group's left side. Another quick flick of the wrist and the whip struck the sixth in the row.

Both men cried out in pain and shook their hands. Their weapons hit the ground.

The group took this as the signal to erupt into action. Terra broke forward, striking the closest enemy on the head with her rifle. They fell face-first, and after Terra followed with a swift kick to the jaw, they stayed down.

Gyles raced beside her, lowering his shoulder and barging into his target. The man was skinny and struggled to take the hit. He flew backward, skidding along the floor.

Santana worked the whip, coiling someone around the neck before dragging them down. She flicked again, this time catching a woman's wrist and pulling her toward Terra. Terra headbutted her in the forehead, then twisted and kicked out at the nearest man who was crouching for the gun.

"I don't think so," Terra stated. Beside him, another of their crew went for the gun, but before she could, Terra stomped on her hands. She casually reached for the weapon, then aimed it at the woman's head. "Still want to try?"

The woman shook her head emphatically. Two of their group peeled off and sprinted down the hall. Terra turned to Santana, who read the message without the need to voice it. She aimed her tranquilizer gun and fired two shots.

They ran for a moment longer, then their bodies froze. They both slammed to the floor.

Gyles had their final member pinned against the wall with a gun pressed to his chest. Terra patted his shoulder, then began working around the group.

"How many sets of cuffs do you have?" Santana was impressed.

"As many as I need." Terra smirked, then tossed a pair to Santana. "Lightweight and compact. They're perfect."

Santana examined the cuffs. They were the very peak of AJS technology, a thin sheet of metal pressed into a loop with no chain to stack between them. As Terra slapped another pair on one of the downed enemies, Santana marveled at how the magnetic systems in the technology acted to bring the cuffs together. It was efficient, allowing cops to carry considerably more restraining devices without adding bulk to their effects.

"Want a turn?" Terra asked.

Santana hooked one of the rings around the wrists of a woman on the ground, then the other. Terra activated the cuffs, and they drew together, pulled by their magnetism.

"Impressive," Santana announced.

"We're full of tricks. Come on. Let's finish rounding up the cattle."

They dragged the group into a room piled high with boxes. Before leaving, Gyles suggested, "Wouldn't it be easier if we wore their uniforms?"

Terra raised an eyebrow.

Santana examined the group. "I suppose I could fit into her uniform. But this isn't *Scooby-Doo*. Does that shit even work?"

Terra nodded. "It could be an idea. Would mean that you'd be less identifiable as strangers in this place."

Gyles turned to the man nearest. "I'm sorry, fella. I'm going to hate this as much as you will."

The man kicked out as Gyles leaned toward him. He recoiled, avoiding the strike. "Stay still."

"Like this," Terra stated. She drew closer. Her rifle's muzzle caused the man to shrink in its presence. "Stay the fuck still. You got that?"

The man glared at her.

Gyles and Santana worked to strip two of the group they'd incapacitated. Soon they were awkwardly shuffling into their black fatigues, stretching the material and testing to see if it fit comfortably.

"Your turn," Santana told Terra.

Terra scoffed. "I don't think so."

"What?" Gyles asked.

"I'm not wearing someone else's sweaty clothes," Terra stated.

Santana raised her eyebrows. "Yet we're expected to? I thought we wanted to blend in?"

"No." Terra smirked. "You two can blend in. I'm wearing protective AJS nano armor. I'm happier wearing this than I will be in a pair of slacks and a friggin' t-shirt. Besides, you two can masquerade as my guards, taking me farther into the ring. If I put up a fuss, we might be able to skate by the other workers unnoticed. I don't know if you've been paying attention, but this place has a distinct lack of security."

Santana cocked her head. "Guess that's one of the downsides of building this so quickly. One thing that does surprise me…"

"What's that?" Terra asked.

"Well," Santana continued. "There's been no more sign of Val."

"I've noticed that, too," Terra replied. "Worrying, yes. That won't stop us as we carry on. Worst case scenario is we flank that bastard and take him by surprise."

"Optimistic," Gyles offered.

Terra met his gaze. "You give me an alternative way to be right now. Now, are you two ready? Because I'm going to put up quite the struggle."

"I'm sorry, this is a secure area," a lab coat-wearing man stated.

Valentina halted. The man had a red goatee, thin and neatly groomed. Wrinkles lined his face, and the top of his head was bald. He had an air of authority that kept the nearby doctors looking at their keyboard, and there was something sour on his breath.

"I have orders to see Archie." Valentina's gaze flickered toward the many naked bodies strapped to the tables. There was a strange smell in the air, like stale sweat and onion.

Rory Hawkins—at least, according to his name badge pinned to the pocket on his chest—lifted his chin. "Archie is busy. He's asked not to be interrupted."

"Then that's at odds with the instructions I have." Valentina's cold stare withered the man's icy exterior a touch. "I have strict instructions to come to him now. Are you going to be the one to tell him that you stood in the way of a direct order?"

A nearby doctor glanced toward them, gaze quickly switching back to his computer as Valentina turned his way.

"Then we're at odds," Rory replied. "Archie told me only moments ago to be left alone. He is *not* to be interrupted. I believe that my latest orders supersede yours in order of hierarchical importance. Now, if you don't mind, this is a secure area."

"Not anymore," Valentina replied. She jerked her thumb at the door. "Your door is broken."

Rory cocked an eyebrow. On a nearby computer screen, Valentina saw a digital projection of a human body mapped in an array of vivid colors. The mass of it was blue, with greens, reds, and yellows sparking over its hands, feet, and head. Beside the image was a series of pulses and charts monitoring the patient. Valentina read the name, and her heart beat faster in her chest: Kit Harris.

Rory frowned, snapped his fingers, and ordered the nearest

staff member to examine the door. Valentina attempted to slip past Rory, but he stepped in her way.

Valentina met his gaze, then drew her pistol. She kept it low, the barrel pressing into the man's stomach, the pair of them standing so close that she could block the gun from sight with her waist.

"Take me to Archie," Valentina crooned.

For a moment she wondered if the man was going to budge or if he was going to choose to be a stubborn fucker who tested her resolve. Thankfully for him, he turned and headed toward the back of the lab. Valentina brought the gun low, hiding it within the folds of her shirt.

She followed as he navigated around the mass of desks, computer setups, and bodies. Occasionally a finger would twitch, or an arm would spasm. The nearby doctors took note of the movement on their digital tablets.

Valentina wondered how they'd set up the network in a place like this. Wires trailed from the desks, then ran in long coils along the walls. Apparently, this base of operations had jumped back thirty years and had everything locally routed. If only she knew where the central server was, she'd be able to take out the whole damn place.

They neared a set of wide glass double doors. Before they could pass through, someone approached Rory.

The woman was older than him. Her dyed brown hair showed gray at the roots. Her back had a permanent hunch, but the keenness in her eyes sparkled behind thick glasses.

She asked Rory to sign something on her tablet. He paused, glanced at Valentina, then obliged. The mercenary moved closer and pressed the gun into his back, reminding him of what he was here to do and not to raise any alarm or suspicion. All it would take would be for him to jerk and try to fight or to call the woman's attention, and the whole place could erupt in chaos.

I'm so damn close...

She rose on tiptoes and craned her head to see the screen. Luckily for Rory, there was only a signature in sight.

The woman asked if Rory was okay. He sated her curiosity and sent her away. Beads of sweat pooled at the base of his neck.

Then they walked through the glass double doors into a sterile corridor. Here the rock walls had been fully covered with clean tiles. The smell of bleach hung in the air. There was no one in sight, and as they walked, their steps echoed loudly.

"You won't get out of here alive," he whispered. His eyes stayed fixed ahead.

"You haven't met me before," Valentina returned, but she knew that getting in was the easiest part, and she hadn't considered her exit strategy.

Please, Kit...be okay. Just do that for me, please.

They took a right, then encountered a solid metal door. Rory stopped. Valentina nudged him. She pressed the gun into his back. He swiped his card. The door unlocked.

"Well, aren't you going to be a gentleman and open the door for a lady?" she asked.

Rory clenched his jaw, then opened the door. A dark staircase descended into shadows.

"You best not be fucking with me, Rory."

"I'm not." Rory motioned. "This area is for priority staff only, secured for Archie and his private work. You wanted him. This is where you go."

Valentina lowered the gun and moved in front of Rory. She stood inches from him, ignoring his sour breath as her gaze bored into his. "Don't think about running off and alerting the others, now. You know the trouble that will get you into, don't you?"

Rory held her gaze.

Valentina smiled. "Do you know who I am?"

"The Red Countess," Rory replied. "Nice costume."

Valentina smiled. She reached up and gently patted his cheek.

His eyes widened as his body grew stiff. His lips flapped like a stranded fish before he toppled back.

He fell against the wall and flopped like an abandoned teddy bear. She crouched before him and held up the small syringe she'd injected him with. "Don't worry. It's nothing too serious. Only a little formula to buy me some time."

Rory stared at her, aghast.

"Minor paralysis," she explained. "Just don't swallow your tongue, and in half an hour you'll be right as rain." She took his badge from his chest. Rory looked at her desperately as though he wanted to fight back and stop her. "I'll take that. Thank you for your help so far."

She reached forward and kissed his nose, leaving a red smear on his face from her lipstick. "If this *is* a trap, I'll be back up real soon, ready to blow your brains out and paint the wall with your life force. So, let me ask once more. Is Archie down here?"

Although his body couldn't move, she read the truth in his eyes. She smiled. "Good boy. Hopefully, I won't see you again."

She turned, then descended the stairs.

CHAPTER TWENTY-FIVE

"Get your hands off me," Terra growled while wriggling to try and free herself from Santana and Gyles.

She was a good actress, Santana had to admit. They walked briskly through the corridors, Terra putting up a struggle when they encountered another in their path. They gleaned strange looks from local staff as they descended ever farther into the den.

Santana met their gaze, silently explaining that they were bringing an intruder to justice. Soon they were deep into the lair's heart.

"Labs this way," Gyles offered as they passed a sign on the wall. They turned, only to find yet another corridor.

"I hope you're tracking this," Santana quietly informed Terra. "APRIL has a built-in SatNav or mapmaker, right?"

"Just focus," Terra replied.

They headed straight, a group of men and women in black a little further ahead. Terra put up her struggle, trying to wrestle free of the others. Santana held her firmly, but Terra pushed in the direction of Gyles, catching him off-guard.

He fell into the nearest door, and the three of them tumbled through. Santana collected herself as the sound of hurrying footsteps grew louder. Her eyes widened as she found a large man, his face battered and bloody, sleeping on the floor beside her.

"Erm...Santana?" Gyles crooned.

Two men were asleep on the couch, lying on top of one another. The room stank of marijuana and an old TV was playing silently.

Terra rose to her feet. "I think we might've found a new sign from Val."

The door darkened as three people stood in the frame.

"Are you okay?" a young woman asked, her hair cropped at a severe angle.

The other two fixated on Terra. "AJS in the unit. Get her!"

They rushed in, two of them aiming for the AJS officer as the woman moved to help Santana get to her feet. "Move, quick."

Santana was hoisted back against the wall. She reached out and slammed the door closed to raise further attention as her so-called protector kept her from harm's reach.

Terra fought against the two men, her punches and kicks coordinated and well-placed. She let them get a few shots in, but soon it was apparent that she had the upper hand.

"Come on," the woman told Santana. "Restrain her before she gets free."

Gyles pushed himself on his ass, moving toward the wall and out of the way.

Santana moved into the fray, narrowly avoiding a blow from Terra. As she joined the group, she spun, turning her attention to the woman. She punched her cheek, sending her spinning to the floor. With a backward kick, she caught one of the men in the stomach. Terra did the rest of the work, maneuvering quickly to restrain them and bind their wrists.

"Shit, running low," Terra complained, holding out the last remaining cuffs.

Gyles stood above her and handed her a roll of duct tape.

"Where did you get this?" Terra asked.

"In the corner." Gyles pointed near the unconscious men.

They slapped some tape on their captives' mouths, then examined the room. With six captives in the space, it was getting pretty crowded. Santana raised the eyelids of the unconscious on the couch. "They're drugged."

"With what?" Gyles asked.

"Hard to say," Santana answered. "Could be several things, but judging from the lack of marks, wounds from an injection, and the smell in here, I'd guess marijuana."

"She's been here," Terra repeated. "We must be close."

"Are they going to be okay?" Gyles looked at those unconscious and bound on the floor.

Terra drew a long breath. "I hope so. They might get in some shit from their leaders, but that's not our problem. Come on, let's get a move on."

Santana was the first out the door, studying the halls. They sidled out, Terra taking the center position again. Gyles closed the door after turning off the lights.

They came to the next turn, then paused. A man in a white lab coat crouched near a door with a glass window, apparently fixing a ripped-out metal panel next to it.

They watched him for a moment. Santana gazed through the window and saw the laboratory on the other side. Her mouth fell open.

The lab-coated man glanced over his shoulder. "Can I help you?"

Santana raised her tranquilizer gun and shot the man in the neck. He flopped over, landing face-first on the metal grate.

Gyles turned her way. "That was a little reactive."

Santana pointed.

The three looked through the window, each of them shaking their head when they saw the numerous bodies strapped to the tables.

"Holy fuck..." Dick gasped.

His face lit up in shades of blue, the pulsing glow from the Atlanticore fragment causing his eyes to sparkle. The fragment was the size of a fire hydrant, half-buried in the wall. Around the main fragment, dozens of smaller cores glowed and pulsed with their mysterious light.

"It's beautiful." Dick shook his head in disbelief. "Stunning..."

He looked around the pocket cave. It was around the size of a small hut or igloo, the walls smooth and carved. In the spaces with no Atlanticore were more of the strange carvings and sketches. This time, they showed men and women excavating the fragments and using them for bizarre technologies. In one painting, Dick could have sworn that he saw a bike hovering above the ground, the blue pulse of a fragment powering it from beneath.

"What the hell is this place?"

The footsteps had led here, fading the moment he stepped into the chamber. It was almost as though the cave led him forward, driving his curiosity to bring him into this room. Now and then he glanced over his shoulder, worried that a door might appear and trap him inside.

A *hum* in the air accompanied the core's pulse. Dick had seen a few raw elements in his time but never had the opportunity to get this close to one before its excavation. The hairs on his arms stood on end. His throat was dry. He found it hard to look away.

"Unlimited power..." he muttered. "Contained in something so beautiful. A gem that has confounded science for decades."

He couldn't help himself. He reached forward, the flesh of his fingers tingling with energy as they drew near to the large fragment. It reminded him of his science experiments at school, holding a Van der Graaf generator and watching his hairs stand at attention or shuffling his feet on the carpet and feeling the static buildup on his skin.

He hesitated, fingers inches from the rock. The fragment's face swam in mystic blue as though there was a liquid energy inside, trapped beneath glass. His lips parted, though he held his breath.

Then he touched it.

The effect was immediate. His skin was on fire, then it doused, a sudden rapid flare and cool. He gasped as the energy raced around his skin, setting his nerves alight. His vision flashed white, exploding like fireworks in the night sky. It snatched his breath, his lungs aching for air. The only good thing was that the throbbing in his broken shoulder subsided.

He tried to pull his hand away, but it was as though he'd become magnetized. Somewhere far away he heard himself crying out, the echoes of the cave surrounding him in his shouts. The light built to a blinding crescendo until Dick was almost positive that he would pass out or end up teleported somewhere exotic, possibly aboard an alien spacecraft that had stolen him, an object of interest for the beings to study.

The light snapped off. He gasped for breath and dropped to one knee. He was tingling all over, but the worst of it was subsiding. He smelled burning and wondered if it was his flesh.

A tunnel unfolded before him. Where the largest fragment had been, there was now a crawlspace. The piece was receding into the opening as though it was floating or maybe burning a path through. Dick glanced over his shoulder, certain that a pair of eyes watched him.

When he found no one, he moved toward the fragment, still not quite able to curb his curiosity and draw himself away.

CHAPTER TWENTY-SIX

The first sound other than her footsteps was the gentle, rhythmic *beeping* of a machine.

Valentina slowed, treading lighter. She approached the bottom of the stairs—flights that had carried her several floors down, it seemed—and was now gifted with light.

She held her breath as she approached the opening. There was no door, only a large arch that led into a space she couldn't yet see.

"…excellent progress. Another couple of days and we'll have solid evidence that this was a glorious success." Valentina could recognize that voice anywhere, remembering Friedrich, the little scientist with the large brain. "Soon we'll have broken all known beliefs of science and will be able to cure so many people the world over."

A dark laugh rang. "Still? After all this time you still focus on health over profit? Don't you understand what we have here? It's a fucking goldmine. A chance to fleece the world and take over Atlantica. With this much coin, we'll be able to make Wendy and Stanley Howard look like peasants." She heard a slapping sound. "Almost there, aren't we, boy?"

Valentina crept closer. She ducked behind the arch, then peeked into the room.

The cavern was monstrous. The ceiling stood almost out of reach of the powerful floodlights that lit it from the surrounding walls. A walkway led to a platform that held a large glass booth. Outside the booth was a single desk with multiple screens. Friedrich sat behind it with Archie Fontana in a La-Z-Boy beside him, reclined and sipping from a glass filled with deep red liquid.

Valentina's blood boiled. The weeks of hatred that had consumed her threatened to spill. Her fists clenched, her lips thinned, her jaw set. She could do it now, could run out and kill him, end it all. It would be so easy.

If not for the miracle lying before them.

Movement drew her attention to the glass booth, which looked similar to the bedrooms she'd seen in old *Star Trek* episodes, only the walls were entirely glass. Inside, a man was sitting on his bed. He was all but naked, his body covered in tubes and wires. He had short stubble as his hair attempted to grow back.

"Kit…" The name leaked from her lips.

Kit Harris was awake, but he didn't look good. His skin was pale. He looked clammy, even from afar. His cheeks were gaunt, and his eyes had a glazed look. He reached out, attempting to grab a glass of water, but his fingers fell short, his hands flopping down weakly.

"We need to stabilize his vitals," Friedrich announced. "Before we can get too excited, we need to ensure that he can survive off-monitor. Every test so far has failed, and he's still refusing to eat and exercise."

"Then pump him with food," Archie returned. "Force him to move. We're on a deadline here."

"Medicine doesn't work that way—"

"Bullshit," Archie snapped. He drained his drink, then got to his feet. He crossed to the glass, staring in at Kit. He hammered a fist, then called, "Get moving, won't you? You're supposed to be our medical miracle. Fucking prove it already."

Kit's head turned slowly, almost mechanically. His blank gaze searched for Archie but didn't find him. Valentina wondered if it was one-way glass.

Valentina had seen enough. She drew her pistol, using it to lead the way. She stepped onto the walkway, noticing that the cave fell into an abyss on either side. *What was it with this guy and dangerous places to keep his equipment?* She allowed herself a moment to search for tracks, wondering if she'd get a repeat of her last encounter with Archie when the entire system had shot into the ground and carried him through the jungle.

"It's over," she announced boldly, her voice magnified.

Archie spun, his face melting through a kaleidoscope of emotions. It took him a moment to see who he looked at, Valentina not in her staple reds.

He flinched, eyes darting to his La-Z-Boy. He made a break for it, but Valentina was quicker, reaching for the gun that rested at the side of the plush chair and turning it on Archie. "I said it's over."

Archie took a step back, hands raised. "Valentina... What a surprise to see you here."

"I guess vanishing into the heart of the jungle would afford you that kind of luxury," Valentina retorted. "Stealing my brother, hiding miles beneath the ground, running your operation beyond any hope of others finding you. It was an effort to get here, but you knew I would make it in the end, didn't you?"

Archie half-shrugged. "I had a hunch. I thought the jungle would beat you, though."

"I'm resourceful."

"Clearly." Archie stared at her, tracking her gaze over to the glass booth where her brother sat. "You can't take him."

"Bullshit." Valentina's lip curled. "I haven't run through stinking bogs and climbed waterfalls to leave empty-handed.

You've played your part. He's back to consciousness. Now, over to me."

To her surprise, Archie started laughing. "No. That's not how it works. We've made leaps and bounds with the subject, but he's far from recovered—"

"Kit," Valentina barked, causing both Archie and Friedrich to jump. "His name is Kit."

"Kit is very much still in recovery." Archie lowered his arms, trying to regain his composure. "All of that equipment in there… without it, he dies. Take one of those out, and his vital organs will shut down. He's connected to technology, Valentina. Without the AI operating his vital systems, he'll be nothing more than a blob of flesh on the ground."

Valentina's stomach fell. She stared at Kit, her brother sitting there like a ghost of his former self. Around his armpits and neck were red patches, sores from lying down for so long, his body forgetting how to move and operate as he woke up. Was he stuck in here? Couldn't there be a way to remove him from his prison?

Valentina lowered the gun, her nostrils flaring. She strode over to the computer system and indelicately shoved Friedrich out the way. His chair toppled, the man's glasses falling from his face as he skidded on the smooth floor.

She turned her attention to the screen, allowing herself a moment to get lost in the information. She was an expert with technology and soon found her way around the interface. She explored the data readouts, little understanding what they told her, but looking for the key information linked to the glass booth in the center of the platform.

Archie moved to help Friedrich up. Without looking, Valentina held up the gun, aimed at his chest. "Don't fucking think about it."

She barely blinked. Her eyes soaked in the information. Her stomach curdled, all information pointing to the same conclusion Archie was relaying to her…

Except...

She stood straight, gun aimed at the frozen Archie. "It appears we're at an impasse."

"It appears so," Archie stated. "You say you won't leave until I've healed your brother, the same way it's always has been. We're on the same page."

"And those subjects outside?" One hand carefully traced the underside of the desk. The bottom was smooth, but Valentina soon found the little button she'd assumed would be there.

"Those bodies? Those staffers of yours strapped to their beds? The others you're experimenting on... What about them? Are they duty-bound to serve until they've been healed, or are they part of a wider experiment?"

Archie smirked. "I'll admit, our research into the AI has yielded some...impressive results. When we first set up in this place, I was...concerned, to say the least. The sub—" He stopped himself at Valentina's glare. "Your *brother* was on the cusp of collapse. Failure seemed inevitable. His heart rate declined at an alarming rate, forcing us to resuscitate him."

Valentina's fingers curled into fists.

"He was on the edge," Archie continued, nodding at Friedrich for support in confirming his story.

Friedrich had climbed to his feet and was busy adjusting his glasses. Somewhere far off, Valentina heard footsteps.

"That is correct," Friedrich stated. "By all accounts, your brother died. It was a fight to bring him back to the land of the living, and for the first few weeks, it seemed as though we'd lost all hope." He drew a deep breath. Valentina wished they would hurry up.

"We checked in every day, but the results were the same. No cognition, no conscious activity. It seemed as though all was in vain." His gaze flickered to Archie. Something unsaid passed between them. Anger, perhaps?

"But your brother became the miracle we needed," Archie

continued, taking over from Friedrich. He clapped, and his face lit up. "Valentina, do you know what your brother has signified? He is Lazarus. He is the revived. The AI...it *works*. From nothing to *everything*. All it needed was time to read the code, to replicate its intelligence, test the boundaries of your brother's nervous system, play with what was available before it could kickstart its processes." He stepped closer to Val. "He's *awake* because of us. Doesn't that please your soul?"

Valentina frowned. "I could get on board with your excitement if it hadn't been for you running away and hiding miles from civilization. I don't know how you'd react about someone stealing your brother and fucking off into hiding, but I imagine probably not terribly well. It doesn't give the best impression. Maybe a call or an update on his wellbeing would have worked well, but you didn't do that, did you?"

She aimed down and pulled the trigger. Archie cried out in pain. His foot exploded in a spray of red. He fell onto his ass, clutching the wound. Friedrich's eyes widened, and he moved to help his boss. Valentina turned the gun on him as she stepped away from the computer and slowly moved toward the booth.

"We had a fucking deal," Valentina declared, her volume increasing. "I fucking trusted you. You held the only thing that was precious to me, and you used him like a goddamn pawn. How dare you talk to me about success? How dare you talk of excitement? You see him as a plaything for your twisted games, but he's my brother!"

She shot again, this time getting Archie's other foot. The footsteps grew louder. Friedrich turned to run away.

"Stay!" Valentina cried and fired another shot. She caught Friedrich in the side of the shin, and though he yelled, he remained standing. He stopped in his tracks, quivering, his hands in the air.

Valentina reached the doorway into the booth. She produced

the card she'd snatched from Friedrich when she shoved him over, then swiped it. The door *hissed* open, sterile air meeting her.

It closed behind her but didn't block her view out the glass windows of the two dozen gunmen heading down the stairs and coming to assist in their call from the desk's panic button.

Valentina dragged a nearby cabinet and let it lie in front of the door. Producing a small pen-like device from her pocket, she jabbed the security mechanism. Blue sparks flew, and the green activation light died. The lights inside the glass booth faded, but those around the cave walls remained.

Definitely not one-way glass. She sighed. *That makes it even worse. He's been sitting in here knowing he's a guinea pig for...how long?*

The only saving grace she had was that inside the booth, all was quiet.

The gunmen filed in, breaking into a sprint to protect their master. They swarmed around him, blocking Archie from sight. A few of their number peeled off, weapons aimed at the booth. One of them shouted something that came through only muffled on Valentina's side. A barrage of bullets sprayed the glass, but they left only minor fractures. Valentina had been relying on this. She knew Archie would protect his asset, ensuring that no one could break in and claim him.

A small group crossed to the door, attempting to break in. Valentina turned back, saw that it wasn't as easy as they'd hoped, then turned her full attention to Kit.

She walked slowly, almost dreamlike. Kit perched at the edge of the bed. A railing rested against his stomach and kept him from falling. Her breath caught, and tears welled in her eyes. She aggressively swiped them away, hating the waves of emotion cresting inside her.

She stopped mere inches from him. She reached out, hesitated, and retracted her hand. "Kit?" Her voice was a mere whisper.

Kit didn't show any sign of recognition. He stared down at the floor, eyes unblinking.

"Kit?" Valentina placed the hand on his shoulder. His skin was cold yet sticky, as though he'd just rolled out of the ocean. "Can you hear me?"

She moved in front of him and crouched before her brother. In her peripheral vision, she noted that the gunmen had stepped back. She wondered if Archie had commanded them in the same way she would, to hold fire and wait for her and Kit to emerge. They couldn't stay in here forever.

"Hey…it's me," Valentina whispered, moving into his line of sight. She couldn't believe how painful this reunion was, how hard she found it to take in what he'd become. To see what he'd been and to know that this was what he was now, what *she* had made him—if somewhat indirectly.

Kit had been in the wrong place at the wrong time. The minions of her target, a rogue human trafficker named Harvey Bergenstein, had somehow discovered that Valentina had a brother, and they came for him.

They made it look like an accident, but it wasn't. Valentina knew better. The car's registration was to one of Bergenstein's men. It had sped around the corner when Kit set off across the road. It was late at night with hardly anyone around. They'd reversed over him for good measure before speeding off into the night.

The impacts had crushed his body. His ribs broke, his femurs fractured, his hips shattered, and he had a bleed in his brain. He was discarded, left as a sack filled with broken tools. When Valentina's alter ego Isabella arrived at the hospital, the doctors told her it was unlikely he'd make it through the surgeries. Three days later, he was still clinging to dear life.

He'd been in his prime back then. His body was athletic. He had friends, dreams, and hopes.

Now he was a husk, connected and bound to his equipment.

Over the years, Valentina had toyed with retirement ideas but had always chosen the thrill and the money over her limited family. Because of that, she paid the ultimate price.

"Can you hear me?" Valentina's heart dropped into her stomach. How was she going to get him out of here?

A flicker of recognition passed beneath Kit's eyes. His head turned, only a fraction. He drew a long breath. Stale, untreated breath filtered from his dry, cracked lips as he whispered, "Izzy?"

Valentina's frown broke. A smile crept onto her face. Her eyes lit up. She removed her trademark crimson wig to reveal long brunette locks. For a heartbeat, Valentina shrank back into her consciousness, allowing Isabella Harris to rise to the surface. She rested her hands on Kit's cheeks and drew him into an embrace, holding him more delicately than she wanted to, fearful that he might break.

"Bella…" Kit croaked. "How?"

"It doesn't matter," Isabella replied, her voice softer than Valentina's, much like her touch. "There isn't much time, okay. We have to get you out of here. We have to get you away from these people."

Kit turned his gaze to the windows, meeting the returning stare of two dozen shooters. His breath came in long, slow hitches. "How? I can't leave this. Not if I want to live."

He spoke as if in slow motion, each word a Herculean effort. Isabella wiped away her tears and turned his gaze back to her. "Listen to me. Do you trust me?"

Kit offered a weak smile. "Of course I do. Always and forever, sis."

"Always and forever…" Her lip quivered. "Listen, you might see some parts of me you don't like, but I want you to know one thing. I'm doing this all for you, got that? Once we're out of here, I can explain everything. I can help you recover. We can get miles away from Atlantica and all of this bullshit, and we can be happy. Do you believe that?"

Kit's gaze grew glassy, but he offered a slight nod.

"Okay, then hold on in there," Isabella replied, her voice already weakening as Valentina fought for dominance.

Valentina rose to the surface, her stance and demeanor hardening. She lowered her hands from Kit's cheeks, then turned her attention to the surrounding equipment.

A single question filled her mind. How the hell was she going to get them both out of this place in one piece?

Her internal reply was almost immediate, backed up by the echo of Isabella in her head. *Because you're Valentina Fucking Winters, the greatest mercenary Atlantica has ever seen, and you've yet to meet a challenge you can't overcome.*

CHAPTER TWENTY-SEVEN

Terra brought the laboratory under her control, if only temporarily.

Doctors were bound to their desks. The subjects lying on their metal tables were untouched. Santana and Gyles helped to wrangle those who put up a fight, but all in all, the captives were too intelligent to fight back.

"Where are all the military units?" Terra asked. "This is seriously concerning me. You'd have thought that the guard level would be higher for a place like this."

"I don't like it," Santana agreed. "I don't like it one bit."

"Over here," Gyles called from the far side of the room. A large glass double door barred their way. "There's a corridor along here."

Santana snatched a nearby staffer's ID badge, then swiped it at the door. The LED light flickered red.

"Doesn't have permission," Santana stated. "This is high-security." She turned back to the captives. "Which one of you can get us through this door?"

Terra marched over to someone nearby, then snatched their

card. She held it up. "You don't need them. Computer in my head, remember?"

The doors parted. As soon as the smell of bleach hit their nostrils, the distant sounds of guns firing met their ears.

"Oh, that can't be good." Terra broke into a sprint.

Santana chased her. Gyles brought up the rear. They ran in the relative direction of the echoes as more gunshots rang out. They reached a cross-section and found a doctor sprawled against the wall. His eyes moved, his brain alert, but his body was frozen.

A door stood open beside him. Terra held up a hand, warning the others to stop. "She's down there." Her tone held such conviction that Santana couldn't doubt her despite having questions. "Quiet, now."

They took their time as the sounds of voices muttering and issuing commands came from ahead. They tried to reduce their noise as they closed on the archway dozens of steps down into the dark.

They were near the bottom when a shadow grew before them. Feet appeared first, two sets of them, carrying something between them. Only when they entered the archway did Santana figure out what it was: two guards carrying a man.

His gaze rose to hers. He wore a sour expression, and blood dripped from the places where his feet had been. Santana had never met the man, but she'd done her research and instantly recognized Archie Fontana.

So, too, did Terra.

The guards dropped him indelicately and reached for their weapons. Terra and Santana were faster, firing and taking down the guards. Archie tried to turn and crawl back to the rest of his men, but before they could react, Terra had her hand on the back of his collar.

With strength that surprised Santana, she hurled him back

toward the stairs. His spine *cracked* against the metal. His eyes closed.

"Stay with him," Terra commanded Gyles. "Don't let him go anywhere."

"What about the others—" Gyles began.

"I said 'stay.'" Terra didn't wait for a response. She pulled a fallen guard and held him in front of her as a shield.

Santana tried to follow suit, but the guy was too heavy. Instead, she ducked behind the door and leaned out enough to watch Terra approach the others.

"Cover me!" Terra roared over the sound of returning gunfire.

"I am!" Santana called.

Terra's heart raced in her chest, but APRIL was doing its best to slow it down.

The world shrank around her. She moved as if in slow motion. APRIL's technology created a display in her vision where she could see each target, locate their weak spots, prioritize who to shoot, and calculate her chances of success.

At the moment her display read **fifty-nine percent,** but it was rapidly declining as the element of surprise faded, and they regained their wits.

Bullets sprayed the chest of the man she held before her. Her nano armor flared with light as bullets rebounded off her suit and fell into the depths below. She gritted her teeth, aimed her rifle, and swept the gathered crowd. Their numbers thinned fast, but they were still firing back, and that was a problem.

She reached the desk. A frail scientist with glasses cowered beneath it. Raising her foot, she booted the desk over, the computer equipment smashing on the floor. She tossed the body of the man before her, then crouched behind the safety of the desk.

For the first time, she could glance back at the entry. Santana was doing her part, her aim impressive as she took out more of their number. Terra employed APRIL's thermal vision, able to see where each target was. Some were retreating, working toward another doorway at the back of the room, across another suspended platform.

It's like these guys read the book on "How to be a Villain."

She peered over the desk and sprayed another barrage of bullets. The scientist groaned and cowered nearby. The assault of sound muffled her hearing, but soon their return fire slowed.

"Are you ready to shut this shit down?" Terra asked the AI inside her head.

Affirmative, came APRIL's reply. **Five remaining.**

Terra stood with her rifle in one hand and her pistol in the other. She leaped to the side, avoiding immediate fire, then took down the last of the group. Bodies littered the platform. A ringing sound filled the cave. She turned back to find Santana walking toward her, pistol leading the way as she kept an eye on the fallen.

Warning. Immediate threat—

Terra shot behind her without looking. One of the guards had half-raised a shaking hand to shoot at her. They fell, leaving Terra and Santana in quiet.

Santana took in the sight before her.

Bodies were everywhere across the platform. Blood pooled around them. She slowly advanced, cautious that it might not be over. Behind her, Gyles and Archie were silent.

"Nooo!" a voice cried. A man near Terra rose sharply to his feet. "Do you have any idea what you've done!"

He ran his fingers through his hair as he stared aghast at the computer equipment on the floor. Smashed screens, chips, and wiring were everywhere.

The man looked up at Terra with wide eyes. "You've broken the connection. All the research, all the information and data we've received, you've destroyed it." He motioned at a glass booth in the center of the platform. "You've single-handedly destroyed the asset. Without him, it's over. Without…this…he's as good as dead."

Santana and Terra looked at the booth. Inside, Valentina stared back at them. A man rested on the bed behind her.

"Oh, shit…" Santana breathed.

Terra's mouth fell open.

CHAPTER TWENTY-EIGHT

The gentle hum of electricity fell quiet in the room. The gunshots died down, and in their wake stood Santana, Terra, and Friedrich.

Valentina couldn't see Archie. At that moment, she couldn't have cared less about him because Kit had fallen.

He lay in the bed, eyes closed, his body limp. She raised his hand, but he couldn't hold it up. She could barely hear him breathe, and now that she was looking out at the chaos, she could see why.

The computer, the central console, was destroyed.

"Fuck..." she muttered as she raced toward one of the metal bars by the wall. She tore it from its moorings, adrenaline surging through her, then attacked the booth's glass front.

A spider web crack appeared. She smashed it again, then again, then again. After another few tries, she drew her pistol and fired it in the same location until the glass finally cracked. She picked up the metal bar, punched a hole through the fragments holding on for dear life, and roared, "What the fuck have you done?"

Terra and Santana froze.

"The equipment," Valentina continued. "It's all that was keeping him alive. You don't understand what you've done...how you've single-handedly killed him."

Santana looked between Terra and Valentina, searching for a hint of regret or panic on Terra's face. After all, she'd been the one who broke the computer. Terra had recklessly destroyed the link that was keeping Valentina's brother alive.

Valentina hopped out of the hole. The glass cut into the palms of her hands, but she didn't care. She couldn't feel it. She crossed to Terra and slapped her. Santana stepped back, her eyes wide. A bloody handprint painted Terra's face.

Terra showed no sign of retaliating.

"What is wrong with you?" Valentina cried. She didn't understand what was happening, the emotion that welled within her. Ordinarily, she'd have it handled, but this...it was all over because of this...cop.

She grabbed Terra's hair. Terra grimaced, then gripped Valentina's wrist with her hand. They wrestled, each woman grunting as they danced around the space. Terra punched Valentina in the stomach. Valentina attempted to sweep Terra off her feet, but she couldn't get enough purchase. The officer was well-trained.

"When you're quite done," Terra replied at last, shoving Valentina away.

Valentina's hair was disheveled. She paid no attention to the fact that her wig was still in the booth as her chest rose and fell. "You've fucked it all up. I don't know why I brought any of you. I should shoot you all now."

She aimed her pistol at Terra. Still, Terra didn't show a sign of remorse. Santana explored her options in her head, hand finding the handle of her whip.

"Your brother is going to be fine," Terra informed Valentina. "If you calm your shit, maybe we can talk this through."

"How?" Valentina returned. "How do you know?"

"Lower the fucking gun, and I'll tell you," Terra stated.

Valentina's arm remained locked in place. After a moment, it started to shake as she lowered the gun.

"Your brother is going to be okay because he's on a similar system to mine," Terra stated, looking down at the computers. "The AI in my APRIL system was the foundation of the software, and they've replaced vital functions of his brain with the technology."

"How do you know this?" Santana asked.

Terra once again motioned at the computers. "Because the AI is sophisticated, it's quick and smart. APRIL read the software as I approached the guards and gave me the read. The AI is already in your brother's system, designed to be independent of the machinery and equipment they've been using to sustain him."

Valentina's shoulders softened. She turned back to the booth. "He's so weak. He...he's barely able to sit."

Terra nodded knowingly. "Likely because your brother was rejecting their help. While the AI can heal his cognitive function and also serve his base needs, without sufficient exercise and food, he'll be a shell of what he was. He's been in bed for months, I'm guessing. Maybe even years. But, if he's weak, it's because he's chosen it."

Valentina headed back to the booth. She reached the sill, then swept the glass away with her sleeve. Hopping back inside, she approached her brother in relative quiet. She sat on his bedside, hand stroking his hair. His eyelids flickered. "Kit...are you really healed?"

Kit was slow to respond. "Hmmm?"

"Here." Valentina helped him back into a seated position with his arm around her shoulder. "You have the building blocks inside you to heal, but you chose to reject their help...why?"

Kit turned his head, the effort apparent in his eyes. "I thought you were dead. I didn't..." He swallowed dryly. "I didn't know where you were. I heard you...in my dreams, but..." His brow creased in pain. "I wouldn't give them the satisfaction..." His voice faded as he almost fell unconscious again.

"You wouldn't give them the satisfaction of winning," Valentina finished with a soft smile on her lips. "You're certainly one of the family."

Valentina waved Santana toward her, choosing to keep Terra at bay. Although Terra had been right, Valentina couldn't help but feel some embarrassment for her attack.

Santana hopped through the gap in the window, aiding Valentina as she brought Kit to his feet. It was easy. He was alarmingly light. They disconnected all the tubes and equipment from Kit, much to Friedrich's chagrin, then led him toward the hole.

Terra waited for them there, occasionally threatening Friedrich with a glare not to move. Together they passed the man through. Terra cradled him in her arms when he was clear of the glass. Valentina followed him.

Kit blinked in the bright floodlights, his gaze barely registering the bodies around him. Valentina extended her arms, silently instructing Terra that she would be the one to carry her brother to safety.

Wherever so-called safety was.

"How do we get out of here?" Santana asked.

Gyles emerged from the archway, dragging the unconscious Archie behind him. "Back the way we came?"

"What's through there?" Valentina motioned to the door at the far end.

Santana turned to Friedrich. The man attempted to shrink within himself so he could hide.

"There is no way out," Friedrich stated. "You don't understand..."

Terra crossed to Friedrich and backhanded him across the face. The man spun, then dramatically collapsed. He pushed back, attempting to get back to his feet. "It's Archie. You don't know the measures he's taken to secure the asset."

"I think we have some idea," Valentina replied. "But your *asset* is ours now."

Terra turned her rifle on Friedrich. "Way out. Instructions. Now."

Friedrich's lip quivered as he extended his hands. "There are a handful of emergency vehicles out that door, but you'll never make it out alive. It's too dangerous."

"Because your other experiments are zombie cadavers ready to give chase and destroy us all?" Santana replied sarcastically.

"No." Friedrich swallowed as if for theatrical effect. "Because Archie rigged this place to blow, and one wrong move will set the explosives in motion."

A beat of silence passed between them. Gyles looked around nervously.

"I'm sorry?" Santana asked.

Terra moved closer, the barrel of her rifle pressed against Friedrich's protesting hands. "Speak faster, speak true." She jerked the rifle away and fired a shot next to Friedrich's body. Metal *clanged* against metal, and a scorched smell hung in the air.

"He rigged the place!" Friedrich blubbered. "Archie was so obsessed with protecting the asset that he…that he…he rigged the place with explosives. They're everywhere, around the entire compound.

"He became *obsessed* with making this operation work, refusing to pay or support his guards, focusing only on Kit. Those outside were an extension of his madness. Archie figured he could create biological supersoldiers if he had enough time and motive."

"The bombs." Santana brought him back to the point.

Archie was quiet behind Gyles, his mouth open.

"They're wired to an electronic signal sent forth by a chip. Once the chip comes within range, the whole place goes up." Friedrich tugged on his collar. "See? I'm fitted with one, too."

At the base of Friedrich's neck was a pink scar, something lumpy and almost visible beneath it.

"You're joking," Gyles marveled.

"Hold on," Santana commented. "You're a prisoner within this place."

Friedrich nodded solemnly. "Unless the sequence is deactivated, there's nothing I can do. I'm stuck here."

"How do we deactivate it?" Terra asked.

"There's only one person who can." Friedrich glanced at Archie.

"Fuck." Santana ran her fingers through her hair.

Valentina scowled and shuffled to support her brother further, whose legs were barely able to take his weight.

"It's fine, though," Gyles declared. "As long as Friedrich stays here, we'll be good, right? We'll all be okay. *We* can go."

Valentina shook her head, picking up the unacknowledged elephant in the room. "No. Because my brother's AI has the same tracker, doesn't it?"

Friedrich nodded. "It does."

They exchanged glances. Santana's gaze lingered on the back door. "Where's the deactivation panel?"

Friedrich drew a deep breath. He walked slowly toward the booth. Gingerly holding the edges of the hole Valentina had made, he scrambled through the gap and inside. The others followed, Valentina waiting with Santana while Terra hopped through. Gyles dragged Archie closer, keeping him within range.

Friedrich moved to the center of the booth. He paused at one of the tiles on the floor, then crouched. He peeled the corner away and lifted the slab to reveal a digital console beneath. "It was the safest place," he explained. "This was the one place where we kept a constant watch on what was going on. No one apart from Archie or me could come in or out."

Terra was silent while examining the panel. Her gaze intensified as she allowed APRIL to scan the system. After a few moments, she announced, "It's a voice activation code. Password and voice signature required."

"How are we supposed to get past that?" Gyles asked.

Valentina handed Kit to Santana, then turned her attention to Archie. Without warning, she kicked him in the stomach. "Wake up."

Archie grumbled but didn't wake.

Valentina struck again, then again, and once more. Archie rolled onto his side, eyelids flickering. She straddled him and grabbed him by the collar. She pulled him up to her, then shook him. When he didn't respond to that, she slapped him repeatedly until faint words began to filter from his lips.

"Wake the fuck up," Valentina demanded.

Archie struggled to consciousness. He blinked stupidly, the pain of his destroyed feet apparent in his features as he let out a tremendous cry. Valentina clamped a hand to his mouth, muting as much as she could as she spoke to him. "The password. You will speak it into your little system, and we will get the fuck out of here, you got that?"

At first, Archie didn't seem to comprehend. She repeated the instruction, this time throwing him toward the booth. He slid along the ground, back smacking the remaining glass.

"Val..." Santana warned. "We need him."

Santana could only see red in Valentina's eyes. She stormed over to Archie and picked him up by the collar again. She lifted him off the ground, shoved him through the hole and into the booth.

"Val!" Santana cried.

Terra moved quickly, catching him before he could smack into the nearby equipment. Valentina hopped in after him. She dragged him over to the panel and held his face in front of it. "Speak your words, dammit. We *will* escape this place."

Archie chuckled, the sound lost amid a racking cough that rattled his body.

"Now!" Valentina demanded.

Archie turned to her, venom lacing the pain in his eyes. He wheezed as he spoke. "You always were a ruthless bitch, weren't you? I always knew it would come down to this, one way or another. It would end up being you or me."

"The password." Valentina ignored his words.

"And still you have no idea, do you?" Archie continued. "You have no idea how this will play out? Of the things I've done to control and maintain the great Valentina Winters."

Valentina drew her pistol and held it to his head.

"Go ahead, shoot me," Archie commanded. "You'll never escape this place. See, destiny has a funny way of playing out, especially when a hand other than God crafts it. You were an easy marionette to handle. Played like a fucking fiddle."

"What's he talking about?" Terra asked.

Valentina shook her head. "It's all bullshit."

Archie burst into laughter. A great blob of red saliva expelled from his lips. "You really don't know! Yet, it's so obvious."

Valentina moved closer to Archie with hatred burning in her gaze. "You're bullshitting. Whatever this is, you're buying time. It's over, Archie. The game is over."

"The game that I began!" Archie roared, his laughter turning to menace. He grimaced as pain jolted his feet. "You relied on me for Kit's health this whole time, obeyed my every command in the interest of protecting your precious brother, but it was I who put him in his situation in the first place."

All humanity that remained in Valentina's gaze dissolved.

"It was I," Archie continued. "I ordered the hit on Kit, knowing that you would *need* me for help. He was the ultimate disposable pawn. The great hook that kept you reeled in, on my side, able to help me to my purpose. The AI in his head, stolen from Deng at Tynamo Inc., the advancements we've made, none of it would've been possible without you, Val. Everything, all of this, it's because of you."

Valentina grabbed a fistful of Archie's hair. "You're lying!"

"No…" Archie grinned. Blood dribbled down his chin. "No, I'm not."

Valentina hit his head against the floor. Red painted the tiles.

She raised his head back to hers. "You son of a bitch. Give me the fucking password so we can get out of here."

"Fine…" Archie coughed, his eyes squeezed shut. "Fine…but know that it was always destined to end this way."

"With your death," Valentina stated.

"With *our* death." Before Valentina could say anything, Archie tapped a button on the console, then uttered, "Code Crimson."

The lights went out. Darkness fell. Silence settled around the room.

"Good luck," Archie declared—not knowing it was the last thing he'd ever say. Valentina shot in the dark, confident that she'd hit her target. As a gasp came from Gyles, an alarm blared. Red lights flashed, lighting up the cave in the color of blood.

Friedrich whimpered, already scrambling to the back door.

"Where is he going?" Gyles asked.

"Run!" Santana cried as the rumbling sounds of explosions came from far off in the caves.

CHAPTER TWENTY-NINE

A flash of gold caught Santana's eyes as the floor beneath her shook.

"Go!" Terra roared, following Valentina through the hole. They hopped clean onto the other side. Valentina relieved Santana of her brother. She threw Kit over her shoulders, then sprinted for the back door.

Terra pumped her arms, moving faster than the others, gaining fast on Friedrich. Gyles stumbled behind them, struggling to find his pace.

Santana froze. That flash of gold... That was...

"Santana!" Gyles called. "Come on!"

Santana jumped into the booth and raced across the tiled floor. She hopped over Archie's body, the world disorienting as it came to her in flashes of red. Rubble crumbled from overhead as the explosions grew louder.

"Santana!" Gyles repeated, hesitating on the bridge.

She saw them breaking ahead. Terra was already at the door, having overtaken Friedrich. She wrenched it open, allowing them to make their passage through.

Santana snatched the gold object and stuffed it into her bag.

She swung the strap back around and vaulted through the space. She landed deftly, then turned her attention to catching up with the others.

An explosion rang from the stairwell behind her. The floor jerked. She toppled, falling to her side.

"Go!" she screamed at Gyles, who still waited for her.

"Not without you," he roared.

"Go!" Santana demanded, pleased to see Terra run back to grab his arm. She dragged him away, the pair of them narrowing their gap to the door.

The platform dropped. Weightlessness overtook Santana. The rock around the door exploded, leaving a gaping chasm. The walls shook, and great hunks of boulders loosened and rained down.

The platform jammed at an angle. Santana pushed herself to her feet and ran.

Her heart raced. Gyles disappeared through the doorway with Terra and the others. She doubled down, her arms pumping at her sides. She cursed herself, wondering if it would prove worth it and why she couldn't leave a shiny object alone.

Explosions sounded around her, muting all other noise. Her eardrums throbbed in her head. Loose debris rained on her, rocks scraping her skin as she neared the door. She was close now, only a few meters away.

The platform groaned. A bomb detonated a short distance away. The anchors holding the platform in place gave way. Santana cried out, her hand moving to her whip. She lashed out, aiming for the rocky outcrop below the doorframe.

The whip found nothing.

Santana tumbled.

Above her, red lights shone intermittently, strobing her fall in shades of crimson.

Terra took the lead, her vision lighting the way ahead in shades of green. Behind her came the desperate footsteps of Gyles and Valentina. Gyles was sobbing, but they had no time to stop, not if they wanted to remain alive.

We need more light, APRIL, Terra urged the AI.

Her chest plate illuminated, bursting forth with light. The tunnel appeared before them, winding in jagged twists and turns.

"You couldn't have done that earlier?" Valentina called.

"I didn't know!" Terra's surprise joined the others.

The way ahead was guesswork, the metal grate flooring fading to rock. Even with Friedrich scrambling behind them, he was useless, his breathing getting in the way of his commands.

Clearly they hadn't given much thought to this side of the tunnel system. Terra kept her focus, ignoring the rain of rocks and debris falling on them. Even when Gyles cried out, she couldn't turn. There was no time. They *had* to escape.

She followed the cave system, taking what she assumed to be the most logical steps toward freedom. There were vehicles here. Friedrich had told them there were.

Eventually, the tunnels widened. The bursts of detonations were all-consuming. Terra spotted the first glint of a vehicle up ahead—a small helicopter. Its metal body caught the glimmer of daylight streaming from a crevice directly above them.

She increased her speed, commanding APRIL to guide her in identifying the system. She hopped inside and started the engine with a touch of a button. The cave filled with the thrum of machines.

"Get your ass over here," she yelled, feeling the craft already beginning to lift off the ground. The rotor spun overhead, kicking more dust into the air until it almost obscured the others.

Valentina was the first to get there. She indelicately threw Kit inside, having no choice but to leap in after him. She cradled him on the floor without strapping herself down.

Friedrich followed, stumbling and holding his chest. He scrambled inside. Terra pushed the thrusters.

The helicopter rose.

"Wait!" Gyles called, struggling to stay upright. Behind him, the walls blasted inward. The helicopter shook from the magnitude of the explosion.

Terra had no choice but to go. She lifted off, aiming for the gap above them, hoping that the detonations wouldn't stop them at the last hurdle. Gyles closed in and jumped. His hands wrapped around a metal landing strut in a death grip. Even above the din, she heard his cries.

They rose higher, accelerating toward freedom. Below them, everything crumbled, exploded, and shattered. Blast after blast after blast rang out...

Then they were aboveground and rising into a day lit by sunshine. It stung their eyes, the intensity of the greens, blues, and browns causing them all to shade their eyes. The helicopter lurched as rocks collided with its underside. They rose higher and higher until they were confident they'd cleared the worst of it.

Terra steered the helicopter away from the blast radius, watching the impact of the bombs below them. An area at least a mile wide sank into the jungle, the trees and ruins above ground collapsing in on themselves. The roar of the blasts was audible for miles around.

Terra hovered for a short moment, waiting for the worst to pass. When she heard Gyles' shouts from below, she searched for a place to land. Her thoughts were with Santana, yet another casualty on the list of those who'd fallen in the rumble in the jungle.

CHAPTER THIRTY

Santana fell.

She didn't know how long she'd fallen or how long remained. She raced the boulders and smaller rocks, fell through a rain of dust and pebbles. She struck out with the whip, hoping to find something to purchase, but no luck so far.

She cried out. The red lights stopped as the final blasts rang. She bashed into a rock below her, struggling to comprehend the physics of velocity as she repeatedly lashed out with the whip.

This isn't how I end. Not like Mom...

She jerked to a sudden stop. Her whip had caught something on the wall. She swung, her side hitting the rock. She reached out blindly and pulled herself in, shrinking away from the worst of the tumbling debris. She found shelter and froze, listening intently as the rubble and dust fell farther.

She had no idea how long she held herself there, hoping and praying that the bombs wouldn't blast even deeper. She had no idea where she was or how far into the earth she could be. All she knew was that she had to hold on. There was nothing else to do.

Her body was slick with sweat. In the darkness, as the world beat its own percussions, she saw her mother, suspended before her. Her smile was once enough to light up a room, but it didn't work down here. Ghosts weren't real. Even Santana knew that.

*Please, please, please...*Santana whispered on repeat, uncertain when everything would stop. She closed her eyes and prayed to a God she didn't believe in, only knowing that survival was key, and this was all she had.

She had no idea how long she waited in the darkness. She felt the air move from falling rubble, heard the echo of it landing some distance below...

Eventually, all fell silent.

Santana waited in the quiet darkness, scared to make a move. She gripped the whip and finally dared to attempt to reach into her bag for light. She drew out her cell phone and activated the flashlight, aware that the power icon was blinking red.

She found no comfort in the sight that lay before her. Even with the cell phone's light, she could only see darkness. She was on a rocky cliff face, unable to fathom the distance below, above, or across.

Her whip had looped around an outcrop. Now that she examined it in the light, it looked much too unstable for her liking. She twisted slowly, exploring the length of the rocky walls. Her stomach jumped when she saw a platform a short distance below her. Not only that, but it appeared to lead inward and away from danger.

How to get there?

Santana turned her attention to the grooves in the wall. Her fingers were sore from holding onto the whip, and a layer of greasy sweat covered her flesh, but she started her descent.

She worked slowly, keeping the whip nearby and using it to anchor herself to any outcrop she could find. Her muscles were corded, shaking from the effort of holding her body close to the rocks. Inch by inch, she made her way down.

This is what you trained for, Sokolov. This is what it was all building toward. You can do this.

Her foot slipped. She recovered. Her hand grabbed crumbling rock. She pulled herself back.

With great effort, she stretched her leg, her toes making contact with the platform. With one last leap, she landed on solid ground...

...or what she thought was solid.

The platform crumbled beneath her. Santana leaped into the tunnel, allowing herself a moment of recovery as the falling rock echoed around the chamber.

She lay there for some time, drawing deep breaths and letting her body rest. She pulled her flask from her pack and drank a swallow of water. There was only a little left, so she drank sparingly. She rifled through her bag and found the last of her protein bars—an emergency one she'd held back from the others, heeding her father's advice to stay prepared.

She thought of eating but decided to put it back in her pack. After some time, she pushed herself to her feet and explored the way ahead.

The tunnel led into the distance, which was some relief. She'd worried about finding an immediate dead end, but luckily it didn't come to that. Shining the light ahead, she entered the tunnels, knowing that there was nothing else to do, and praying that she wouldn't hit *her* dead end.

"We have to go back!" Gyles was frantic. He remained in the helicopter while Terra stepped out to get some air.

They'd found a flat, open crest of a hill not too far from the destruction. In the distance, the volcanoes loomed like giant's teeth. She propped her hands on her hips and drew in great lungfuls of air, waiting for APRIL to stabilize her vitals.

"We can't just leave her there!" Gyles protested, turning to

Valentina for support. Kit lay on her lap with his eyes closed, his chest barely rising and falling.

"She's gone," Valentina offered softly, saying what Gyles didn't want to hear. "She's gone, Gyles. No one could've survived that blast."

"No." Gyles' eyes sparkled. His breath hitched. "No...she can't..."

Terra met his gaze, then turned away, only confirming the thought.

"It's over," Valentina repeated. "There's no going back in there. Everything Archie had worked toward. It's gone... It's... She's..."

Friedrich shuffled uncomfortably in his seat, the only one to employ his seatbelt. He looked down at his toes, sadness in his eyes. "Such a waste." He glanced at Kit. "At least the asset survived."

Valentina glared at him.

Friedrich shrank back.

"Terra," Valentina called. "We need to go. He needs medical attention."

Terra drew a few more lungfuls of clean air, then returned to the pilot's seat. She strapped herself in and encouraged everyone to do the same. The helicopter rose as each person on board silently thought the same thing: aircraft that fly over the jungle generally crash.

She veered off toward the foggy distance, taking her best guess at the city's direction. Gyles and Valentina fixed their gaze on the forest, both of their heads filled with thoughts of Santana Sokolov and Dick Chambers.

A staircase appeared in the darkness before her.

It was roughly hewn, but there were clear signs of human interference. Santana paused to examine the area with her flashlight. On the wall were a few scratches and dabs of ancient paint. She frowned, not wanting to head farther into the depths of the earth but unable to stop her curiosity. If there were signs of civilization down here, maybe there could be resources, shelter, even a way out.

She descended into the dark. The staircase wasn't straight but wound in the tunnel's natural direction. As she walked, the paintings and sketches grew more sophisticated until she stared at tapestries on the wall, great storyboards of past events. She saw extinct creatures, hunters with spears, a whole timeline of human activity.

Her heart leaped into her mouth. In the shadows ahead, her mother followed.

She reached the bottom of the stairs and stepped into a chamber that took her breath away. The walls were straight and carved with a smooth brick design. There were seats of rock lining the walls, and in the center of the room was an ancient stone dais, its borders glittering with patterns of gold.

Santana stopped, drinking it all in. She couldn't believe what she saw. How hard had she hit her head on the way down? What was this place, and who was it built for?

Multiple tunnels sat at intervals around the room. On the walls glittered fragments of Atlanticore, casting the room in a ghoulish light. She turned off her flashlight, wanting to preserve the little power that remained as she examined the room.

"An ancient battle..." she breathed, reading the nearby painting of dozens of fallen soldiers scripted on the walls. "An advanced civilization... How can this be?" She stroked an image of a woman riding a hovering craft of some kind with its bottom painted in blue light. "Atlanticore?"

She turned her attention to the dais, a modest structure decorating the room's center. It appeared to be a fountain with a large bowl at its bottom and the faded carving of a figure in the center. She couldn't recognize its face, the features all but worn away.

The only defined parts were two arms spread out wide and two legs caught in motion.

Santana whirled at the sudden sound echoing through the tunnel. The roar was loud and rich in tone, reminding her of the territorial roars of brown bears. She wondered if cave bears and other creatures could survive this far down in the earth, especially when she had yet to find a water source or other signs of life.

That same roar came again, louder this time. Santana went to draw her pistol but discovered it was no longer there.

Dammit, must have fallen when I did...

She readied her whip, the lash trailing at her side as she looked between the tunnel entrances. The acoustics warping it made it impossible to detect which tunnel the sound emerged from.

She took a step back, eyes darting between the spaces, only able to make out the edges of the entryways in the glow of the pulsing Atlanticore. Padding footsteps accompanied the roar, and in the darkness Santana saw the shape of something approaching. The being coalesced, the large shadow that Santana's mind had conjured shrinking as the shape of a man emerged.

"Hello, Santana."

CHAPTER THIRTY-ONE

"You?" Santana's disbelief rang in her voice.

The man stepped into the limited light, the gloom making his thin frame harsher. Connor's beard was blue, the kindly mask he wore slipping as his eyes grew wide with wonder. "I didn't expect to see you here."

Santana frowned, struggling to comprehend what she was seeing. "What are you doing here? How did you... You left?"

"No," Connor stated. "I left *you*, but I didn't leave my purpose." He motioned around the space. "This...this is what I've been looking for."

Santana cocked her head. "*This* is Atlantis?"

Connor nodded with excitement in his eyes.

"Hold on. You left..."

"No," Connor repeated. "I left you all in the cave system, but I didn't leave entirely. I shrank into the dark, searching for alternate routes.

"I found the way ahead to your missing companion and followed in her tracks, letting her lead the way farther into the tunnel. When I found the ravine, I saw the way down and climbed into the darkness, stumbling across the first clues of the lost civilization."

He stared up at the ceiling. "It's here, Santana. I can feel it. Lost in the folds of the earth beneath the Covenrane Peaks. I know it."

Santana processed this information. "You followed Val... So it was *you* who removed the grappling gun?"

Connor shrugged. "I didn't want anyone to follow us."

Santana took a step forward. "You climbed down to the falls? Did you see anyone down there? Was there anyone...hurt, or... did you see John?"

Connor evaded the question. "How are *you* here, Santana? I suppose that doesn't matter. It could be a good thing. Two hardcore explorers following the trail to the hidden city." He shuddered. "I have goosebumps just thinking about it."

"Wait..." Santana looked back at the tunnel Connor had arrived through. "So there's a way back to the surface? I'm saved... There's a path?"

"There is," Connor agreed. "But if you think I'm leading you toward it, you're wrong. I didn't come this far only to come this far."

He strode toward the dais, his eyes wide as he examined the statue. "The lost gods of Atlantis..." He skirted the figure. "A clue...a waypoint to guide us farther into the magician's den..." He rubbed his hand over the stone. Dust fell from his fingers. "But, where to next?"

Santana looked back toward the tunnel entrance, part of her wanting to find a way back to the surface. The other part...

I have to see this through.

She joined Connor in examining the statue. Although something in the back of her head niggled her about the fact this man had tried to stop their progress, she knew that two heads would be better than one.

"What's the key?" Connor asked. "What's the system? Are you guiding us toward a new tunnel? A way through the rock? What's the significance of the Atlanticore stars?

Santana gripped the statue and attempted to spin it. The grooves she'd noticed around the base gave a little, and the statue began to move. "Help me, would you?"

Connor did so. They rotated the statue until it dropped an inch into the ground and stopped entirely.

"The statue *is* the key," Connor stated. "Clever."

They waited for something to happen. After a moment, the glowing blue fragments grew more intense in their brightness. The cave juddered and cast Santana back to her experience on the bridge.

The statue sank into the ground, spinning as it did so. After a few more moments, a hole replaced where the statue had been. Another chamber opened beneath them.

They stared into the opening, not needing to shine a light now that the glowing blue intensified.

"After you," Connor stated.

Santana scoffed, then latched her whip around the edge of the hole. She lowered herself until she was a few feet from where the statue now stood. With a gentle swing, she hopped into the space.

She left the whip where it was, letting Connor work his way down. Her eyes grew wide as she examined the space, the smooth floors of large rock tiles, the carved walls decorated with ornate embellishments lined with gold, and thrumming with blue energy. Another staircase appeared before them, wider than the others, at least the width of a school bus.

Connor hopped down. His laughter filled the air. "My God…" His mouth fell open, not needing to say anything else. Santana felt it, too. There was a change in the air, an electric thrum of excitement and power. The walls showed more paintings of the ancient civilization, sketches that she'd only glimpsed before.

Now they looked flawless and untouched, as though freshly painted.

"It can't be..." Santana breathed.

"It can." Connor was practically giddy with excitement. "Oh, Santana...can you imagine what this means?"

"It's nothing." Santana lied to herself, not wanting to get too excited. "Paintings and energy cores. That's all. We're not there yet."

"Spoken like a true adventurer," Connor shot back, already moving toward the stairs.

He ran down them two at a time. When he reached the tenth step, something shifted. The step he trod on lowered, and a *snapping* sound exploded from the walls.

"Duck!" Santana shouted.

Connor fell to his stomach just in time. Arrows fired from the walls in volume, dozens upon dozens flying over his head and into holes on the opposite side. Connor clapped his hands to the back of his head while Santana watched from where she stood.

After a minute, the arrows ceased firing.

Santana slowly worked her way to Connor. She helped him to his feet. "Keep your wits about you. This place is protected."

"Roger that." Sweat peppered Connor's forehead.

The rest of their descent was slower. The stairs rolled down, deeper and deeper into the earth. Santana had keener vision than Connor and kept them both protected as she guided them around the traps and plots on the ground.

At the bottom of the stairs, they came to a doorway twelve feet high and equally wide. The door was gold, its front ornately carved with images of people, gods, oceans, and sea creatures, the linework pristine and with an aura of something that made Santana's flesh tingle.

"The doorway to Atlantis..." Connor offered, drifting toward it as if in a dream. "It's...it's here..."

He pressed his hands to the door, eyes wide as globes as he

drank in every last inch of its surface. Santana took out her cell phone, documenting the find with a picture. At the camera's flash, Connor whipped around to her. "What are you doing?"

"Documenting."

Connor cast her a mistrusting glance. "Before you do that, shouldn't you help me find a way to open this?" He shoved against the door. The gold gave nothing in return. Santana came to his side and pressed her shoulder against it, but it stood firm.

"Here," Santana offered, pointing at a small hollow beside the door. It was carved and deliberate. "Something goes in here."

"A key. Fuck. Where are we supposed to have found a key?" Connor turned his head to the stairs and sighed.

Santana stared at the slot, unblinking. She reached into her bag and withdrew the golden object she'd snatched from the glass booth where Kit had been. Had Archie known about this? Did he have a clue about what they would find directly underneath the compound?

The object was a sextant, an ancient navigational tool that sailors used in the Old World. It was still in perfect condition, its golden body glinting in the blue light. She placed it inside the lock, the shape perfectly matching the hollow. She pushed it until it stopped, then stood back.

She waited for something to happen. Her mind went back to her time in the Temple of the Sun and the activation of the strange Old World magic that had swallowed their senses and brought the place to ruin. She expected the door to light up, for something to click into place and for the golden doorway to begin moving by itself.

No such luck.

"Well?" Connor looked at Santana expectantly.

"I...I don't know," Santana replied. She removed the sextant, then replaced it in the hollow. She fiddled with the item, wondering if it wasn't in right.

Still, nothing happened.

"Let me take a look," Connor commanded, storming over and indelicately ripping the sextant from its home. He turned it over in his hands a few times.

"Wait," Santana stated. "There."

She took the sextant back, pulling it from reluctant fingers. She brought it to eye level, looking at the strange oval hollow inside the sextant. "It can't be…"

"What?" Connor rose on his tiptoes to see over her shoulder.

The hollow was small, around the size of the end of her thumb. Santana knelt and put the sextant down. She reached inside her collar and drew out the chain around her neck. The pendant swung at the end of it.

She unclasped the necklace in silence. Bringing the pendant to the hollow, she set it inside.

It fit perfectly.

"Mom…" Santana breathed. "What were you trying to tell me?"

She turned back to the keyhole and slid the sextant inside. With a final, confirming *click*, the device was in place.

A mechanism ground. Something was happening behind the door. The reams of blue light running along the ways traveled from the rock into the door. The linework of an extinct artist illuminated as the Atlanticore power surged around the door frame, flooding it with light. Santana and Connor stepped back in awe, taking in the full breadth of what they saw.

"Marvelous," Connor exclaimed.

Santana couldn't speak, her eyes hot with tears as her thoughts turned to her mother.

The light shone brightly as the Atlanticore completed the tapestry. When every line and crack had filled, a final *click* confirmed the opening.

Santana's skin felt electric. There was static in the air. She took another picture, the cell phone lighting up once more.

The world went blurry. Pain flared in Santana's cheek. She fell to the ground, the phone slipping from her grasp and cracking on the stone.

CHAPTER THIRTY-TWO

"What are you doing?" Santana asked as Connor's boot slammed down on her phone.

"Finder's keepers," Connor crooned, his smile unfaltering. "No documentation from you, no proof that anyone else was here. This was my find and mine alone. You wanted Atlantis... It's here."

His foot found her cheek. Santana caught the boot on the upswing, causing Connor to stumble. He pulled free of her, then ran to the door. With one bold push, the doors swung inward, and the only reality Santana had ever known cracked in two.

The rush of water met their ears. The lost city unfolded before them in a magnificent display of architecture and technological prowess. A single pathway followed the door, its edges illuminated in blue. Pools of crystal clear water ran along either side. The causeway rose steadily toward the gargantuan building, a lost fortress hiding in the depths of the largest cave Santana had ever seen.

And still, lights were activating. All around the edges of the colossal space, blue lights illuminated. They disturbed a nest of bats, and a black cloud flew over the space. Santana pushed herself to her feet as her mouth fell open. The silver of fish swimming in rich shoals flashed in the waters, the banks covered with weeds and moss and plants of all colors.

She walked as if in a dream, one hand straying to her cheek. Already she'd forgotten Connor's attack as her eyes drank in the sights. Connor had begun his walk across the causeway with his eyes fixed ahead as he laughed. The sound traveled into the enormous space.

"Atlantis..." Santana breathed, the word alien on her tongue. How hard had Connor hit her? How hard had she hit her head when she fell? She couldn't be seeing what she saw. It couldn't be. It just couldn't.

Connor ran to the edge of the causeway and stared into the water. He dipped a hand in the pool, disturbing the mirrored surface. Fish curiously rose to his touch, and still he laughed, looking like a clown with a coat hanger in his mouth. He jumped up and down, excitement coursing through him. He spun in place, chuckling...

...until he saw Santana.

Realization dawned on them both. The magnitude of what they'd found covered them like the weight of a dark phantom. Santana held her whip by her side, already charging at Connor. Connor reached for his gun but was unable to get a clear shot. Santana's shoulder slammed into his chest.

"You don't understand the work I've put into finding this," Connor grunted as they rolled on the floor. Santana grabbed his wrists, wrestling to twist the gun out of his hands. "What I've been through."

"We can share the find," Santana lied, knowing that in history only one name would ever be remembered. "This doesn't have to be this way."

He threw his head into her. Santana's eyes rolled back. He turned the gun on her and fired.

The slug passed over Santana's shoulder and hit the rocky

wall. Rocks chipped down, raining into the pool. Santana dug her elbow into his stomach. Connor raised his knee to shield his chest but was too late. He gasped as the blow winded him.

Santana grabbed the gun. Connor fought back. Their momentum spun the weapon from his control, sending it skating across the causeway. Santana rose to her feet, then kicked him in the side. "Enough!" she cried.

She broke for the gun. Connor caught her foot. She tripped and turned, cracking the whip onto his hand. He yelled as red blood streaked across his skin.

Santana dove for the pistol, clutching it tightly in her hands. She rose to her feet, then turned the gun on Connor. He was undeterred as he ran for her. She hesitated. Connor struck her.

They both fell back. This time the pistol flew into the waters and slowly sank into the depths. Fists and kicks flew. Santana grew breathless but knew she could beat this man if she tried.

They broke apart. Santana took a fighting stance as Connor whipped something silver and sharp from his pocket. He came at her, the knife blade aiming for her stomach…

Thunder roared, and Connor fell. He flopped onto his stomach before reaching her, his arms extended, almost pushing Santana into the water.

She stared down at him in disbelief, the thunder still loud in her ears. Blood pooled from beneath his body. Droplets worked their way into the water where small silvery insects gathered around the liquid.

Santana turned to the doorway, in the direction of the gunshot.

Toward Dick Chambers.

She blinked stupidly. Dick stood there as if waiting for permission to enter. His gun smoked. He lowered his arm. He waited, his gaze darting around the fortress.

"Sokolov," he announced at last.

Santana ran to Dick, her footsteps clattering loudly on the

causeway. Tears streaked from her eyes, but she didn't want to slow down and let her body take the lead for a change. She closed on him, then threw her arms around his neck. She buried her face in his shoulder as he stumbled, trying to absorb her momentum.

He folded one arm around her and let Santana process her emotions. He hid his pain, not wanting to distract her from the moment.

Santana didn't understand it. She'd found Atlantis…she'd nearly died…and now, this?

"Santana…are you…"

Before he could get further, Santana's lips were on his. She kissed him deeply, the tears staining her cheeks becoming sticky on his. His stubble was scratchy but not unpleasant. She cupped his cheeks in her hands, tongue playing with his, the pair losing themselves in the moment. Right then, all that existed was Dick and Santana, and that was fine.

Eventually, she pulled back with embarrassment coloring her cheeks. She couldn't meet his gaze. Instead, she looked down at the makeshift sling. "John, are you okay?"

"Only a little broken shoulder. Nothing to worry about."

Santana's hands went to her mouth. "I'm so sorry."

"It's fine," Dick lied. "Nice place you got here."

Santana turned to the fortress, to Atlantis. "Yeah… Can you believe it?"

"Is it…"

"Atlantis?" A whimsical smile bloomed on her lips. "I think so."

"And Connor?"

Santana gave him a "do you need to ask" look.

"This is impossible."

"No." Santana beamed. "No, it's not. And we're the first ones to make it…the first ones here. Come. Please, Dick, come. I want to see what's inside."

She passed through the door and retrieved the sextant and pendant. Depositing them in her bag, she closed the doors behind her. She took Dick's hand, leading him along the causeway. When they reached Connor, they wove around his body, their amazement showing as they caught sight of strange insects, mammals, and fauna around the place.

The fortress allowed them passage with a mere touch of the hand. At first contact, blue lights flared on either side of the door, and they swung up. The lights inside illuminated as they approached. The place appeared to run as though on an automated system, although they saw no wires or signs of electrical boxes as they passed.

They swept through the place, passing from room to room in the fortress. Signs of former life littered the area, but there were no bodies or skeletons visible. The entire place was vacant and desolate.

They climbed the stairs to the upper turrets. There were paints and signs of woolen materials creating woven tapestries. There were empty jugs and golden cups, sewing machines, and sophisticated armories stacked with weapons.

They reached the highest turret and stepped out into the open once again. From here, they had a full view of the surrounding area, and Santana's eyes misted at the sight. It was more than a fortress. On the other side of the building was an entire city with houses scattered in irregular patterns and fields the size of soccer pitches fenced off and filled with plant life. Somewhere in the distance, she thought she could see cattle and sheep roaming around.

"What the hell is this place?" Dick's voice was a mere whisper.

"I don't know." Santana wiped a tear with the back of her hand. "But it's beautiful."

"It stretches for miles," Dick stated. "That water, it's clearer than anything I've seen. The plants, the trees, how is it possible that all of this exists underground?"

"Maybe that has something to do with it?" Santana pointed at a lone white structure in the center of the city. Its spiral tower rose toward the ceiling, poking high above the other roofs.

"Only one way to find out."

They made their way slowly onward. Their stomachs rumbled as they passed through the vacated streets. Dick found a bushel of something that looked like raspberries, and as they each popped a handful in their mouth, their eyes lit up. The taste was sweeter than anything Santana had imagined. The juice brought her senses alive. She woke up, tiredness washing from her.

"This place is amazing." Juice ran down Dick's chin.

Santana couldn't argue.

When they arrived at the building, they knocked on the door. No one answered. The pair didn't expect anyone to reply.

They pushed the door open and discovered an area akin to Roman baths Santana had seen before, only the water inside was glowing brightly with light.

"What's in there?" Dick asked.

"Atlanticore?" Santana suggested.

"I don't know. Look."

Around the edges of the pool, a vibrant orange light joined the blue. Lava mixed with whatever source was in the pool, creating a strange mystic glow. They explored the space, finding a series of channels and pathways where the energy ran out of the building and into the town.

"This must be some sort of energy center," Santana stated. "It branches to the outside. Maybe this is how it creates Atlanticore? Or maybe…I don't know…"

"Go on," Dick encouraged.

"Maybe this is where the power is," Santana mused. "We must be beneath the volcanoes, which would explain the lava—not that I can guess where the rest of it is. Maybe…maybe the Atlanticore is drawing power from the Earth's core, but…that would mean…" She groaned in frustration. "I don't know."

"One thing I do know," Dick commented. "This might be the first moment of peace and quiet I've had in some time."

They sat beside the pool and finished the last of the berries they'd grabbed. Santana asked Dick about how he ended up here, and he told the story as well as he could remember it. Santana filled Dick in on the parts that he was missing. A smile reached his face as she told him about Kit.

A few hours later, they returned to the front entrance, looking for a way back out. Santana's pack was full of items taken from Atlantis, her mind tracking each step so she could find her way out.

For hours they searched for the path to the surface, each time winding up back where they started. The detonations had revised the passage beneath the earth, and soon enough they grew hungry and thirsty once more.

They returned to the lost city, feeding on the fruits until they sated their hunger. Dick drank from the pools, the cool water racing through him. Santana's tiredness once more lifted at the taste of the berries.

As they sat and discussed their options, neither of them noticed the most miraculous thing of all.

Dick was moving his shoulder without pain.

CHAPTER THIRTY-THREE

One week later

The world was quiet and blue.

Santana stretched and pulled her feet from the pool. They were cool now. The fish that were schooling around her feet were disappointed as they swam off into the depths. Behind her, woven baskets were full of berries and fruits of all kinds from the strange array that grew in the ground.

Footsteps came from behind. Dick Chambers approached, the body of a goat slung over his shoulder. At first, the sight frightened her until she remembered the smell of the cooked chicken he'd managed to rustle up the night before.

"Should last us a few days." Dick flopped the goat to the ground.

Santana gave an appreciative nod.

"Any luck on the outside?" Dick asked.

Santana shook her head. Over the last week, she and Dick had taken it in turns to explore the tunnels, trying to map their way back to the surface. So far, every branch had led to yet another dead end.

"Nothing," she declared. "I'm beginning to think we're trapped down here forever."

Dick sat beside her and removed his boots. He dipped his feet into the pool, his skin prickling at its chilly touch. "Would that be the worst thing?"

Santana met his gaze. In truth, she'd been wondering that, too. In their last few days of being stuck down here, they'd uncovered so much more of the city. That included stores of paper, armories filled with hunting equipment, and weapons powered by Atlanticore.

They'd even found agricultural vehicles and strange motor-bikes that ran on the blue power source. Everything they needed was down here—everything they needed to survive.

Santana absently stroked the pendant hanging around her neck. She thought of her mother, of her search for lost treasures. If they could get back to the surface, they could share this gift with the city. They could share Atlantis with the world, become famous the world over. It was their one-way ticket to fame, and they were sitting on it.

"I don't know," Santana admitted. "I always promised myself that if I found something of this magnitude, I'd share it with the world. That's what Mom would've wanted, anyway. But...the more I think about it, the more simple life could be down here. There's so much to discover still, so much to document. I suppose that staying a while wouldn't be the worst thing in the world. It's not like I have much to go back to."

"What about your father?" Dick asked.

Santana smiled. "He's not been the same since Mom passed. I don't recognize him anymore. He's...he's changed..." Tears rose in her eyes. She turned the heat back at Dick. "What about you? What are you going to do if we can't get out of here?"

Dick smiled and leaned back on his hands. He'd removed his jacket and looked rather handsome out of his typical PI attire. "I don't have anything to get back to. No family to speak of. I have

Doug, but I mean... He's good by himself. Down here it's quiet. It's nice. Away from the filth and the scum of the city. I can't say I miss it."

"Me neither," Santana admitted.

She scooted a little closer to Dick and rested her head on his shoulder. He lifted her chin and kissed her. Before they knew it, they were lost in the throes of lovemaking, their clothes discarded as they fooled around by the water.

When they finished, Santana lay naked beside Dick. Nearby, a fish leaped from the water. Dick's shoulders shook as he began to laugh.

"What's so funny?" Santana asked.

"Oh, remembering something funny you once said to me."

Santana looked up at him. Their eyes met. "What's that?"

"That you wouldn't sleep with me, even if I were the last man on Earth." Dick smirked. "Turns out you were wrong."

Santana rolled her eyes. "Turns out that we might be the last two people on Earth, at least down here." She smirked and added, "Dick."

Dick looked down at her in surprise. Santana chuckled. As she rested her head on his chest, her body basking in the after-glow of their activity and the pulsing blue of Atlantis, Santana thought back to the cave she'd found and the single entrance leading up toward a shaft of light on the surface.

An opening that she wouldn't tell Dick Chambers about. At least not for a while, anyway.

The church grounds were foggy, cast in a dense mist. Those gathered around the two gravestones could barely be distinguished, only their dark figures remaining on the edge of vision.

Isabella Harris, known more commonly by her alter ego, Valentina Winters, crossed her arms and stared down at the engraved stone. Beside her, weak and skinny but stronger than he'd been in years, Kit Harris leaned on his crutches. The reverend spoke solemn words and threw a handful of dirt on the ground where a body should lie but didn't, then completed the service.

Isabella made the sign of the cross, instructing Kit to do the same. His hair was growing, the gaunt look in his cheeks already beginning to wear off as he ate and healed and grew.

"We would never have found you without them," Isabella stated softly, looking between the two graves. "They gave their lives for you."

She stepped away, taking Kit with her, allowing the next group to pay their respects. Rain began to beat down, dampening their clothes as well as their spirits. She made her way to the church gates, unsurprised to find a woman in a long dark jacket waiting for them.

"Terra," Isabella offered.

"Val," Terra returned.

Isabella glanced at her brother. He smiled.

They remained silent a while until Terra finally spoke. "Are they…"

Isabella nodded. "They are."

"Damn shame," Terra replied. "They were good ones. Even Dick Chambers, as much as he made it hard for us to admit."

Isabella smiled.

"How are you doing, Kit?" Terra asked.

"Better. One day at a time."

Terra nodded. "One day at a time." She drew a long breath and offered a weak wave at Gyles, who lingered on the edge of the fog before disappearing in the opposite direction. "Where you headed now? Want to stick around for a drink? Toast in their honor?"

Isabella shook her head. "We have a plane to catch, ain't that right, lil brother?"

Kit nodded.

"Oh?" Terra asked. "A plane to where?"

Isabella tapped her nose. "My crimson friend told us to tell no one."

"Well, a promise made is a promise kept." Terra smirked and turned away from the gate. "You look after yourselves, okay?"

Isabella nodded. "Always."

Kit waved.

Terra dug her hands in her pockets and headed down the street.

"A promise made is a promise kept," Isabella mused, wondering how many promises Valentina had made and broken. "Come on, Kit. Time to start a new life. There's nothing left for us here."

Little did she know how much she echoed the sentiment of two of her closest comrades, hiding miles down in the ground beneath her feet.

AUTHOR NOTES MICHAEL ANDERLE

DECEMBER 2, 2021

Thank you for not only reading this story but these author notes as well.

So, this is it, right? The end of the four trilogies...the story of ATLANTICA.

Or is it?

Of course not!

While we have a bit more to tell in this timeline, I'm jumping ahead and backward in time now. In essence, I told you these stories so I could tell you these other stories!

I guess that's similar to how I got the ZOO Universe going.

Let's go backward. How did the Executioners get started? Well, read *The First Executioner* to find out how they got started and why ATLANTICA built the...umm, *unique* legal system they have in these stories.

Here is the book: The First Executioner

Next, I'll take you into the future. A future where the cataclysm that mankind tried to stop tens of thousands of years ago… happened. Here, we find ourselves in a new future where mankind used the technology of ATLANTICA to save themselves from the results when one abuses the technology from ATLANTICA.

Beware the hand that feeds you.

Check out our new stories about the future of Earth. You will notice that we do not brand it ATLANTICA. That is because those who haven't read these stories will uncover this truth through the stories.

I hope!

I don't have a link for the book, but here is the cover for the first story of HELLCAT.

Thank you for trusting us with your time. I hope to talk to you again in both these series!

Ad Aeternitatem,

Michael.

P.S.

I'm typing these author notes sitting in my office in Cabo San Lucas, Mexico. About a mile from me is the resort I was visiting when I originally came up with the idea for ATLANTICA.

The resort's name is Pacifica. Coincidence? I don't think so.

That was a LONG time ago, it seems. Maybe two years? Either way, I appreciate you being here for the author's notes at the end of the first four trilogies, which were built to tell four arcs forming one story.

We have barely scratched the surface. If you enjoy these stories, please give us a good review of the books. It helps more than you know!

BOOKS BY MICHAEL ANDERLE

Sign up for the LMBPN email list to be notified of new releases and
special deals!

https://lmbpn.com/email/

For a complete list of books by Michael Anderle, please visit:

www.lmbpn.com/ma-books/

CONNECT WITH THE AUTHOR

Connect with Michael Anderle

Website: http://lmbpn.com

Email List: http://lmbpn.com/email/

https://www.facebook.com/LMBPNPublishing

https://twitter.com/MichaelAnderle

https://www.instagram.com/lmbpn_publishing/

https://www.bookbub.com/authors/michael-anderle